'Oh, James, I knew I could rely on you.'

She grasped both his hands in hers and stood on tiptoe to kiss his cheek. 'Thank you.'

'Vinny.' He held onto her hands and raised them one by one to his lips. There was no sign of the bantering, carefree young man who loved to tease. 'You shouldn't thank me. I have brought you nothing but grief.'

'How can you say that? You are my dear—' She stopped and looked up at him. He was waiting for her to continue, but she could not. The word 'brother' stuck in her throat.

He said it for her. 'Brother?'

'No. Not brother. Not even stepbrother. That was a game we played to amuse everyone.'

'And the time for games is past,' he said quietly, holding her hands to his chest, where she could feel his heart beating almost as quickly as her own. 'You know, I have been waiting for you to grow up...'

Born in Singapore, **Mary Nichols** came to England when she was three, and has spent most of her life in different parts of East Anglia. She has been a radiographer, school secretary, information officer and industrial editor, as well as a writer. She has three grown-up children, and four grandchildren. You may find that some of the characters in this story are familiar to you, as *Lady Lavinia's Match* follows on from Mary Nichols's most recent novel, *The Incomparable Countess*.

Recent titles by the same author:

THE RELUCTANT ESCORT
THE WESTMERE LEGACY
THE HONOURABLE EARL
THE INCOMPARABLE COUNTESS

LADY LAVINIA'S MATCH

Mary Nichols

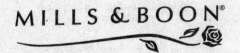

First published in Great Britain 2002
Harlequin Mills & Boon Limited,
Eton House, 18-24 Paradise Road, Richmond, Surrey TW9 1SR

© Mary Nichols 2002

ISBN 0 263 83129 9

Set in Times Roman 10½ on 12 pt.
04-0702-87547

Printed and bound in Spain
by Litografia Rosés S.A., Barcelona

LADY LAVINIA'S
MATCH

Chapter One

1820

The canvas was huge, several feet long and seven high, propped against a wall in the ballroom of Stanmore House, the London mansion of the Duke of Loscoe. Beside it, on the floor, were several pots of paint and, on a table nearby, a selection of brushes, cloths and a jar of water.

Lady Lavinia Stanmore, a huge apron covering her spotted gingham gown and paint brush in hand, stepped back to appraise her handiwork, which was so large that it had to be viewed from a distance to see the whole. It was a rustic, fairy-tale woodland scene with several gnarled old trees, wound about with columbine, giving shade to half a dozen rabbits at play, some colourful toadstools and a bank of wild flowers.

'Heavens, Lavinia! I know you like the broad view, but this is monumental.'

She turned to face the man who stood nonchalantly leaning against the door frame. James, Earl of Corringham, was dressed to a shade and only managed to escape being a fop by a whisker. His hair was fair and as beautifully cut as his superfine green coat. His biscuit-coloured pantaloons tucked in tasselled Hessians and his precisely tied cravat proclaimed him a Corinthian of the first water.

'Oh, it's you, James.'

He grinned, his grey eyes alight with humour. 'Whom else did you expect?'

'I didn't expect anyone in particular.'

He stepped forward to inspect the painting more closely. 'Where on earth are you going to put it? Where in this house, large though it is, is there enough wall space to hang such a monstrosity?'

'It is not a monstrosity!'

'I beg your pardon. I did not mean it is ugly,' he retracted quickly, knowing her temper could be volatile. 'I meant monstrous in the sense of very big.'

'It has to be big. It is a scene.'

'I can see that.'

'I mean a scene for a play. It is a backcloth for *A Midsummer Night's Dream.*'

'Oh, I see. Tell me more.'

He only asked her for details because he loved looking at her, loved the sound of her voice, the light of enthusiasm in her green eyes when she talked about things that interested her, the way her chestnut curls lay so lovingly on her slender neck, the way she held herself with a natural grace that had nothing to do with her aristocratic antecedents. He loved everything about her and it was a pity she looked on him as an older brother and not, as every mama of the *ton* viewed him, an eligible man in need of a wife.

He was not her brother, they were in no way related, except through the fairly recent marriage of his stepmother to her father, the Duke of Loscoe, distant enough to make no difference at all to the way he felt about her, the way he had felt ever since meeting her three years before. She had been a high-spirited, wilful sixteen-year-old, up from the country to sample the delights of London for the first time, not yet come out and far too young to be thinking of marriage. When the Duke had married his stepmother the following year it was easier to treat Vinny as a sister and they had fallen into an easy relationship that he had no idea would be so difficult to change.

'We are going to put on a play to raise money for Stepmama's orphanages,' she explained. 'The cost of running them is rising all the time and the need for them increasing day by day, and I hit on this way of finding the blunt.'

Homes for children orphaned by the late war were one of the Duchess's favourite charities. It was that more than anything else which had changed Lavinia's initial resentment of her to grudging admiration which, when her father declared his intention of marrying Frances, soon turned to love.

She had become more of a mother to her than her own mother had ever been. If it had not been for her brother, her childhood would have been a lonely one. Miss Hastings, her governess, had provided a modicum of education along with lessons in manners, but Lavinia had escaped as often as possible to roam the fields, ride her pony or find mischief with Duncan. It was little wonder she had grown up knowing more of the ways of little boys than young ladies. The only time she saw her mother was when she was sent for to be punished for these misdemeanours and that usually meant being confined to the schoolroom and more isolation. It was almost as if her mother could not bear the sight of her.

'I suppose it was Little Mama's idea.' James's name for his stepmother had been coined when Frances first came to their home in Essex as his father's bride, when he was

seven years old and she was seventeen. It had stuck even
after his father's death and her subsequent marriage to the
Duke.

'No, it was mine. There was a company of touring players who came to Risley earlier this year. They put up a
huge tent and everyone went to see them, so I thought,
why not do something like it ourselves? I would have done
it at Loscoe Court, but I realised it would not attract a
large enough audience, and, as we were coming to London,
I decided to have it here. We are going to convert the
ballroom into a theatre for one night.'

'Who is ''we''?'

'Oh, anyone who is interested. You can take part, if you
wish.'

'Can I, now? What makes you think I have any talent
as an actor?'

'We won't know until we hear you try, will we? And if
you are *quite*, *quite* hopeless, as I suspect you may be,
why, then you may help us behind the scenes...'

'Shifting the scenery,' he said, nodding towards the
painting.

'If you like.'

'And if I don't choose to do it?'

'It is of no consequence. There are others who are willing.'

'Who?'

'Duncan. Perhaps Benedict Willoughby.'

'You cannot rely on those two. Your brother is a sloth
and young Willoughby is wild and unreliable.'

'Duncan can rouse himself when he wants to. I thought
it might divert him.'

'From falling into more scrapes? You will only do that
if you manage to separate him from Willoughby.'

'I do not think you should belittle him, James.' She

defended her eighteen-year-old brother out of habit, not because James was not right. 'I collect you were always in scrapes when you were young. Now you are grown old and staid, you have forgotten what it was like.'

'Old and staid!' He laughed. 'Is that what being seven and twenty is? And I thought I was only now reaching my prime.'

'You know what I mean.'

'Do you propose to act in this little entertainment yourself?'

'Yes, if I am good enough.'

'Who else?'

'Lancelot Greatorex.'

'Lancelot Greatorex? Who is he?'

'The manager of the Thespian Players and a very fine actor.'

'That accounts for the preposterous name. I assume it is a pseudonym?'

'I do not know, do I? I never asked him. The players have other engagements round the country for the next few weeks, but he has promised to come to London at the end of the summer with some of his company to direct us.'

'Good Lord! Do you mean to say the Duke has countenanced you associating with *play actors*?'

'Why should he not?'

'Oh, Lavinia,' he sighed. 'Have you even asked him?'

'Not yet, but I will.'

He laughed. 'Then I wish you luck, but forgive me if I am not present when you do. I have no fancy to be at the receiving end of his temper, nor even to witness it.'

'Papa doesn't have a temper—not a bad one, that is. He is always prepared to listen.' And that had come about since he married Frances. Before that he had been a remote and unreachable figure, seen only occasionally, someone who inspired awe rather than love. Not until her mother died and he had brought her to London did she even begin to know him. And that had been a revelation. He was far from the ogre she had always supposed him to be.

'And having listened, will pronounce judgement and that will be the end of it. His Grace, the Duke of Loscoe, is a benevolent papa who puts up with a great deal more from his daughter than many men would, but that does not mean he will allow you to do as you please.'

'We shall see,' she said blithely.

'Five guineas says he will not hear of it.'

'Done,' she said promptly. 'I will get Stepmama on my side. He can never refuse her anything.'

'And if he does agree, who do you hope will come to witness the performance?'

'Everyone. All our friends and no doubt some who are not truly our friends, but I do not care why they attend, so long as they pay for their tickets.'

'And you think your papa will allow that? And in his ballroom, too.'

'I don't see why not. Don't you remember that ball Stepmama arranged at Corringham House three years ago for that first orphanage in Maiden Lane? The most unlikely people came, some not *haut monde* at all, and she did not turn anyone away who was prepared to pay the entrance price.'

'That was before she married your father and it was not the same thing at all. A ball is not a play.' He paused, watching as she picked up another brush and dipped it in paint to put the finishing touches to a spotted snake shedding its skin. There was no doubt she was a very talented artist, a talent which had been nurtured by their mutual stepmother, herself a highly acclaimed painter.

'Am I to suppose from that, that you will not be favouring us with your presence?'

'Oh, I shall come, if only to watch.'

'And laugh when things go awry, I shouldn't wonder.'

'Oh, Vinny, I would never do that.' He watched her deft strokes, hating to act the devil's advocate, but he could see her riding for a fall and wanted to prevent it if he could. 'And there's another thing that might divert the *ton* away from your play: the King's efforts to rid himself of his wife.'

Caroline, after living abroad for the last six years and making herself the subject of notorious gossip, had, on the succession of her husband to the throne, suddenly decided to return to London, expecting to be acknowledged as Queen. Her furious husband ignored her, but she enjoyed the plaudits of a fickle populace, who cheered her to the echo whenever she went out.

'I know that, but I do believe that will help our cause rather than hinder it. Anyone who is anyone has come to town this summer, either to attend the coronation or view the procession from some vantage point and the Season will go on much longer, considering it is not to be until the first of August. It is why we are here. Nothing would have kept Stepmama away from Loscoe Court and little Freddie unless Papa was obliged to attend.'

'If there *is* a coronation. The whole thing is like to turn into a huge farce and make the King look more ridiculous than ever.'

'So Papa said, but it will make for a very interesting Season, don't you think?' she said, with a mischievous smile. 'Just think of all those people who have not been to town for years and years, all bringing wives and daughters, who will doubtless wish to be amused.'

'You think they will come to see your play?'

'I do not see why not. You never know, you might find yourself a bride among them—'

'Heaven forbid!'

'Why not? You know it is high time you married.'

'Oh, Vinny, not you too. It is bad enough having Little Mama giving me jobations over it without you adding to it. I will marry when I am ready. And for love.'

'No, really?' She laughed. 'For love? Who is she? Do tell...'

'Certainly not. And you have no reason to roast me. I collect you had a Season two years go that cost the Duke a fortune, and you turned away every eligible who so much as hinted he was interested.'

'It was not fair to encourage them when I had no intention of accepting them, was it?'

'But why not accept one of them?'

'For the same reason you have given. I will marry when I am ready.'

'And when will that be?'

'When I fall in love.'

'And how will you know when you are in love?'

It was a question which had occupied Lavinia ever since her come-out, but one she could not satisfactorily answer. Her friends and contemporaries seemed not to be able to answer it either, notwithstanding that many of them were already married, some even with families. 'I shall know,' she said airily, rinsing out her brush, then changing the subject abruptly, added, 'You have not told me why you are here.'

'Do I need a reason? I heard you had arrived in town and decided to pay a call.'

'A mere courtesy call, then. I will tell Stepmama you came. She is out shopping.'

'I wanted to see you too. I have something to show you.'

'What is it?' She turned from her work to face him and a spot of paint-stained water flew from her brush, narrowly missing his pantaloons.

He stepped back adroitly. 'Vinny, put that brush down or you will ruin my clothes and then I shan't tell you anything.'

She did as she was told while he picked up one of the cloths from the table and bent to clean the watery paint from the toe of his boot.

'Come on, James, let me see.'

'Go to the window.'

She hurried across the polished floor to one of a long row of windows that looked out over the street. The road was busy with the usual traffic of carriages and riders going about their business, but immediately below the window was the carriage James had arrived in, its pair of matched horses being held by a young urchin to whom he had given a copper or two. 'Oh, James, a high-perch phaeton! Have you just bought it?'

'Yes. Do you like it?'

'Oh, I must look at it properly.' She whipped off her apron and hurried from the room, down the grand staircase, across the tiled floor and out of the front door, followed by a smiling James.

'My goodness,' she said, stopping beside the phaeton. 'Those wheels must be at least six feet high.'

'So they are.'

'But it is a horrid colour. Yellow and black is far too ostentatious. It's the colour a newly rich industrialist would choose to flaunt his wealth.'

He laughed. 'Probably because I bought if from a newly rich industrialist. He turned it over and his wife made him get rid of it, said it was dangerous.'

'And do you think it is dangerous?'

'Not in skilful hands. Would you like to come for a ride in it?'

'Now?'

'Why not? You can leave that painting for an hour or two, can't you?'

Lavinia did not hesitate. She was always ready for mischief and the thought of parading in Hyde Park, head and shoulders above everyone else, amused her. 'I will go and change. Wait for me in the drawing room. Ten minutes, no more.' She was dashing back up the stairs to her bedroom before she finished speaking, leaving him to amble slowly into the drawing room to wait.

She was back within the stipulated time, dressed in a blue taffeta carriage gown and matching pelisse, her unruly curls tamed under a fetching straw bonnet trimmed with blue ribbons tied beneath her chin. That she should have been chaperoned did not cross her mind, or, if it did, was immediately dismissed on the grounds there was no room for more than two in the carriage; anyway, James was like a brother.

He helped her climb up into her seat, sprang up beside her, flicked the reins and the horses began to trot steadily towards Piccadilly.

'It's like being on top of the world,' she said. 'Papa had a high-perch once, but he didn't keep it long. When he married Stepmama and little Freddie came along, he decided it was no longer a suitable conveyance. I only ever rode in it once; he said it was vulgar and unstable and he didn't know why he had been persuaded into buying it.'

'Perhaps I should not have asked you to accompany me until we had asked him.'

'We could not.' She paused, watching him skilfully negotiate the turn into Piccadilly. 'He is gone to the Lords and like to be there all day. He is being asked to give his advice over the question of the Queen's coronation, though I wonder at the haste. The Prince Regent—I mean the King, I keep forgetting—has been married to Caroline and living apart from her for years. Why has he left it until now to do something about her?'

'Because, in case it has slipped your attention, my sweet, she has arrived back in England expecting to be crowned with him. And he is determined that will never happen.'

'How is he going to prevent it?'

'Divorce her, I suppose.'

'But his behaviour has been every bit as bad as hers. Would he dare risk it?'

'I suppose he thinks the risk worth taking. If he can divorce her, he might remarry and beget an heir.'

She laughed. 'But he is too old and fat, surely?'

'He might not think so. And who else is there? His brothers have not been exactly helpful in the matter of legitimate heirs, have they? Plenty of little Fitzes, but none the law can recognise.'

'There's the late Duke of Kent's baby.'

'Victoria, yes. But she's a girl.'

'So what?' she said sharply. 'The only reason women are considered inferior is because men have made them believe they are. And I am not the only one to think that. Stepmama believes it too, as you very well know.'

He laughed as they turned in at the gates of the park and turned along the carriage ride. 'Vinny, are you looking for an argument?'

'Not at all, unless you are dying to give me one, in which case—'

'Argue with you! Never! It is more than my life is worth.'

'Good, because I want you to let me drive.'

'Certainly not!'

'Why not? You know I am as good a whip as any man. All you need to do is hand over the ribbons.' She reached out and laid her hand upon his, hoping he would relinquish the reins. He felt himself tense at her touch, but brought himself quickly under control.

'No, Vinny. There are far too many people about and it would not be just you and me who might be hurt if you upset us.'

'Very well,' she conceded, knowing he was right. 'We will come out very early one morning when the park is deserted and you shall let me try.'

'Your papa would not allow it. Nor Little Mama, either.'

'Then we will not tell them. Oh, go on, James, it will be fun and what harm can come of it when you are there to look after me?' She looked up at him, dazzling him with her smile. 'Will you?'

'I will think about it. Now, I think you had better acknowledge Lady Willoughby before she reports to your mama that you cut her dead.'

From the height of her seat, Lavinia could look down on the occupants of the other carriage and smiling, she turned and bowed to her ladyship. From then on, she was kept busy bowing and bidding 'good day' to dozens of ladies out for an afternoon drive and not a few gentlemen on horseback who knew James and envied him his attractive companion.

There was Lord Bertram Haverley, a widower of middle years, known to be looking for a second wife to give him the heir his first wife had failed to do, though she had provided him with two daughters. Sophia, the older, was not quite of marriageable age, and Eliza was two years younger. They were both pretty, bright girls dressed in white gingham. Soon after parting from them, they stopped to speak to Mr Martin Drew, stiffly correct, who only just managed to conceal his disapproval of her going out unchaperoned; and there was handsome Lord Edmund Wincote, who was a stranger to Lavinia, but greeted James so enthusiastically he was obliged to pull up and present him to her.

He was a young man of perhaps four and twenty, fashionably attired in a riding coat of good Bath cloth, a yellow waistcoat, deerskin breeches and tasselled boots. When he swept off his tall riding hat to Lavinia, he revealed short dark hair that sprang into tight little curls.

'I am happy to make your acquaintance, my lady,' he said, appraising her with eyes so dark they were almost black. 'Are you in town for the Season?'

'Yes, my lord. And you?'

'Oh, most assuredly, London is the place to be at this moment.'

'Oh, you mean because of the coronation?'

'Not at all.' He smiled into her eyes, making her stomach give a sudden lurch. 'Because Lady Lavinia Stanmore is here.'

She laughed a little shakily. 'Flatterer!'

'I speak from the heart, my lady. I hope to have the pleasure of meeting you at some of the entertainments being held this year.'

'Oh, undoubtedly, should we both be invited to the same function,' she said airily, pretending to be unaffected.

'Then I shall look forward to them all the more.' He smiled and replaced his hat before wheeling his horse round. 'Until we meet again, my lady. Corringham, good afternoon.'

'That was pitched too bold by far,' James said, as they pulled away and made for home. 'He must be desperate.'

'What do you mean, desperate?' she snapped, turning

on him, green eyes flashing. 'Am I such a poor catch? A
ninny no man could possibly want unless he be desperate?
You may be my brother, but that does not mean you may
disparage me—'

'Vinny, that is the last thing, the very last thing, I would
do. It is the man I disparage, not you. And I am *not* your
brother.'

'Thank goodness for that for, if you were, you would
wrap me up in so many prohibitions I should not be able
to breathe. Good heavens, the man was only being polite.'

'I am sorry, Vinny,' he said. 'I did not mean to upset
you. You are miles above him in every way and, by desperate, I meant he was trying to find favour even when he
must know he has no hope.'

'And how do you know he has no hope? He is handsome and very polite and—'

'But for all we know he might be a fortune-hunter, looking for a rich wife and they don't come richer than the
daughter of the Duke of Loscoe.'

'How do you know that?'

'What, that your dowry is likely to be more than gen-
erous?'

'No, silly, that Lord Wincote is pinched in the pocket.'

'A guess,' he said. 'I haven't seen him in years and now
he turns up out of nowhere, bold as brass. It makes me
cautious.'

'Fie on you, for your suspicious nature. I'll wager his
coat was tailored at Weston's and the boots came from
Hoby's. Besides, that horse of his is no broken-backed
hack. Men without feathers cannot fly so high.'

'There is such a thing as credit. And debt, as I should
know.'

She was diverted from the subject of Lord Wincote to

turn and look searchingly into his face. 'James, surely you are not—'

'No, of course not. I was referring to my green days. I am a reformed character, as you are perfectly aware.'

'So you do not need a rich wife?'

He smiled, unable to resist teasing her, knowing she never took offence and would give back as good as she got. 'Oh, I would not turn one down simply because she was rich, all other considerations being in her favour.'

'What other considerations?'

'Her temperament. She would have to be beautiful and biddable too. I could not abide living under the cat's paw.'

Surprisingly she did not rise to his bait. Instead she said, 'And do you not think Lord Wincote might have the same sentiments?'

'I am not privy to his sentiments, Vinny.'

'Nor, as far as I can tell, to his true situation. Not that it matters, money is not important...'

'Only because you have never felt the want of it.'

'I told you before, I shall marry only when I fall in love. And if I fall in love with a pauper, so be it.'

'Not with him, surely? He is not worthy of you.'

'I shall say who is worthy and who is not.' Her temper was up and he ought to have known better than goad her, because it only made her more determined to further the acquaintance of the young man in question. Too late, he realised the wisdom of silence and drew up at the door of Stanmore House without saying another word.

He jumped down and strode round the phaeton to help her alight. She jumped from the last step and almost fell into his arms. He caught her and held just a fraction longer than he ought to have done, but the feel of her lovely body so close against his sent tremors of desire through him and he wanted to savour the feeling as long as he dared.

'Will you come in?' she asked, looking up into his grey eyes and seeing there a look which she could not fathom. It was sadness and tenderness and humour all mixed up together and it confused her. And there was a strange twist to his mouth as if he wanted to smile, but could not, which made her want to ask him what troubled him and to comfort him. 'Mama might be back.'

He released her reluctantly. 'Does that mean I am forgiven?'

'Of course it does, silly.' The fleeting moment of intimacy was gone. 'But you must make recompense.'

'Oh?' He raised one eyebrow. 'And what might that be?'

'Take me out in the phaeton again.'

'Of course. It will be my pleasure.'

'Tomorrow. Early. Seven o'clock.'

'Now, Vinny, I never said—'

'You said you would think about it and now you have thought and have decided that there cannot possibly be any harm in letting me take the ribbons in a deserted park. You think you might even enjoy teaching me, always supposing you manage to rise early enough.'

'Oh, so you are privy to my thoughts, are you?'

'Of course. You are an open book to me.'

He did not think so, or she would have read the love in his heart, a love which had grown and matured ever since that day, three years before, when he had been introduced to her. His stepmother, who had an unerring sixth sense where he was concerned, had warned him that Lavinia was far too young to be thinking of marriage and, as he was often in one sort of scrape or another, the Duke would never countenance him as a son-in-law until he mended his ways.

Mending his ways had been easy; after all, his misdemeanours had been minor ones, all part of the process of growing into manhood. Changing the way Lavinia looked at him was far harder. She was as elusive as a butterfly, there to be seen and admired, laughing with him, sharing confidences, expecting him to pull her out scrapes, but likely to flit away without warning, leaving him empty-handed. He sighed, just as the Loscoe barouche drew up beside them and the Duchess alighted.

'James, I had no idea you were in town.' Almost thirty-eight years old, Frances, Duchess of Loscoe, was as elegantly beautiful and as full of life as a girl half her age.

'I arrived yesterday, Mama, and, hearing you were here, I came to pay my respects.'

'And found only Lavinia at home. I am sorry. If I had known…' She paused to look at the phaeton, while her groom unloaded armfuls of parcels from her carriage and took them into the house. 'Did you arrive in that?'

'Yes. I bought it for a song. Its first owner grew tired of it.' He could not rid himself of the habit of justifying his purchases to her. If it had not been for her careful supervision when he was growing up, he would have dissipated his inheritance before it had been in his hands five minutes. Now, long after he had learned more sense, the habit remained.

'I am not surprised. It looks very dangerous.'

'No, it isn't, Mama,' Lavinia put in. 'But it is very exhilarating to ride in.'

'By that am I to assume you have been for a ride in it?'

'Only a very little one to the park and James drove very sedately, I promise you.'

Frances made no comment as she led the way into the house and ordered refreshments to be brought to the drawing room. Then she took off her gloves and hat, carefully stroking the long curled feather into place before handing them both to a footman.

'Now, tell me all your news,' she commanded her stepson when all three were sitting comfortably with cups of tea in their hands. 'There is nothing wrong at Twelvetrees, is there?'

'No, but being a country landlord can be very trying at times, especially with the economy in the state it is. I felt like a little diversion.'

'You would not feel like that if you were married.'

'I cannot see how being married would make any difference to the work of the estate.'

'No, but you might not find is so trying if you had a wife and children to fulfil you.'

'Oh, Mama, not again, please. I promise to make a push on the matter this Season, will that satisfy you?' He looked at Lavinia as he spoke, but she was smiling to herself and stroking the tortoiseshell cat which had climbed on to her knee, apparently completely unperturbed. If the Duke were to enter the room the cat would be gone like a streak of lightning.

'For the moment. I do not suppose you have been in town long enough to receive any invitations yet.'

'No, but I do not doubt word will soon go round and I will be besieged. Tell me what is planned and where you will be going, then I shall know whom to accept.'

'Lady Graham is holding a ball…'

'Don't tell me Constance is not off her hands yet. This must be the third year she has tried to fire her off.'

'James, I wish you would not be so vulgar,' Frances said. 'Poor Constance cannot help being plain, but I am sure some young man will recognise her worth before long.'

'Well, it will not be me, so you may put that idea from

your mind. But if I am invited, then I shall go, if only to dance with you.'

'And me,' Lavinia put in.

He inclined his head towards her. 'That goes without saying, my dear. Now, what else is there?'

Although the Season was half over, the Duchess reeled off a catalogue of events, from musical soirées and routs to balls and picnics, not to mention a visit to the opera and another to Vauxhall Gardens. 'That is, if this wretched business with the Queen doesn't upset everyone's plans.'

'Then I shall look forward to seeing much more of you both.'

Lavinia began to laugh and they both turned to her in puzzlement. 'What have I said that is so comical?' he asked.

'You have just said the same thing as Lord Wincote and in him you condemned it as bold and desperate. Are you desperate, my lord?'

'Certainly not.' Unwilling to enter into a discussion on the topic, he stood up. 'Now, if you will excuse me, I must leave you both.'

Lavinia sprang to her feet. 'I will come to see you off, James.'

He smiled, took his leave of his stepmother, then left the room, followed by Lavinia. At the outer door, she took his hat and gloves from the footman and handed them to him. Her eyes were alight with mischief. 'I shall see you tomorrow at seven round the corner in the mews,' she whispered. 'We do not want to wake the household, do we?'

'Vinny, I do not think—'

Before he could go on, she had pushed him towards the door. 'Good afternoon, my lord.' He suddenly found him-self on the step and the door firmly closed behind him. It was a situation he would never have put up with from anyone else; any other young lady treating him in that cavalier fashion would have been dropped immediately. But Lavinia was different. Lavinia was Lavinia, self-willed, to be sure, but there wasn't an ounce of malice in her body; she had not meant it as a put-down, simply a way of preventing him from arguing.

He clamped his hat on his head, strode to the phaeton, climbed in and drove off, smiling to himself at the prospect of teaching her to drive it.

'Vinny, what was all that about?' Frances asked when Lavinia rejoined her. 'Have you quarrelled with James?'

'No, Mama.' And Vinny, who did not see the need to hide it, told her about the encounter with Lord Wincote and James's reaction.

'He was only trying to protect you,' her ladyship said. 'You know he is very fond of you.'

'That does not mean he may act as a substitute father. I am not such a ninnyhammer as to fall under the spell of the first man who pays me attention.'

The Duchess laughed. 'No, for you demonstrated that very clearly when you had your come-out. Your dear papa thought you were being too particular.'

'But you did not, did you? You know how important it is to feel comfortable and at ease with one's choice.'

'Of course. But there are other things to consider.'

Lavinia laughed. 'Oh, I know. Good looks and mutual interests and money. I have heard it all before. But I want to be in love. You and Papa were in love, weren't you?'

'Yes, of course. We still are.'

'Then you will understand.'

'Yes, but you have only just met Lord Wincote. You surely do not think you are in love with him?'

'No, how could I be? I have barely exchanged half a dozen words with him. I simply wanted to tease James.' What she did not say was that Edmund Wincote had the most mesmeric eyes she had ever come across. They seemed to have the power to turn her usually iron will to jelly. She wanted to see him again to be sure she had not dreamed it. And if she had not, to explore where the feeling would take her, James's disapproval notwithstanding.

'Teasing people,' Frances said slowly. 'has been known to rebound on the one doing the teasing.'

'I know, but James asks for it. He is so…so…*stiff* sometimes.'

The Duchess laughed. 'That is the last word I would use to describe him. What is it you do to him to make him behave so out of character?' The question was a rhetorical one; Lady Loscoe had a very good idea, but it was not for her to point it out. She decided to change the subject. 'When I left the house this morning, you were intent on doing some painting. How did it go?'

Lavinia scrambled to her feet, her eyes alight with enthusiasm, James and Lord Wincote both forgotten. 'Come with me and I will show you.'

She led the way down to the ground floor ballroom and flung open the door. 'There! What do you think of it?'

Frances stood and surveyed the great canvas in surprise for a full minute, then she said, 'Lavinia, why is it so big?'

'It is a backcloth to a play.'

'Oh. Have you been commissioned to paint it?' Frances herself took commissions for all sorts of subjects, most of them family portraits, pets, horses and vistas of people's estates, the proceeds for which she donated to the orphanage fund. Not surprisingly, she had never been asked to make scenery.

'No, I just did it. It is meant for *A Midsummer Night's Dream.*'

'Yes, I can see it would do very well for that, but that doesn't explain why you decided to do it.'

'Mama, you remember the Thespian Players coming to Risley earlier this year?'

'Yes. The Duke allowed them to put a tent up in one of the meadows, I recall.'

'It gave me an idea. I should like to put on a play for our friends and acquaintances and donate the entrance money to the orphanage fund.'

'Oh, I see. It is very commendable, Vinny dear, but have you thought about all the work involved? Where would you find a tent, for a start, and where could you pitch it, considering we are in London, quite apart from providing costumes and seating and finding people to act in it?'

'They are not insurmountable problems. And I did not think we should need a tent, we could use this ballroom...'

'Vinny, I am not at all sure your father would allow that.'

'He would if you asked him. It would only be for one night and we would charge an astronomical amount to come in, so it would be very select. No riff-raff. I have worked it all out, expenditure and income, just as you taught me.'

Frances smiled. 'Oh, I have no doubt you have and now you think you can wind me round your thumb and make a conspirator of me.'

'Oh, it will be such fun! Do say you agree.'

'I shall have to think about it. Whom else do you plan to involve?'

'James—'

'James?' she queried in surprise. 'Has he agreed?'

'Not exactly, but he will,' she said confidently. 'And

then there is Duncan and Constance…' She reeled off a list of her friends, being careful not to mention Lancelot Greatorex. 'Augusta and her two little ones, who would make beautiful fairies, if they can be schooled in their parts…' Augusta was James's sister. She was married to Sir Richard Harnham and had two delightful children, Andrew and Beth.

'*A Midsummer Night's Dream* is a difficult play for amateurs, Vinny.'

'Oh, I plan to condense it. If I leave out the play within the play and stick to the love story, I shall not need so many players. I might even try and simplify the language and set it in modern times.'

'Might you, indeed!' Her stepmother laughed. 'You are certainly not lacking in pluck if you imagine you can improve on Shakespeare.'

'So you do agree?'

'Vinny, I commend your enthusiasm, I really do, but you know there is so much going on in town this summer, I cannot help but feel you will be playing to an empty room.'

'No, for we shall do it after all the fuss over the coronation is over.'

'But that is not until the first of August—the Season will be over by then and everyone will start going home to the country.'

'If there is a coronation. James is not at all sure there will be but, in any case, no one will leave town until something is resolved. Everyone will still be fired up with nothing to divert them. There will be a kind of vacuum and we shall be there to fill it. Oh, please say yes.'

'I shall have to talk to the Duke.'

'Of course,' Lavinia said, hoping that her father would be too distracted to pay much attention to what his wife was asking and would give the nod without thinking too deeply about it. And once rehearsals were under way and it became apparent that they needed professional help, she could introduce the idea of asking Mr Greatorex to step in. She decided to let the matter rest for the time being and began talking about Lady Graham's ball.

'You owe me five guineas,' Lavinia said as soon as she had climbed into the phaeton beside James the following morning. It was very early indeed and there was little traffic on the road: a couple of milkmaids were driving their cows from Green Park to the houses where the milk would be sold direct from cow to kitchen maid's jug; a chimney sweep was striding down the street, his poles and brushes over his shoulder, followed by his tiny assistant scampering to keep up with him; a hackney cab carried a late reveller home; a marauding mongrel and a pair of spitting cats were determined on disturbing the peace.

James took his attention from his driving long enough to turn and look at her. Early as it was, she was looking gloriously vibrant. Her gown was covered by a long cloak whose hood was flung back to reveal her thick chestnut-coloured hair. Not wanting to involve her maid, she had endeavoured to tie it back with a ribbon but several shorter strands had escaped and curled about her ears and neck. Excitement made her green eyes sparkle like emeralds and the early morning air, so much fresher than the heat in the middle of the day, had made her cheeks rosy.

He was almost breathless with longing, but he managed a cool, 'By that, am I to assume you turned your papa up sweet and he has agreed to allow you to use the ballroom for your play?'

'Yes, I told you he would, did I not?'

'There must be a proviso or something of the sort.'

'No, not at all,' she said, smiling broadly, revealing perfect white teeth. 'I told you he would not stand against Mama, didn't I? She asked him when he came home last night.'

'Then you did not speak to him yourself. I am not sure that doesn't invalidate the wager.'

'I did not undertake to ask him myself. I distinctly remember telling you I would get Mama on my side.'

'Then I suppose I had better pay up.' He sighed and turned into the park gates. There was no one about except a few horsemen, galloping across the grass, and a drunken reveller rolling home on foot, his top hat over one eye and his cravat awry. 'But I cannot help feeling there is something you have not told me. What about this play actor, Lancelot the Great or whatever he is called? Is he to be made welcome?'

'He will be.'

He laughed suddenly. 'You did not even mention him, did you?'

'No, one step at a time. And we didn't make any stipulations about him in the wager, either.' She paused. 'Come on, James, admit you have lost.'

He pulled the horses to a stop, extracted a purse from his coat pocket and gave her five guineas from it. 'There, does that satisfy you?'

She dropped the coins into her reticule. 'No, for it was not the wager that brought me out this morning. Did you think you could make me forget that you promised to hand over the ribbons?'

'I made no such promise.'

'Oh, come along, James, you know it is what I want to do above all things.'

'What! Even above acting in one of Shakespeare's plays?'

'At this moment, yes.'

'Very well.' He gave her the reins. He did not relinquish complete control, but laid his hands over hers to guide her. Even that small touch sent desire coursing through him and made him wonder how he was going to be able to hold on to his self possession. 'Slowly, now, and keep the inside horse away from the verge. It is running wheels over bumps and slopes that turns these things over.'

'I know. You do not need to guide me.'

Reluctantly he took his hand away and they proceeded along the carriageway at a walk which soon became a brisk trot, but when she would have set the horses to canter, he put a hand out to restrain her. 'That's enough for today, Vinny. Even I would not be such a bufflehead as to go faster here.'

Reluctantly she slowed the horses. 'Thank you, James. You are the dearest of men.'

He did not reply. He knew she did not mean the endearment in the way he wanted her to mean it, but it gave him a glow of satisfaction, even so. And then his smile faded as he saw Edmund Wincote riding straight towards them.

He would have liked to pretend they had not seen him, but his lordship was determined he would be acknowledged and reined in almost across their path, startling their horses. Fearing Lavinia would not be equal to the task, James grabbed the reins, which Lavinia was reluctant to relinquish. For a moment it confused the horses and they began pulling in different directions. It took all his considerable skill to regain control of them. As it was, Lavinia was jolted almost out of her seat and her hat went flying.

'You fool, Wincote!' James said, hauling the horses to a stop. 'You could have had us over. As it is you have frightened Lady Lavinia half to death.'

'Have I?' the young man said, addressing Lavinia and doffing his riding hat, apparently unperturbed. 'Then I beg your pardon, my lady.'

'Think no more of it,' she said smoothly, though she was shaking. She was not sure if it was caused by what could have been a nasty accident or meeting him again so soon. 'I should have pulled up sooner.'

He dismounted and retrieved her hat. 'I did not expect to see a carriage in the park so early, especially one with so dexterous and decorative a whipster.'

'Why not?' She favoured him with a smile. 'I like to rise early. It is the best time of the day, before the heat becomes unbearable, don't you agree?'

'Oh, indeed.' He gave her back her hat and watched admiringly as she put it on and tied the ribbons. 'May I call on you and your mama later? I would wish to assure myself you have had no ill effects from the fright I gave you.'

'That will not be necessary,' James put in quickly. 'You can see her ladyship has come to no harm.'

Wincote grinned knowingly. 'Oh, I understand. Rest assured your secret is safe with me, Corringham. I wish you good day, my lady.' And with that he wheeled away.

'What did he mean by that?' Lavinia asked, as they continued on their way.

'He imagines we crept out for a secret assignation.'

She laughed. 'Then he was not so far wrong, was he?'

'He was a very long way from being right,' he said grimly. Far from their secret being safe, he had a notion it would be all over town by evening.

Chapter Two

Lord Edmund Wincote was not in the least put off by James's antagonism; he arrived at Stanmore House that afternoon, only to discover that the Duchess was 'at home' and the house was filled with callers, all taking tea and all talking at once.

Lavinia, clad in a pale green silk gown, its high waist delineated with a band of cream velvet, heard him being announced above the noise and hurried over to make him welcome. 'Lord Wincote, how nice to see you. Do let me present you to the Duchess.'

She led him forward to where the Duchess was talking to a group of ladies, together with Sir Percival Ponsonby, who always dressed flamboyantly in glaring unmatched colours, but was, for all that, held in great affection and esteem by the Duchess. Today he was in a very old-fashioned puce coat and green breeches. His grey hair was worn long and tied in a tail with a narrow black ribbon.

'The King is playing least in sight while his wife is seen everywhere,' Lady Willoughby was saying. She was enormously fat, though apparently unaware of it. Frances had once painted a portrait of her, which she loved because it depicted her flatteringly rounded and without her many chins. The Duke, however, had said the Duchess had be-littled herself and her art to do it. 'I do believe she enjoys putting the King to the blush.'

'I really do not know how she has the effrontery to come back to England,' Lady Graham put in. 'I heard the King had offered her thousands of pounds to stay away…'

Percy laughed, at home among the female company. 'Well, if he did it has made no difference; she is here.'

'I heard the King will not allow her to live in any of the Royal palaces and the Lord Mayor has offered her his home,' Mrs Butterworth added her contribution to the gossip.

'More fool he. It will do him no good.'

'Mama,' Lavinia said, taking advantage of a lull in the conversation. 'May I present Lord Edmund Wincote?'

'Why, of course.' The Duchess turned to him at once, smiling a welcome. 'How do you do, Lord Wincote?'

He took her hand and bowed over it with precise courtesy. 'I am honoured, your Grace.'

'Are you come to town for the festivities?'

'That was my intent, my lady. I have a friend whose house overlooks the route of the procession and he was kind enough to invite me to join his guests. In the meantime, I have taken lodgings in Mount Street and plan to enjoy whatever London has to offer in the way of entertainment. I was riding in the park yesterday when I chanced upon my old friend the Earl of Corringham and Lady Lavinia. He was so good as to present me to her ladyship. I came to pay my respects. I hope I do not intrude.'

Lavinia was relieved when he did not also mention their second meeting when she had been driving the phaeton. She did not want a scolding over her hoydenish behaviour.

'Not at all, my lord,' the Duchess said. 'You are welcome. May I present Lady Willoughby, Lady Graham and her daughter, Miss Constance Graham, Mrs Butterworth and Sir Percival Ponsonby.' She indicated each in turn. 'Lord Edmund Wincote.' He bowed in acknowledgement, repeating their names politely as he did so.

'Wincote?' Lady Willoughby queried. 'I am not sure I know that name. Where are you from?' Lord Willoughby was the first of his line to be elevated to the peerage and, though very wealthy, had no country estate, so the family lived in London the whole year round. Lady Willoughby was convinced that gave her a special knowledge of who was who and how often they visited the capital.

'Cumberland, my lady,' he answered, not put off by her forthright manner. 'After my father died, my brother John and I lived with our grandfather. He was in poor health the last few years of his life and rarely travelled. And since the demise of my elder bother, he liked to keep me by him to look after the estate. Sadly, he died earlier this year.'

'That accounts for it,' the lady said, apparently satisfied. 'Is your wife with you?'

It was obvious to all that if his wife was in London she would have accompanied him on afternoon calls, but it was Lady Willoughby's way of ascertaining if he were married, a most important consideration.

'I have no wife, my lady. But perhaps I shall soon remedy the deficiency.'

'We must take you round and introduce you to people,' Lavinia said to cover the uncomfortable silence that followed this. 'Perhaps we can contrive invitations for you.'

'Thank you, my lady.'

'I wonder if the Queen will attend any functions,' Lady Willoughby said. And then said to Lady Graham, 'Do you expect her to make an appearance at your ball?'

'Good gracious, no.' Her ladyship affected a shudder of

revulsion. 'I cannot imagine anything worse than the up-heaval that would cause. Constance would hate it, wouldn't you, my love?'

'Yes, Mama,' the young lady said. She had mousy hair, and a pale face rather devoid of animation, although she had good bone structure and an enviable figure beneath the plain blue gown she wore.

'And what about you, Duchess?' Lady Graham went on as if her daughter had not spoken. 'Are you expected to entertain Royalty this Season?'

'I think not. It would compromise the Duke, who is trying very hard to be impartial, though we are obliged to attend the King's official birthday reception at Carlton House tomorrow evening.'

During all this chatter Lavinia was acutely aware of the handsome figure standing beside her. Although he stood quite still and smiled occasionally as one or the other spoke, there was a kind of aura of energy about him. It was almost as if he were longing to make some point in the conversation, but was holding back for fear of giving offence. And after Lady Willoughby's grilling, she admired him for it. 'Lord Wincote, do you like to act?' she asked.

'Act, my lady?' he queried, taken by surprise.

'Yes, play acting. I am going to put on *A Midsummer Night's Dream* to raise money for the Duchess's favourite charity. I would welcome more people taking part.'

'I have no experience of acting, my lady.'

'Oh, that does not signify. I am sure you must have played charades…'

'Why, yes, in my youth.'

'There you are, then!' she said triumphantly. 'Do say you will join us.'

He bowed. 'I shall be honoured, my lady.'

'Thank you,' she said, giving him one of her dazzling smiles. 'Constance, will you take part?'

'If you think I have anything to offer, I will.' Constance spoke quietly as she always did and Lavinia wondered how she could be persuaded to project her voice so that an audience could hear her. Perhaps Mr Greatorex would school her.

'Of course you have. And you, too, Sir Percy.'

'Me?' he queried. 'Why, my dear, I can act nothing but the part of Sir Percival Ponsonby.'

She laughed. 'That is all I ask, but Sir Percy might need a new name for an evening. How does Theseus, Duke of Athens, sound to you?'

'But I am useless at getting words by rote.'

'Oh, you do not have too much to say and Stepmama will rehearse you, won't you, Mama?'

Before the Duchess could answer, the butler announced the arrival of the Earl of Corringham and James sauntered into the room, dressed in light wool fawn-coloured frock coat, cream brocade waistcoat and white lawn cravat in which a diamond pin gleamed. He came forward to bow over his stepmother's hand, then turned to greet the ladies and Percy, all of whom he knew well.

He left Lavinia until last. 'Lady Lavinia, your servant,' he said, bowing formally and making her want to giggle. He could be so pompous at times.

'James, I did not expect you,' Frances said, looking quizzically from stepdaughter to stepson. 'Twice in two days is so out of the ordinary that I begin to wonder what the attraction might be.'

'Why, you, Mama. And the delightful company you keep.'

'Gammon! Now ring for more tea, for this has gone stone cold.'

He did as she asked, pretending a nonchalance he did not feel. He wanted to know what Wincote was up to. He could feel the tension in the air and knew it had not been occasioned by his arrival; it had been swirling about before that. 'Did I hear you talking about Lady Lavinia's play?'

'Yes,' Lavinia said. 'Lord Wincote has agreed to take a part in it.'

'Indeed?' He turned to Edmund and managed to convey a wealth of meaning in the tone of his voice and the way he lifted one eyebrow. 'I hope you realise what you have undertaken, Wincote. Lady Lavinia can be a dreadful bully, you know.'

'I find that difficult to believe, but if it be so, then I shall feel honoured to be bullied by so charming a director.'

'And what part have you been given?'

'None yet, but it is of no consequence. I will try my utmost in whatever part I am asked to play.'

'I do not doubt you will,' James murmured under his breath. Aloud he addressed Frances. 'Has the Duke really given his blessing?'

'Yes. Why should he not? It is only for the amusement of family and friends.'

'Oh, is that all?' He turned and grinned at Lavinia, sharing her secret; not for a moment would he betray her by mentioning Lancelot Greatorex. 'So you will need a scene shifter?'

'Yes, but do not think you can escape so lightly, James,' she said. 'You must take a role.'

'Oh, no.' He watched as the maid returned with freshly made tea and the Duchess filled a cup and handed it to him. 'I would be no good.'

'Why not? If Sir Percy and Duncan and Constance can do it—'

'Hold your horses,' Percy put in. 'I never said I would. I am too old for such capers.'

'But I need one or two older people. Someone must play the Duke of Athens and Egeus, Hermia's father. It would look silly if they were young boys. That is why I need you and James.'

'You need me because I am *old*?' James said, affronted.

'No, but you can *act* old, you do it all the time,' she said, a statement which made the Duchess laugh aloud. 'And we can paint your face with a few wrinkles.'

He turned to Edmund and spread his hands. 'See what I mean about being a bully.'

'Her ladyship would not need to bully if you were more willing,' Edmund said.

'True, true,' he admitted with an exaggerated sigh. 'But I do not subscribe to the view that the ladies should have their own way all the time.'

'Which is, I am persuaded, why you are still single,' Lavinia retorted. 'Now, do not be a spoil sport, or I shall not speak to you again for…for at least a month.'

'Good,' he said promptly.

'James!' Frances chided him.

'Oh, very well, Mama. I suppose I will have no peace until I agree.'

He had never had any intention of refusing her, especially knowing that Edmund Wincote was to be in the cast, but he could not resist teasing her. He did not know why he did it; it certainly did not promote his cause. If he were more serious, more careful of her sensibilities, and treated her more like a woman instead of a mischievous child, she might look at him differently. Almost every time they met he began with the intention of acting like a proper suitor, but something always intervened: either they roasted each other, or she said something to affront him, and they ended brangling.

'Splendid!' Lavinia said, smiling at him and quite over-turning his bad mood. 'You can begin learning Egeus's lines, ready for our first rehearsal.'

'And when is that to be?'

'I do not know yet. I will let you know when I have all the characters decided on. Duncan has agreed to be Oberon. I asked him yesterday.'

'Is that all you have so far? It is years since I read the play, but surely there are many more characters?'

'Yes, there are, but leave them to me.'

'And are you to direct us, my lady?' James asked, still unable to refrain from teasing her. 'As well as acting and painting the scenery and no doubt sewing all the costumes—'

'James, you know very well I cannot sew. You must all be responsible for your own costumes.'

'I do hope you are not going to begin these rehearsals before our ball,' Constance said doubtfully. 'I do not think I could concentrate on anything else before then.'

'No, of course not. We have plenty of time. The performance is not to be until after the coronation.'

'Oh, then it will not interfere with the Season.'

'No, except that it would be advantageous if everyone knew their parts.'

'Which part would you wish me to learn?'

'Do you think you can manage Helena?' It was a large role and might be beyond Constance, but so far Lavinia could think of no one else to fill it.

'If it is a big part, I would as lief you found someone else and let me stay in the background.'

'I know you are not one to put yourself forward, Miss

Graham,' James said, with a gentle smile. 'But I am quite sure you are equal to the challenge.'

Constance blushed crimson, but could find nothing to say except to thank him without daring to look at him.

'Corringham, I did not know you were coming to town or I would have sent you an invitation to the ball with all the others,' Lady Graham said, tapping him on the arm with her fan. 'You will be able to come, won't you? It is to be on Wednesday, the fifth of July.'

He bowed. 'I shall look forward to it. Now, if you will excuse me, I shall take my leave. I have some business to attend to.' He was reluctant to go while Wincote remained but he had undertaken to look over a couple of horses at Tattersall's and was expected. There were to be some races on Hampstead Heath in a couple of weeks' time and he had been foolish enough to enter and make a wager on the outcome. The stakes were minimal; he had no intention of falling back into his old ways; it was more a question of pride, but he needed a prime mount to win.

It was only after he had left that Constance drew her mother to one side and whispered in her ear, which resulted in Lady Graham finding an opportunity of speaking to Frances when Edmund was engaged in being pleasant to Mrs Butterworth. 'What do you know of Wincote's background, my lady? Is he a proper kind of person to invite to a gathering like our ball? Constance seems to think we should include him…'

'I really know nothing about him, except that he is known to James. Perhaps you should have taken the opportunity to ask James while he was here.'

'Oh, I could not do that. It would have looked so obvious that I was checking on him. But he has delightful manners, has he not? And I can see no harm coming from it. And Mount Street is a respectable address, don't you think?' Without waiting for a reply, she went on. 'I think I shall go and ask his exact direction so that I can send him an invitation. Poor Constance is so anxious...'

'No more anxious than her mama,' Lavinia whispered, as the lady hurried away in the direction of Lord Wincote. 'I do feel sorry for Constance. Lady Graham sets her sights so high, is it any wonder she is constantly disappointed? James said it is because Lord Graham is in dun territory and must have a wealthy son-in-law.'

'James does not know everything, Vinny, and it is unwise of you to repeat it.'

'I only said it to you, I would not dream of repeating it to anyone else.' She stopped speaking as Edmund, having stayed the customary time, approached to take his leave. The other ladies, having heard Lady Graham extending her invitation, had decided that he must be acceptable in Society and had besieged him with their own offerings, which he had accepted with great politeness and due gratitude.

'Your Grace.' He bowed. 'I cannot remember when I spent so agreeable an afternoon. And to be received by your friends is indeed an honour. I shall perhaps see you at Lady Willoughby's on Friday evening?'

'I shall look forward to it,' her ladyship said, offering him her hand, which he took and bowed over, before affording Lavinia the same courtesy. And then, smiling, he was gone, leaving a babble of conversation behind him.

'Such a pleasant young gentleman.'

'And so handsome.'

'Perfect manners,' Lady Graham added. 'He may have come from the north country, but his address cannot be faulted.'

'How did James come to know him?' Percy asked Lavinia.

'He did not say. I imagined they were at school together.'

'But James is at least three years older than he is. I
would hardly have expected them to be associates.'

'Well, I do not know. If you are so curious, why didn't
you ask him?'

'Not polite to quiz him in your mama's drawing room,
don't you know?'

'No, but it does not stop people from talking about him
behind his back. Just listen to them!'

It seemed the whole room was buzzing with talk of the
new arrival and Lavinia felt a certain sense of triumph that
she had seen him first. The faint mystery about him served
only to intrigue and excite her. That James did not like
him she was well aware, but put it down to the fact that
the man was young and handsome and everyone was falling over themselves to be agreeable to him. James's nose
had been quite put out of joint, though why he should care
she could not fathom. He had always been laconically indifferent to what others thought of him.

'Yes, and I think it is time the party broke up,' he said.
'Fanny, I shall set a good example and take my leave.' He
bowed to the Duchess and left. Very soon everyone else
drifted away, leaving Lavinia and her stepmother to dress
for dinner and await the arrival of the Duke.

Lord Wincote appeared at Lady Willoughby's soirée on
Friday, his dress and manners as impeccable as before,
though the day had been hotter than ever. Having been
greeted by his hostess and exchanged pleasantries with the
Duchess, he made a beeline for Lavinia and stayed by her
side most of the evening, engaging her in small talk and
pretty compliments.

'The last three days have certainly been worth the effort

of making the journey to London,' he told her. 'Such pleasant acquaintances I have made since my arrival and none more agreeable than your good self. I am overwhelmed by your kindness to me.'

'I have not been particularly kind,' she said. Unable to meet his gaze, she was pretending to look about her at the company, though the tension in her body was enough to tell him she was not indifferent to him.

'Allow me to disagree, my lady. For someone who is a stranger to the capital with nothing but my good name to commend me, I have been made most welcome. And it is all down to you.'

'Fustian!' She turned then and smiled at him. 'Please do not be so formal. I shall begin to think you are as stiff as James.'

'The Earl of Corringham,' he said thoughtfully. 'A very agreeable gentleman, though I collect he likes to tease.'

'Yes, but I take no note of it. He is like a dear brother, though of course we are not related.'

'Oh, are you not?'

She looked sharply at him. 'No. The Duchess was his stepmother before she was mine. I am surprised you did not know that.'

'I must have done, but I had forgot. Living so far from London, I am not up to date with events, you understand. My grandfather was something of a recluse.'

'Then where and when did you meet James?'

'My brother introduced us when I went up to Cambridge, seven years ago now. Henry, like the Earl, was three years older than me and they were almost at the end of their time there. They were friends, but so far above me as to be indifferent to my presence. I was surprised his lordship even remembered me. Henry died the following year, which made me my grandfather's heir; after Henry's funeral, I did not return to my studies but stayed at Grandfather's side until I came into my inheritance earlier this year.'

'I see. And you never came to London while you were at Cambridge?'

'No, as I said, I was not there very long. My last visit to the capital must have been…goodness, I have forgotten the date, it was so long ago.'

'You must find it much changed.'

'Oh, yes, indeed. There are so many new buildings and more being built; whole streets have disappeared and new ones put in their place, all in excellent taste. I particularly like the use of trees to line the roads and the gas lighting which makes moving about at night so much safer.'

'Yes, that is one thing I suppose we must thank his Majesty for.'

'I have seen articles and caricatures in the newspapers, of course, but until I arrived here, I had not realised the contempt in which he is held…'

'Only by some. And it is not so much contempt as ridicule. He is so very, very fat.'

'I saw the Queen yesterday as I was leaving my lodgings in Mount Street. There we saw so many people crowding round and cheering her, I was unable to make a way through them until she had entered her carriage and been driven away.'

'I believe it happens every time she stirs outside. If it were not for Stepmama being here and needing my company, I should return to our country estate in Derbyshire.'

'I do hope you will not. I have been looking forward to furthering our acquaintance.'

'Really?'

'Yes, but you must know that already.' He paused, then went on, apparently plucking up his courage. 'Having but lately arrived, I have not yet acquired a carriage, or I would have begged the favour of being allowed to drive you out.'

She laughed suddenly. 'What, at seven in the morning?'

'No, not at all, that would be highly improper and if I did not know you are incapable of the slightest unkindness, I might be tempted to believe you were making a May game of me…'

'Oh, no, my lord, I beg your pardon—I am so used to roasting James. It *was* very unkind of me. Please forgive me.'

'Of course. How could I refuse?' He smiled. If James had been there he would have described it as a smile of triumph, but Lavinia took it at face value. 'I had in mind a gentle hack along Rotten Row, at a suitably respectable hour,' he went on. 'Shall we say, half past ten, tomorrow morning?'

'Are you always so careful of protocol, my lord?'

'I am a stranger in your midst, my lady, I cannot flout convention until I am established and then I would do so with the greatest care not to upset those whose regard I value.'

She was reminded of his comment when meeting her driving James's phaeton, that their secret was safe with him, and wondered if he was referring to that. 'My lord, if you are implying that I should not have accompanied Lord Corringham in his phaeton—'

'No, indeed not, my lady. You have explained he is regarded as your brother and none but the worst gabble grinder would infer anything else. I simply meant I wished to be correct.'

'In that case, you will want to ask the Duchess for her permission to take me riding. It is no good speaking to Papa, he is never at home these days.'

'Naturally, I will, as soon as you give me leave.'

'You have it. I shall be delighted to ride with you.'

He hurried off to importune Frances, leaving Lavinia, smiling to herself at his seriousness.

'Lady Lavinia, your obedient.'

Lavinia turned to find Benedict Willoughby at her elbow. She did not like the young man, who had tried forcing his attentions on her years before. She had been saved by Frances and James, but not before she had slapped his face and his cheek had been cut by her ring, an injury that kept him indoors for a week. He had only been seventeen at the time and trying his wings, but she was sure he had not forgotten it any more than she had, even though he had apologised and she had forgiven him for Duncan's sake.

'Mr Willoughby.'

'I came to ask if I might take a part in your play. Duncan says it is going to be great fun and, if he is much occupied with rehearsals, I shall see nothing of him all Season.'

'Yes, I can quite imagine you would expect to find some fun in it and possibly at my expense.'

'Oh, my lady, you wrong me. I have wanted to do something of the sort for an age.'

'Oh, Vinny, let the young shaver have a part.' James had strolled over to join them and heard the young man's request. 'You cannot afford to be particular, you know.'

'James, I did not expect to see you here.'

'Must I always give notice of where I intend to be, so that I may always be expected?'

'No, don't be silly.'

He looked from her to Benedict, who was still waiting for his answer, then back to her. Whether it was the warmth of the room or the glass of wine she had consumed or simply that he had flustered her, he did not know, but she had a delightfully heightened colour and her green eyes sparkled with vivacity. Her gown of cream Michelin lace over a matching silk slip followed the lines of her figure so that he was hard put not to stare. 'Well, are you going to keep him in suspense all night?'

'Oh, very well,' she said. 'You can be Bottom, Mr Willoughby.'

'Bottom!' Benedict exclaimed. 'Isn't he the one who wears an ass's head?'

'Yes, but it is a good part and you will have Titania fall in love with you.'

'Who will be Titania?'

'I don't know yet.' She smiled suddenly. 'I will find someone young and pretty for you. So, will you do it?'

'Very well,' he said, bowing and leaving them.

'Vinny, you vixen,' James said. 'You enjoyed tormenting him, didn't you?'

'No, I am completely indifferent to him. But you were right, I cannot afford to turn anyone away. You are not going to let me down, are you?'

'Vinny, you know I would never do that…' He paused, watching Lord Wincote threading his way through the throng towards them. 'And I sincerely hope others will not either.'

She noticed the direction of his gaze. 'Surely you do not mean Lord Wincote?'

'I meant no one in particular, but if by chance he should do anything to upset you, he will have me to contend with.'

'Why should he upset me?'

He did not have time to answer before the gentleman in question arrived before them. Wincote was smiling broadly. 'My lady, her Grace has been so kind as to say yes, providing you are properly chaperoned, of course.'

'Yes, to what?' James demanded.

Lavinia turned and looked at him in surprise. His question was so abrupt and really it was no business of his. 'Since you ask,' she said levelly. 'I have arranged to ride in the park with Lord Wincote. Now, if you will excuse us, I am going to introduce his lordship to some more of the company. I see Lord Haverley and Mr Drew over there. Perhaps they can be persuaded to join our little production.' And with that, she laid a hand upon Edmund's sleeve and went off with him.

James cursed himself for not watching his tongue; now she was taking a perverse delight in being extra-agreeable to Wincote and that young man was lapping up all the attention. He stood and watched them for a few moments. Wincote was handsome and well dressed, as Lavinia had pointed out to him, and his manners were exquisite. If he had been paying his addresses to Constance Graham or any of the other young ladies, he would have said good luck to him. But Lavinia—no. And was that fair? Lavinia's happiness was all that should matter.

James did not like where his thoughts were taking him and, pushing them from his mind, walked over to talk to his stepmother. 'They make a handsome couple, do they not?' he said, endeavouring to keep his voice neutral.

'Yes, but I am a little uneasy. What do you know of him, James?'

'Nothing at all. After his brother, Henry, introduced us at college, I never saw him again until yesterday. I really cannot vouch for him.'

'Could he be a fortune-hunter? The Duke is so busy nowadays, I do not like to worry him, but it means I must be extra-vigilant on his behalf...'

'Would you like me to make some enquiries?'

'Could you? He has asked to take her riding tomorrow

and I could not withhold my consent for no reason, could I?'

'No, but I assume she will be chaperoned. And the town is so packed with people they will be in someone's view the whole time. Besides, if he is looking to the main chance, he will not do anything to compromise that, will he?'

'No, you are right, but all the same, I would be happier if you were to accompany them.'

'*Me?* You mean me to play the chaperon, Mama?'

'Please.'

'Lavinia will not like it.'

'I am sorry for that, but I will have her protected from her own folly.'

'Very well,' he agreed, but he was not happy about it.

At a quarter past ten the following morning, Lavinia, dressed in a lightweight blue riding habit, nipped into her tiny waist and frogged with silver braid, tripped lightly down the stairs. She sent a servant to the mews to ask Tom Bagshott, one of the grooms, to bring her mare, Misty, to the front of the house.

Riding out with a young man escorted by Tom was nothing unusual; over the last three years there had been many young men of the *ton* anxious to be seen with her and it amused her to set one against the other with a little flirtatious teasing, but today was different. Today there was a sense of anticipation which made her a little breathless, heightened the colour in her cheeks and caused her eyes to sparkle. She was aware of it and yet she did not want to admit that it was because Edmund Wincote had asked her to ride with him.

After all, she told herself, what was he but another young man, one of many trying their luck with the Duke of Loscoe's daughter? Not for the first time, she longed to be a simple country girl, someone who did not have to think about dowries and marriage settlements and fortune-hunters. She wished she could be sure that any young man paying court to her did it out of love.

But if the young man in question was himself rich enough for such things not to count with him, then did it mean she could accept his assurances and allow herself to fall in love? But that was silly, one did not allow oneself to fall in love, it just happened, didn't it? You could not control it. And wasn't she rushing ahead too fast? She had only met Lord Wincote three days before and not by the wildest leap of imagination could she say she knew him.

She had no idea of his likes and dislikes over food, art and literature, whether he was kind or unkind, passionate or dispassionate. But those dark mesmeric eyes were deep enough to hide great passions, she was sure of it, and mysterious enough to hold her in thrall. But how did he truly feel about her in his heart? Standing before a long mirror in the hall, she smiled at herself as she set a plumed riding hat on her chestnut mane; time would tell and, in the meantime, she would enjoy herself.

She heard a knock at the door reverberating through the hall, and only just managed not to run and open it herself. Instead, she turned and went into the drawing room to wait as calmly as she could for Lord Wincote to be announced.

However, it was not Lord Wincote but the Earl of Corringham who entered the room, doffed his tall hat and swept her a bow. 'My lady, your servant.'

She laughed. 'Why the formality, Corringham?'

'It seemed the thing to do, seeing I am here as a formality…'

'Formality?'

'Yes, the Duchess has asked me to be your chaperon this morning.'

'She never has! You are making it up.'

'I am not making it up and, believe me, it was not an errand I sought or wanted, but she asked me and I could not say no, could I?' He had managed to find nothing against Wincote and ought not to judge him on instinct alone; his instinct could very well be at fault. On the other hand, the Duchess's rarely was.

'But why? Tom Bagshott always accompanies me when I ride out. Mama has always been happy about that before.'

'I believe the Duke had an errand for Tom this morning.'

'But why you? There are other servants.'

'My lady, you have cut me to the quick. Am I such a monster that you do not want to be seen out with me? You were ready enough when you wanted to drive my phaeton.'

She leaned back and surveyed him from head to toe. He was dressed in a riding coat of Bath cloth and breeches in the softest tan buckskin tucked into his riding boots. His neckcloth was purest white and tied in a mathematical knot which filled the space between the top of his yellow waistcoat and his smooth, firm chin.

Any young lady would be proud to be seen with him and she was no exception. If it had been anyone but Lord Wincote she was going riding with she would have welcomed him; she might even have invited him to accompany her. But she sensed he and Lord Wincote did not like each other though, as far as she could tell, there was no cause for it. Instead of having a pleasant ride with amusing conversation, they would be trying to score points off one another and she would be pig in the middle.

'I am sorry, James, I love to ride with you and you know

it, but I cannot help thinking there is something smoky going on.'

'Not from me there is not. Nor Mama. If you have a bad conscience—'

'I certainly do not!' They both heard the door knocker at that moment, though neither moved. 'I am going out riding with Lord Wincote. You may come if you please, I cannot stop you, but should you say one word to spoil it, I shall never forgive you.'

'I will remain as silent as the grave.'

'And that will not do either. You will have Lord Wincote think you are sulking. Try to behave naturally.'

He executed an exaggerated leg, denoting his acquiescence without actually saying anything, just as the butler opened the door and announced Lord Wincote.

He strode in, smiling unctuously, and bowed. 'Lady Lavinia.'

'You are punctual, my lord.' She held out her hand which he took.

'No doubt that is down to impatience to be in your company again, my lady.' He glanced round, noticing James for the first time, and his expression darkened momentarily. 'Corringham, good morning.'

James inclined his head. 'Wincote.'

Lavinia looked from one to the other and her heart sank. If this coldness was what she had to put up with for the next couple of hours, it was going to be hard work instead of fun. 'Mama has asked James to accompany us,' she told Edmund, deciding to make the best of it. 'I shall be the envy of the *ton*, having two such *agreeable* escorts.'

James smiled at her. It was a friendly smile, which told her he approved of the way she was handling it and would not let her down. At least, that is what he meant to convey. As long as Wincote acted in a gentlemanly fashion and

Lavinia behaved with decorum, he would remain in the background, difficult as it would be. At least he would be able to observe Lord Wincote's behaviour.

'Come along, then, let us be off,' he said, leading the way to the front of the house where he had left his horse and Lavinia's mare in the care of a groom. Lord Wincote's own mount stood close by. Watched by a fuming Lord Wincote, James cupped hands for Lavinia to mount, which she did, settling herself in the saddle with consummate ease. The two men mounted and, riding one each side of her, they set off for Hyde Park.

The crowds were so thick they found it difficult to do make their way at all; the Ride, when they turned into it, was no better. It was thronged with riders, from men on spirited thoroughbreds, and ladies dressed in the latest frogged habits and plumed hats, right down to toddlers on tiny ponies. They certainly could not trot or canter, which is what Lavinia wanted to do. And the carriage way was even more packed with vehicles of every description: lumbering old-fashioned coaches, barouches, landaus, tilburys, phaetons and curricles. It seemed everyone in town was determined to see and be seen.

'Where have they all come from?' Lavinia asked. 'I never saw so many people out and about.'

'Oh, I expect it is the presence of the Queen in town,' James said, forgetting his intention to remain in the background.

'Well, whatever it is, it has quite spoiled my ride,' Lavinia said. 'Do you think it will be like this all summer long?'

'Undoubtedly it will, at least until after the coronation,' Edmund put in. 'Perhaps we should arrange a day in the country to get away from it all.'

'What a splendid idea! I shall put it to Stepmama as soon as we return.'

'In the meantime, do you think Green Park will be less crowded?'

'Let's go and see,' she said, turning her horse towards the nearest exit which happened to be Hyde Park Gate. It took no time at all to cross the road and enter Green Park which was, as Edmund had predicted, far less crowded. The park was more informal than Hyde Park, with areas of grass on which cows grazed, little copses of trees and winding paths.

'Oh, this is better,' Lavinia said, throwing back her head so that the plume on her hat tickled her cheek. She lifted a gloved hand to brush it away. 'But I really think if one wants to ride properly, it will have to be very early in the morning. To have a good gallop one needs space, do you not agree, Lord Wincote?'

'Now, Vinny,' James murmured. He did not want Wincote reminded that he had met Lavinia out with him at what polite society would consider an unholy hour. As far as he was aware nothing had been noised abroad and he supposed Wincote had decided it would not do to sully the reputation of the young lady on whom he had fixed his attention. But he did not want Wincote to conclude that Lavinia was ready to meet anyone who took her fancy at that early hour.

Although she had had three years' schooling in the ways of the *haut monde*, she was not always aware of the consequences of flouting convention. For James, it was part of her charm and he loved to indulge her, but that did not mean he would sit back and allow her to meet Wincote, or any other young buck, before breakfast.

'Indeed, yes, my lady,' Lord Wincote said. 'But in London, space is at a premium, especially this summer.

Now, up in Cumberland, on our estate near Windermere, it is mostly heathland—'

'I thought it was for the most part water,' James put in, mischievously. 'I do not know about you, but I for one cannot ride on water.'

'James, do not tease,' Lavinia said, then, turning to Lord Wincote, 'Take no note of him, my lord, he is in a very strange mood. Tell me about your estate. What is it called? How many acres does it cover?'

'The house is called Ridgemere, but I am not at all sure of the exact acreage. It used to cover several miles in all directions, but my grandfather reduced the holding before he died. I think there might still be five hundred acres.'

'Heathland?' James queried.

'Three-quarters of it is. It supports a prodigious number of sheep. And below ground there are mines.'

'You own the mining rights?' James queried.

'Yes.' Forestalling more questions, he turned from James to Lavinia. 'One may gallop for miles and hardly meet a soul. I should like you to see it.'

'Perhaps one day I shall,' she said. 'But until then, I must make what I can of the space available.' And with that she dug her spur into Misty's flank and galloped off across the grass. 'Race you to that group of trees,' she shouted behind her and then crouched over her mount and concentrated on riding.

It was a moment or two before the men gathered themselves to follow her and it was James, more used to her ways, who was first off the mark. She could hear the hooves of his stallion behind her and laughed at the sheer exhilaration of it. Not that she could win, she knew she could not. James had the swifter horse and she was handicapped by having to ride side saddle. He overtook her easily and Edmund was drawing abreast as they reached the trees and pulled up.

'You would not have done that if we had been at Risley,' she said, dismounting to rest her horse. 'I would have been riding astride and given you a run for your money.'

'Hoyden!' James laughed as he slid from his horse, followed by Edmund. 'I will put that to the test next time we are there.'

'Done!'

'I am sure I could not take advantage of a lady by beating her,' Edmund said pompously.

'Fustian!' she said.

'Tell you what, Wincote,' James put in. 'If you are so averse to riding against a lady, why not pit yourself against your own sex? Join us on Hampstead Heath in a fortnight's time for some racing. Nothing formal, just a few friends competing against each other for ha'pennies.'

'Very well. I shall be honoured.'

'Oh, good,' Lavinia said. 'We shall organise that day in the country we talked of. The ladies can come and watch. Or,' she added with a chuckle, 'we could hold our own events.'

James sighed. It was just like Lavinia to take what was to have been a purely masculine occasion and turn it into a big event, but she was in such a good humour, her apparent annoyance over his presence dispelled, that he could not remonstrate with her. Lavinia at her sunniest was irresistible.

Chapter Three

'"*I do entreat your grace to pardon me,*"' murmured Lavinia to herself, consulting the text in the small book she carried. '"*I know not by what power I am made bold—*"' She stopped suddenly, jostled by a passer-by, who did not stay to apologise.

'My lady,' Daisy entreated her fearfully, 'I do think you should put that book away and hurry home. I have never seen such crowds.'

Lavinia had been so absorbed in *A Midsummer Night's Dream*, one of several copies she had just bought at a shop in Oxford Street, she had not noticed the press of people in the street, all coming towards them. They were shouting, 'Hurrah! God bless the Queen!', running alongside an open landau, filling the road and the pavement.

Lavinia stopped to stare, knowing she was looking at the Queen and experiencing at first hand the adulation in which she appeared to be held. Her Majesty was stockily built and dressed in mourning for the late king, who had been her uncle as well as her father-in-law, but what surprised Lavinia more than anything was the huge black wig whose long curls hung each side of her rouged cheeks and the thickly painted black eyebrows which made her large

head look even bigger. She was accompanied by the Lord
Mayor, Alderman Wood, and Lady Anne Hamilton, her
lady-in-waiting.

The carriage was going at little more than walking pace,
but its chief occupant was revelling in the adoration, smiling and bowing first to one side and then the other, while
from the houses and shops of Oxford Street more and more
people emerged to add to the crowds, many of whom
waved white ribbons or wore white cockades and shouted,
'The Queen! The Queen! Long live the Queen!'

Lavinia and her maid, with Tom Bagshott walking a few
paces behind them carrying the other books, were intent
on going in the opposite direction, but it was impossible
to force a way through the throng and they found themselves being pushed willy-nilly along with everyone else.
It was like a great tidal wave, carrying all before it. Lavinia
heard Daisy cry out behind her but she could not see the
little maid, nor the tall figure of the groom, because she
could not go back or even turn round.

She dropped her book, her hat came off and then a shoe
and, as she hobbled along, pressed in on all sides, she
began to wonder how much further she could go without
falling down. And that she must not do, for it would mean
being trampled to death. The whole procession had
reached the corner of Portman Street and she was limping
badly when she was suddenly grabbed from behind and
held in two powerful arms.

'Let me go!' she shouted, wriggling to try to free herself. Her hair escaped its pins and cascaded round her
shoulders and over her eyes, so that she could not see
properly. 'Let go of me at once!'

'I fear, my lady, that if I do you will be knocked down
and be trampled on,' said a quiet voice which she instantly
recognised as that of Lord Wincote.

Still held in his arms, she squirmed round to face him, while the multitude followed the carriage into Portman Street, which relieved the press of bodies about her, though he did not release her. 'My lord!'

He lifted a hand from around her waist to brush her hair out of her eyes. She gazed up at him, so overwhelmed with relief that she did not notice that his fingers still stroked her temple and that his other hand was still firmly around her waist. His dark eyes were searching hers, making her feel weaker than ever. If he released her, she felt sure her legs would not support her and she would crumple to the ground. 'My lady, are you all right?'

'Yes, yes, now that you are here,' she said, pulling away from him at last and endeavouring to push her hair behind her ears and replace a few of the pins. 'I thank you for your timely intervention.'

'It was my privilege, my lady, but tell me, what were you thinking of to come out alone on such a day?'

'I was not alone. I had my maid with me and a groom, but I lost them in the mêlée.' She looked back, searching for a sight of them in the sea of heads. 'I was carried along, quite unable to make headway, and had to go with the crowd. I had no idea it would be like this.'

'I advise you to avoid going out on foot while the Queen is in Town.'

'And how long will that be, do you suppose? I do not like the idea of being confined to the house by a mob.'

'You need not be. I will be pleased to escort you, whenever you wish to go out. In the meantime, I will see you safe home.'

'Thank you.' She took off her other shoe and carried it, as they began walking back down Oxford Street, quieter now, with everyone resuming whatever it was they had been doing before the Queen passed. 'But I must find Daisy and Tom.'

'I do not doubt they will find their own way home, my lady. I think you need to be safe indoors before anyone of consequence sees you.'

She laughed. 'Yes, I must look a mess.'

'Not a mess in my eyes, my lady, only delightfully un-ruly, but perhaps others might see the matter differently. Is the Duke at home? Or the Duchess?'

'No. Papa has gone to another of those interminable meetings to try to resolve the problem of the Queen, and Stepmama has gone to the orphanage, which was why I could not have the carriage.'

'Perhaps it is as well. You will be able to change and tidy your hair before anyone sees you and then, with your permission, I will return this afternoon to make sure you are none the worse for your little adventure.'

'Thank you. You are very kind. I must be causing you great inconvenience.'

'Not at all.'

They were just turning into the end of St James's Square when they were spotted by James, arriving on horseback to call on her. He leapt from the stallion and strode to intercept them, his expression furious. 'Vinny, whatever has happened to you?' And then, without waiting for an answer, turned to Edmund. 'Wincote, if you have harmed a hair of her head, by God, you will have me to answer to.'

'James, do not be such a gudgeon,' Lavinia said, putting a restraining hand on his arm. 'Lord Wincote has just res-cued me from being trampled to death by a mob and I am very grateful to him.'

'Oh.' James was only slightly mollified. The sight of Lavinia with her hair all over the place, her dress and stockings torn, with her shoe in her hand, accompanied by a man he did not trust, had frightened him half to death and his immediate reaction had been that Wincote had compromised her, if not actually molested her. It was not easy to change that image of the man instantly into one of knight errant. 'What happened?' he demanded. 'Why were you out unchaperoned?'

'I was not. I had Daisy and Tom Bagshott with me, but we were separated. I was carried along by the mob; if Lord Wincote had not arrived when he did, I do not know what might have happened.'

'If that is the case, I beg your pardon, Wincote.' He turned his mount to shield her from the gaze of the by-standers who were showing more than a little curiosity at the scene being played out before them, and began to escort her towards her home, leading the horse.

'Granted,' Edmund said pleasantly, falling into step the other side of her. 'I think I might have been inclined to the same conclusion if our roles had been reversed—'

'*I* would never do anything to hurt Lady Lavinia.'

'Nor I, Corringham.'

'Lavinia, I think that you must not go out again on foot,' James said as they reached the front door of Stanmore House. 'Not until these troubles are over.'

'Just what I said,' Edmund put in, almost triumphantly. 'I have offered my escort whenever it should be needed.'

'But you have no carriage.'

'No, but I intend to acquire one very soon.'

James did not reply to that, as a footman opened the door and stood holding it, his mouth gaping.

Lavinia smiled at him. 'Dobson, have you seen Daisy or Tom?'

He recovered himself quickly. 'Yes, my lady. They came home some time ago, but as you had not preceded

them, they went out again to look for you. We have all
been most concerned and wondering if his Grace should
be summoned…'

'I am glad you did not do that,' Lavinia said, imagining
how angry her father would be at her foolishness. 'But we
must go and look for Daisy and Tom.'

'Oh, no, you don't,' James said. 'You must go and
change you clothes before the Duchess comes home. Lord
Wincote and I will go. That so, Wincote?'

If Edmund had been hoping to be invited in, he did not
show his disappointment, but bowed to Lavinia and
smiled. 'Of course, my lady. We will bring them both safe
home.'

They turned and left together and Lavinia, who had recovered from her fright, burst out laughing. James and
Edmund certainly did not like each other and, as she
climbed the stairs to her room, she wondered why. Surely
they did not see each other as rivals for her hand?

James had never given her the slightest hint that he felt
anything more than a brotherly interest in her, and she had
only known Lord Wincote a few days, certainly not long
enough to form an abiding attachment. But that was not
to say she could not or would not do so in the future. His
eyes had held hers so that she was unable to look away
and his touch sent fire through her limbs. If the romantic
novels she was constantly reading were right, that was how
love was supposed to strike you, wasn't it? Is that what
Stepmama meant, when she said Lavinia would know
when it happened?

But what about James? She adored him, knew she could
rely on him without reservation; it did not matter what kind
of a scrape she landed herself in, he would be there to haul
her out of it. Even today, though he had not been present
in the crowd, he had been ready and willing to defend her

honour. But surely that did not mean he wanted her for a wife, or that she could view him as a potential husband?

She went into her room, flung her odd shoe on to the floor and sank on to her bed, trying to imagine James married to someone else: to see a woman's figure beside him, holding his arm possessively, looking up at him with shining eyes and him returning that look as if no one else in the world existed for him. How she hated this imaginary wife of his! It was something she had not thought about before and this feeling was so strong it took her by surprise. 'You are selfish beyond redemption,' she scolded herself. 'If anyone deserves to be happy, it is James.'

Not one to give way to the dismals for long, she left her bed and went to look in the long cheval mirror near the window. The sight which greeted her made her gasp and then laugh aloud.

She looked like a street urchin; her hair was in a tangle where the coils which had looked so shiny and neat when she left the house had become unpinned. Her light spotted gingham gown was decked with more than embroidery and ribbons; it was covered in dust and daubed with mud. The skirt was torn, too, and one white stocking was in tatters, revealing a leg which had several lengthy scratches. She did not know when that could have happened; she had no recollection of being hurt, except that her feet were very sore. Unlike an urchin's, they were soft and unused to going without shoes.

Stripping off, she flung everything in the corner, then washed in the cold water which stood in an ewer on her washstand, finishing by sitting on a stool and paddling her feet in the bowl. It was such a hot day it was refreshing and soothing. After patting herself dry, she sat in her shift in front of her dressing table and picked up her hairbrush. She had almost restored her hair to shining strands when

Daisy appeared, hot, dusty and worried. 'Oh, my lady, we thought we had lost you. We searched everywhere and all we found was your bonnet. Someone had trodden on it and it was ruined. When we came home and found you had not returned, we were really afraid. I was so relieved to see the Earl and know you were safe.' She flung herself on her knees in front of Lavinia. 'Please forgive me. Please don't turn me off.'

'Oh, Daisy, do get up, there's a dear. No one is going to turn you off.'

Daisy scrambled to her feet. 'Lord Corringham was very angry. He said it was no thanks to me that you were safe and well and, if I wanted to keep my job, I should look after you better and not leave you to be picked up by any Tom, Dick or Harry.'

'Did he now?' Lavinia said, with a smile. 'And was Lord Wincote present when he said that?'

'No, my lady. Why?'

'No reason. Now, you are to take no notice of Lord Corringham. It is not his place to reprimand you and I do not blame you for what happened. We were separated, which could not be helped, so we will say no more about it. I do not think I shall even bother the Duchess with it.'

'Oh, thank you, my lady.'

'Now, go and clean yourself up and throw those clothes away.' She indicated the pile in the corner. 'Is Tom safely back?'

'Yes, my lady. He brought your books back, except the one you were carrying. They are on the table in the hall.'

'Good. I must remember to thank him.'

'The Earl is downstairs, my lady. He said he wanted to speak to you.'

'I've no doubt he means to ring a peal over me, but he will find himself mistaken if he thinks I will pay any attention,' she said. 'Daisy, pass me the blue silk pelisse-robe and a fresh pair of stockings. Then go to your room and rest for a while, you must be exhausted.'

Five minutes later, with the robe tied about the waist with a wide sash and her hair lying loose about her shoulders, she went down to the drawing room on the first floor. There, James stood with his back to the room, gazing out on to the parched garden.

He turned on hearing her enter and caught his breath at her creamy loveliness. Her green eyes sparkled and her hair shone from its recent brushing and hung in a curtain of rich chestnut brown, which contrasted beautifully with the pale blue of her gown. The wonder of it was that she seemed totally unaware of the devastating effect she had on her beholder.

'Vinny, are you all right?'

'Yes, of course.'

'I am sorry I was angry with you.'

'And I am sorrier still that you should have redirected that anger at Daisy, my lord. You have frightened the poor girl to death. She is under the impression you have the authority to turn her off.'

'I apologise for that, but when I came upon her and that groom, they had their arms about each other and were laughing immoderately. I told them it was not a joke that their mistress was missing.'

'I was not missing, James. It was an unfortunate incident, but no harm has been done and I would as lief forget the whole thing…'

'By that, I suppose, you mean I am not to mention it to the Duchess.'

'No, nor Papa. They both have too much to concern them at the moment without having to worry about me.'

He came towards her and, stopping in front of her, took both her hands in his own. 'I will not say a word, my dear, but only if you promise not to go out alone until this business with the Queen is over.'

She looked down at their hands clasped together and wondered at how small her hands were in his and yet how tenderly he held them safe, just as he would always hold her safe from harm. He was a dear, dear man and she was lucky to be so protected. 'And when do you suppose that will be?'

'I don't know. Until she tires of it, I suppose. Or she is divorced. Whichever it is, I hope it will be soon, for I am heartily sick of the way the population forgets her transgressions and hails her almost as a saviour of the country.'

'And you are a cynic, James. But I promise not to go out without an adequate escort in future.' She smiled and reached up to kiss his cheek. 'There, will that do?'

He smiled ruefully, rubbing the spot her lips had touched. 'It will have to. Now, unless you intend going out again today, I will take my leave of you.'

'No, I shall stay in. I am going to read *A Midsummer Night's Dream* right through and see if I can cast the main characters; by then Mama will be home. We are going to the play at Drury Lane tonight. You may join us in Papa's box, if you wish.'

'No, thank you. I have other fish to fry.'

'Oh, and am I permitted to know her name?'

'It is not a lady, it is business which cannot wait.'

'Very well. But can you be here tomorrow afternoon? I want to give everyone their parts.'

'I thought there were to be no rehearsals until after Lady Graham's ball.'

'It isn't a rehearsal, simply a preliminary meeting, so

·that people know who they are to be and can begin to
learn their words.'

'I will be at your service,' he said, describing a flourish
with his right hand while bowing from the waist, making
her laugh. '"By all the vows that ever men have broke/In
number more than ever woman spoke/In that same place
thou hast appointed me?/Tomorrow truly will I meet with
thee."'

She laughed. 'I did not know you were so familiar with
the play, James, but those are Hermia's lines.'

'I once took the part when I was at school. There were
no ladies and the boys had to take the female parts too.'

'Which they did in Shakespeare's day, but I cannot
imagine you as a woman, James.'

'No? I was young and slim then. A few petticoats and
a wig and the transformation was effected. But I sincerely
hope you had no such plans for me now. I am grown tall
and broad-shouldered and have hairs on my chin. Besides,
I can no longer speak in a falsetto voice.' He attempted it
as he spoke, making her laugh.

'No, I will not embarrass you, James. You will come,
won't you?'

'Of course,' he said, bowing over her hand. 'Until tomorrow.'

After he had gone, she sat on a sofa for a little while,
thinking about him, the conversations they had had, things
he had said, the offhand manner with which she treated
him and the way he took it all in good humour. She pondered on the strange feeling of restlessness which assailed
her when he was near, making her want to shout, to laugh,
to pace about, even to quarrel with him. She had not been
aware of it before but perhaps it signalled that she was
now a woman and ought to be wary of too much familiarity with a man, even one she knew and trusted.

She stood up abruptly and hurried to the ballroom to begin on a new piece of scenery, telling herself she was being fanciful. She was still there when Frances returned.

'Vinny, there you are. I have been looking for you.'

'Sorry, Mama, I did not hear you come in.' She stood back, paintbrush in hand. 'What do you think of it?'

'Very good. But you know, I begin to wonder if it is such a good idea. By all accounts, the bother over the Queen and the coronation has yet to be settled and no one can think or talk of anything else. I am quite worn out with it all and as for your papa…'

'I know, Mama, but it will be resolved soon, surely?'

Frances sighed. 'Let us hope so.'

They were interrupted by the butler who came to inform them that Lord Wincote was in the hall, enquiring if her Grace was at home.

'What, again?' the Duchess murmured, then, aloud, 'Very well, John, show him into the drawing room. I will be there directly.' She turned to Lavinia. 'No doubt when he asked for me, he really meant you, my dear, so go and ask Daisy to put your hair up and come and join us.'

When Lavinia returned to the drawing room, she found Frances and Edmund ensconced over the tea cups. He sprang to his feet when she entered and sketched her a bow. 'Lady Lavinia, your servant.'

'Good afternoon, Lord Wincote. How do you do?'

'Very well, my lady, and you?'

'Excellently, my lord.' She suppressed the urge to smile at this coded repartee as she sat down beside Frances and indicated, with a wave of her hand, that he should return to his seat. 'To what do we owe the pleasure today?'

'I have acquired a light carriage and pair, my lady, and came to beg the favour of your company on a short ride.

With her Grace's permission, of course.' He turned to Frances. 'Perhaps you might care to accompany us.'

The suggestion put the Duchess in a fix, as he well knew. Going with them would solve the problem of a chaperon, but to do so would certainly give the tabbies something to talk about; it would be tantamount to telling the world she approved of Lord Wincote and sanctioned his pursuit of her stepdaughter. And all that without the Duke having met the man. She could not take so much on her own shoulders.

'Thank you, but I am otherwise engaged this afternoon,' she said. 'And I need Lady Lavinia's company. Perhaps another time.'

'Of course,' he said. 'It was only a whim to ask her ladyship to be the first to try the phaeton. It is the latest model.'

'A phaeton?' Lavinia queried. 'Is it a high-perch one like James's?'

'No, my lady, it is more modest than that and safer. Perhaps tomorrow?'

'Fie, my lord!' she said. 'You will have the tattlemongers commenting on the frequency of your visits.'

He bowed. 'I would not wish to make your ladyship the subject of gossip.'

'But call tomorrow, by all means,' she went on. 'Indeed, I wish you would.' His look of pleasure made her smile and the Duchess frown. 'We are going to have a meeting to allocate the parts for the play.'

'Oh.' His disappointment that he was not to have her to himself was quickly stifled. 'I shall look forward to it, my lady.'

Lavinia stood up, obliging him to get to his feet and bringing the interview to an end. He took his leave of both ladies and left, slightly subdued.

'Vinny,' the Duchess said after he was out of earshot and Lavinia had resumed her seat. 'Do I detect a slight tease on your part?'

'He is so serious, Mama, and so correct.'

'Is that not good?'

'Yes, but is it real?'

'Possibly. But time will tell. I am glad you have not been entirely bowled over by him.'

'Why, Mama?'

'We know nothing of him. And until we do, you would be wise to hold back a little.'

'I am not such a ninny as to fall for the first young man who pays me compliments, Mama, but he is so considerate and attentive. He is also very handsome, do you not think?'

'Yes, I believe he is.' Frances smiled. 'Perhaps it would be as well to find out more about him before he makes his intentions any more obvious than they are already. What has he told you?'

'Only that his older brother, who was James's friend, died in tragic circumstances and he stayed at home with his grandfather to help run the estate. It is quite extensive, I believe.'

'That, I suppose, is a start. It may be that the Duke knows more, though I hesitate to trouble him at the moment.'

'Mama, there is no need for that. I should hate Lord Wincote to hear you were making enquiries and assume from that I was setting my cap at him. I am sure we shall learn more little by little as the Season progresses; after all, there will be rehearsals when we are bound to meet in company.'

'Speaking of rehearsals, Vinny, exactly how many people have you invited here tomorrow?'

'Only a handful. Lord Wincote, James, Lord Haverley,

Sir Percy, Mr Martin Drew, Mr Benedict Willoughby and Constance. I have yet to find more ladies, but Lord Haverley said he would bring his daughters.'

'You had better warn cook to prepare some refreshments for everyone.' She stood up. 'Now, it is nearly five o'clock and we had better go up and change for dinner. The Duke has promised to try and be home in time to escort us, otherwise he will meet us at the theatre.'

Lavinia left to obey. Daisy, once more her usual bright self, brushed and arranged her hair in a Grecian style that showed off her long neck and narrow shoulders, before helping her to dress in a rose-pink taffeta gown, trimmed with silk roses along the line of the high waist and around the hem. Slipping her still slightly sore feet into white slippers and picking up her fan, gloves and reticule, she made her way down to the drawing room, to find her father already dressed for dinner, discussing his day with the Duchess.

'She positively refuses to budge,' he was saying. 'She will not leave the country for any consideration.' Marcus Stanmore, third Duke of Loscoe, was, in his forties, still a very handsome man, but tonight he looked tired and his face bore signs of strain. 'Brougham pretends he is speaking her words, but I fancy it is the other way about and she says what he tells her to.'

'But Sir Henry Brougham is her attorney, is he not?' Frances put in gently. 'He is bound to advise her as to the proper course she should take.'

'If I could believe that he was not trying to make political capital out of the poor woman, I might agree with you. It could bring the government down.'

'Shall we try and forget it for a few hours, my dear?' Frances said rising. 'Let us go and have dinner and see the play.'

'And that's another thing…' he said, offering his arm for his wife to lay her hand upon his sleeve.

'Marcus,' Frances said sharply as they moved towards the dining room, followed by Lavinia. 'That is to be your last word on the subject. I intend to enjoy my dinner and the play, which means you must forget the politics and enjoy it too.'

'Very well, my dear,' he said, patting the hand on his arm. 'We will quiz Vinny on her day instead.'

'Well?' he enquired of his daughter when all three were seated at the dining table and being served the first course of turbot in a shrimp sauce. 'What have you been doing today?'

'I bought several copies of *A Midsummer Night's Dream*, ready for the allocation of parts tomorrow,' she said, carefully omitting mention of her little mishap. 'I painted a little more of the scenery. James came to call and later Lord Edmund Wincote.'

'Wincote—who is he?'

'A young man who seems to have attached himself to the *ton*,' Frances explained. 'I can see nothing wrong in him, and he seems very popular…'

'On account of being very handsome and particular,' Lavinia put in, then laughed and added, 'And unattached.'

'I wonder if you know the family?' the Duchess asked. 'He comes from Cumberland. His elder brother, Henry, was at Cambridge with James and he seems to think that gives him entry into Society.'

'Wincote?' he repeated. 'I knew of a Charles Wincote. Years ago now. He committed some indiscretion or other and had to leave town—not at all sure exactly what it was though.'

'Can you find out? I am not sure that I ought to receive him quite so frequently until I know his antecedents.'

The Duke looked at his wife with affectionate humour. 'It is not like you to brand someone because of what their forebears did, Fanny.'

'Ordinarily I would not, but he is showing an uncommon interest in your daughter.'

The Duke turned to Lavinia. 'Is that so, my dear?'

'No more than any other young man, Papa. And you may be sure James is determined to protect me. He is like a mother hen.'

The Duke smiled. 'And who is protecting you from the Earl of Corringham?'

'Oh, I do not need protecting from him, Papa. I can manage him.'

'Do not be so sure, miss. I hope I do not need to tell you to be careful.'

'No, Papa. But James behaves like an older brother and so I treat him.'

She noticed her father lift his eyebrows towards his wife and smile. The Duke and his Duchess were so comfortable together, so loving and understanding that she could not imagine them ever having a falling out. That was the kind of marriage she wanted and she would not settle for anything less.

'Then I will say no more for the moment. Now, tell me about this play.'

Relieved of the subject of her suitors, imaginary or otherwise, Lavinia launched into an enthusiastic account of what she had done and what she intended to do, to which he appeared to listen, but she could tell by his eyes that he was not giving her all his attention and that his mind kept wandering elsewhere. Still he kept his promise not to mention the Queen and her troubles and they finished the meal in good spirits.

* * *

But it could not last. The audience at the Drury Lane
theatre, fuelled by a rumour that Caroline meant to attend
the performance, were unruly and noisy, shouting that they
wanted to see the Queen and laughing and making rude
jests against the King. Lavinia, sitting between her father
and stepmother in the Loscoe box, was reminded of the
noisy demonstration of the morning and began to feel fear-
ful that the Duke would be taken for a King's man and
they would turn on him.

It was just as the orchestra was beginning the overture
that Lavinia saw Lord Wincote take his place in a box on
the opposite side of the auditorium, beside the elderly
Countess of Jersey, a known sympathiser of Caroline. She
nudged the Duchess and nodded towards the opposite box.
'Mama, look,' she said in a whisper so that her father could
not hear. 'Do you suppose he knows what he is doing?'

'I have no idea, but I do hope he does not bring her to
our box during the interval.'

The noisy audience quietened down when it became apparent that the Queen was not going to appear and the
performance was permitted to begin. Lavinia sat through
the first act so tense with apprehension she could not take
in a word of the story or appreciate the acting, which was,
in any case, not first rate, and by the time the curtain fell
for the intermission she was a bundle of nerves.

However, it was not Edmund who knocked on the door
of their box during the interval, but a messenger from the
Prime Minister, requiring the Duke's immediate attendance.

'I'm sorry, my love, I must go,' he said to Frances.
'Shall you stay?'

The Duchess looked at Lavinia. 'Do you want to stay,
Vinny?'

'No, Mama, it is a very poor performance and I had as lief go home if you do not wish to stay.'

'Then we will go.'

Marcus had the carriage summoned and saw them into it, before joining the messenger in the cab he had arrived in.

By the following afternoon, it was all round town that negotiations with the Queen had been abandoned, that she was to live in Brandenburg House on the Thames between Fulham and Hammersmith and the coronation had been postponed for a year. All the work on preparing the Abbey had been halted and the arrangements made for the reception and feasting afterwards cancelled.

'Thank goodness for that,' Lavinia said. 'Now perhaps we can get on with our play.'

Taking the copies of the play into the ballroom, she arranged a semi-circle of chairs facing the woodland scene she had painted and sat down to wait for the cast to appear. Lord Wincote was the first to be announced.

'Good afternoon, my lady.' he said, striding into the room and bowing over her hand. He wore a mustard-coloured superfine frock coat and cream pantaloons, a brown-and-lemon striped waistcoat and a white cravat tied in what she believed was called a waterfall. 'Here I am, as instructed, and at your command.' He seemed remarkably cheerful.

'Good afternoon, Lord Wincote,' she said, aware that he had not released her hand and she was going to have to wrest it from him. 'You are punctual. No one else has arrived.'

'Good, then perhaps we may have a little private conversation before anyone else comes.' His dark eyes were searching hers, his gaze flickering from her eyes to her lips and back to her eyes. And therein lay her problem. She did not seem able to look away.

'Private conversation, my lord?' she queried breathlessly, retrieving her hand and putting it behind her out of his reach.

'About when you will come out in the carriage with me. The park will not be so crowded now that the Queen has moved out of town.'

'And who told you that? Could it be Lady Jersey?'

'Oh, you saw us.'

'So did everyone else. Does that mean you align yourself with the opposition?'

'Not at all. Living as I have done so far from the capital, I am not *au fait* with the partisanship of the *haut monde*. My grandfather once knew the Countess of Jersey and often spoke of her, so I felt obliged to call on her. She has lost so many of her friends and begged me to accompany her to the play. I could not, in conscience, refuse her.'

'Oh, I see.'

'Have I offended you, my lady? Because I would cut off my hand before I did anything to upset you, you must surely know that.'

'Lord Wincote, you should not say things like that.'

'Why not, when they are true?' Somehow he managed to possess himself of her hand again. 'I have known you but a short time, but the esteem in which I hold you cannot be measured in time, only in depth...'

'Oh.' She was thoroughly confused. It could be his idea of playful flirtation, the playing of pretty compliments as acted out between members of the *ton* to amuse themselves. But he had spoken with such fervour, as if the words came from the heart, that she found herself blushing. It was a moment or two before she recovered enough to reply with what was meant to be a light laugh, but sounded more like a cracked gasp. 'My lord, I think that is an improper remark to make on so short an acquaintance—'

'Indeed it is,' said a voice from the doorway. 'Wincote, you should not take liberties just because her ladyship is so trusting as to receive you without a chaperon.'

'James, you are coming, after all.' Lavinia was unsure whether she was relieved or annoyed by the interruption.

'Of course.' He came into the room at an amble, deliberately not hurrying, because if he did he might feel tempted to give the other fellow a facer. And that most certainly would not do. 'I said I would, did I not? You know you may rely upon me.'

Edmund looked as though he would like to make some cutting remark, but he bit it back and smiled. 'Good afternoon, Corringham.'

'Good afternoon, Wincote. Is that your phaeton outside the front door?'

'Yes, I acquired in yesterday from Robinson and Cook, they have their premises only a few doors from my lodgings, and in passing yesterday, I decided to see what they had to offer. Lady Lavinia has been so kind as to agree to try it out.' He paused to see the effect his words would have, but as James's expression registered nothing, he added, 'We shall not require your services as a chaperon.'

James smiled, knowing he had rattled the gentleman. 'And for that relief, much thanks,' he said lightly. 'I cannot think of anything more uncomfortable that riding three in a carriage meant for two.'

'James!' Lavinia remonstrated.

'Don't mean to give offence, my dear,' he said. 'But you must see my point.'

Lavinia was glad the arrival of more of the cast brought an end to the conversation before it could become any

more acrimonious. They came in ones and twos and the
semi-circle of chairs was soon filled.

They were all very restless and talkative, more inclined
to gossip about the latest news of the King and Queen and
speculate on future developments than pay attention. She
had to rap hard on a table to make herself heard. 'Let us
get on, shall we? We can have a cose when refreshments
are served.'

'What did I tell you, Wincote?' James said. 'A positive
Captain Hackum.'

'I am listening, my lady,' Edmund said. 'Though I am
unfamiliar with the play.'

'It is a love story,' she said, giving James a venomous
look. 'It is about a young girl, Hermia, who refuses to obey
her father and marry Demetrius, the young man he has
chosen for her. She is given four days to obey or she must,
according to Athenian law, suffer death or go into a nun-
nery.'

'A harsh punishment, my lady,' Edmund said. 'Though
I have heard of such things happening. Not death, of
course, but lockings up and other threats. It is a cruel father
who would do such a thing. I sincerely hope the Duke of
Loscoe is not so unbending.'

'My lord, this is a fairy tale,' Lavinia said. 'You are not
to make comparisons with real life.'

'I should hope not,' James interjected. 'Since you would
have me learn the part of the cruel father.'

'I have changed my mind,' she said. 'You are too young
for Egeus, after all, and since Lord Haverley has consented
to help us, he would play the part so much better.' She
turned to Lord Haverley, who sat on the end of the row.
'Will you do it, my lord?'

'If it please you, my lady,' he said, with a slight bow.

'Then you will not need me,' James said. 'I will be prompter.'

'No, you will not. I need you to play Demetrius. Lord Wincote can be Lysander and Constance has already said she will be Helena.'

'Only if you cannot find anyone else,' Constance said.

'At the moment, I cannot. Do say you will. Lord Corringham will help to school you, won't you, James?' A statement which made the poor girl blush to the roots of her fair hair.

'Of course,' he said, realising Lavinia had selected him for the task in order to commit him to the project. He grinned at her, letting her know he knew what she was about. 'It will give me the greatest of pleasure.'

'Do go on, Lady Lavinia,' Sophia said. 'What happens?'

'Hermia and her lover, Lysander, decide to run away together,' Lavinia explained. 'They are pursued by Demetrius who, in turn, is followed by Helena who loves him and wants him to turn away from Hermia. They all end up in the woods where the fairies take a hand in the proceedings. They have a magic potion which, when anointed on someone's eyes while they sleep, will make them fall in love with the first person they see on wakening.'

'But they get it all wrong,' Duncan said gleefully. 'I read it yesterday. They all fall in love with the wrong person.'

'I see,' Sophia said. 'But there is a happy ending?'

'Of course. It is supposed to be a comedy.'

'And who is to play Hermia?' James asked. If Lavinia took the part, she would have several love scenes to play with Wincote and he could not pretend he was not jealous. It occurred to him that she might be doing it on purpose, but then he realised Lavinia did not have a mean bone in her body and, in any case, she had no idea how he felt about her. It was her openness, her transparent honesty he loved most about her. She had not even been able to keep her secret about Lancelot Greatorex, but was compelled to tell someone. He felt flattered that it should be him, even if it was likely to put him in a spot of bother with her father.

'For the moment, I shall,' she said, then, addressing Sophia, 'Miss Haverley, will you be Titania, the Queen of the fairies?'

'Oh, do,' Benedict put in. 'I am to be Bottom. Titania falls in love with Bottom.'

'Only because Puck makes a mistake with the magic juice,' Duncan said, grinning. 'He is one of the fairies and a mischief-maker.'

'Then you will be well qualified for the part,' his sister put in. 'Sir Percy has agreed to be Theseus, the Duke of Athens.' She smiled at Percy, who smiled back a little wryly. 'And that leaves Oberon. Mr Drew, would you oblige?'

He nodded his assent and began leafing through his copy to see how much he had to say.

'You have forgotten Hippolyta, the Duke's bride,' James said. 'Not to mention a whole host of journeymen engaged to entertain the Duke on his wedding night, and a handful of fairies.'

'No, I have not. There is no hope of us being able to return to the country at our usual time and Mama misses the children. She has asked Miss Hastings to bring them to London so we shall have our Hippolyta and our fairies, especially if Augusta can be persuaded to allow Andrew and Beth to appear as well. Perhaps you will lead them, Miss Eliza?'

'Yes, if I do not have too much to learn.'

'And we can dispose of the court entertainment. At least for the moment. Is everyone happy?'

There were few moans which signified rather less than total enthusiasm, but all agreed to try and learn their lines. Then the refreshments were brought in and everyone left their seats to mill about and talk to each other and admire the scenery.

'You will make an excellent Hermia,' Edmund said, finding Lavinia standing alone, deep in thought. 'I shall enjoy our scenes together.'

'Oh, so shall I,' she said, almost afraid to turn and face him for fear of what that searching look of his would do to her. She had heard of people who could bend someone to their will simply by staring at them and talking softly—was he one of those?

'Perhaps we shall have an opportunity of private rehearsal,' he said. 'I am at your disposal at any time.'

'Thank you, my lord.'

'And will you do me the honour of taking a carriage ride in the park with me tomorrow?'

'I shall be delighted.' Then, remembering her stepmother's advice to hold back a little, added, 'But not tomorrow. Wednesday would be more convenient.'

'Then Wednesday it shall be. I shall call for you at two o'clock.' He bowed and left, beaming with satisfaction.

'He looks pleased with himself,' James said, coming to stand beside her.

She laughed. 'Yes, I have agreed to go for a ride in his carriage on Wednesday.'

'Oh,' His pause was only momentary, and he quickly brought himself under control, bent over her hand and smiled. 'If you remember, Wincote and I are to go to Hampstead Heath next week. Have you spoken to the Duchess about joining us?'

'Yes. She is in favour. I should have told everyone.'
She stepped forward and clapped her hands for silence and
repaired the omission, which, she had to admit, was received with more enthusiasm than the prospect of learning
a Shakespeare play, and then one by one, they began to
leave.

'Sir Percy, are you going in the direction of White's?'
James asked. 'I have something I particularly want to discuss with you.'

The older man nodded and they set off together, walking
in companionable silence until Sir Percy broke it. 'Well,
what is it?' he demanded. 'I had been hoping to see the
Duchess and be asked to dinner, but you must needs drag
me away.'

'I am sorry for that,' James said, guessing that Sir Percy
had been in love with the Duchess for years and would
rather die than admit it. 'But it is because of something
Little Mama asked me to do that I need your help.'

'Fire away.'

'What do you know of Lord Wincote?'

'Nothing, my boy. I heard that his family come from
some outlandish place in the north of the country and live
on mutton, no more than that.'

'The Duke of Loscoe has said he remembers something
about someone called Charles Wincote, who had to leave
Town over some indiscretion years ago.'

'That has no bearing on Lord Edmund Wincote, surely?'

'Perhaps not, but for some reason, I do not trust him.'

'Do not trust or do not like? Oh, I am an old fool, but
not such a clunch as not to see what is under my nose.
You love the little lady and he is making a play for her.
Stands to reason you'd be jealous.'

James smiled wryly; Sir Percy might act the buffoon,
but he missed nothing. 'It is not only me. The Duchess is

uneasy too, which is why she asked me to find out what I can. Trouble is, no one seems to know anything against him.'

'Then perhaps there is nothing to discover.'

'I overheard him telling Vinny that his grandfather had known the Countess of Jersey years ago.'

Percy suddenly clapped his hand to his forehead. 'Lor, now I remember. It was decades ago. Charles Wincote was said to be one of her ladyship's lovers, but when the Prince of Wales took her under his wing, so to speak, he gave Lord Wincote some inducement to leave the field clear. Of course, Prinny tired of her as he always does, which is why, I suppose, she sides with the Queen now.'

'And Lord Wincote visits her. Do you suppose it can have any bearing on the King's case against the Queen? If he has been brought to London to give evidence…'

'What evidence? Oh, you mean if Brougham decides to bring in counter-claims against the King, as he has threatened to do. He wouldn't, would he?'

'I do not know and in truth I do not care,' James said. 'Except that if Lavinia becomes involved with him, it cannot fail to affect the Duke and Duchess.'

'What do you suggest we do? Tell them?'

'I don't know. I may be following the wrong scent entirely. And becoming embroiled in the King's business is dangerous at any time, but especially now. I would rather find some other way to discourage the man.'

'You will never do it by acting the jealous suitor, my boy. Have quite the opposite effect, don't you know?'

'Then what do you suggest I do?'

'Stand off a bit and let him cook his own goose.' He tapped the side of his nose with his forefinger. 'I have an idea. Leave it to me.' They arrived at the door of White's, a gentlemen's club to which they both belonged. 'And since you deprived me of a good dinner at Stanmore House, you may buy me one here.'

'Gladly,' James said. It was not going to be easy to stand back and watch Lavinia and that man together, but he would try, at least until Percy told him what he planned to do. He might even flirt a little with other young ladies, but not too much. Lavinia was too important to him.

Chapter Four

Edmund arrived promptly on Wednesday afternoon to take Lavinia out in his carriage. The day was almost unbearably hot and she wore the coolest dress in her wardrobe, a spotted poplin gathered into a high waist, with a scooped neck and short puffed sleeves. Her arms were covered by long cotton gloves and her head with a large brimmed cottager hat tied beneath her chin with blue ribbon. In her hand she carried a fan and a parasol whose edge was trimmed in ruched silk. The Duchess had declined to accompany them and she was chaperoned by Tom Bagshott, who rode beside the carriage.

'It is hotter than ever,' Lavinia said, snapping open her fan, though once the horses were moving, the slight current of air over the open carriage brought some relief. 'I wish we did not have to stop in London, but Papa has to stay because of the business over the Queen and while he is here my stepmama is determined to stay with him.'

'I am glad of that,' he said. His shirt points and cravat were as immaculately starched as ever, when everyone else's seemed to be wilting in the heat. 'I know it is selfish, but I could not bear to be deprived of your company.'

'My lord,' she whispered, glancing swiftly at Tom, who

was busy looking straight ahead and pretending not to hear.

'It is no more than I would say in front of a drawing room full of people, my dear. By now everyone must know my sentiments towards you and that my hopes are that they might be reciprocated. I make no secret of them.'

She stared down at her hands, unwilling to turn and look into his eyes. 'My lord, it is too soon to speak of such things.'

'Your reticence is to be commended. I would not expect, nor even want, you to rush into answering me, but I would have you know my intentions.'

'But we hardly know each other. I do not know anything about you, your likes and dislikes…'

'I am sure they accord most exactly with your own.'

She laughed rather shakily. 'But you do not know what those are.'

'Then let us put it to the test, shall we? I know you like the countryside, which is certainly my preference too. It is one of the reasons I have not come to town before now.'

'Why did you come this year? It was surely not just to see the coronation.'

'No, I had business to attend to. I am glad that I did or I should never have met you.'

'Thank you, sir,' she said and found herself wondering what that business might be. 'What else do we have in common?'

'A love of horses, riding and driving. I collect the Earl's was not the first carriage you have driven, is it?'

'No, I drive a curricle around the estate at Risley, but it is not only horses I like. I love all God's creatures, dogs, cats, birds, rabbits, foxes, badgers. I have a menagerie of them at Risley and I would never love anyone who could harm an animal.'

'Then you do not hunt?'

'No, my lord, I do not.' She spoke very firmly. 'I once told Mama that I would have it written into my marriage contract that my husband should not hunt. She thought I was joking.'

'And were you?'

'Only partly, considering I am unlikely to have any say in the making of the contract, apart from giving my consent, of course. Papa would never force me.'

He made no reply to this but went on with his catalogue. 'Painting and literature, those are two more interests we share. I have no talent for painting, but I appreciate it in others.'

'And what do you most hate?'

He smiled. 'Anyone and anything that makes you frown.'

'Am I frowning now?'

'No, you are not. You are your sunny self, the most beautiful and bewitching young lady I have ever met. Did anyone ever tell you your eyes are the windows to your inner self? They could never lie, even if your tongue were to attempt it, which I know it would not.'

'Oh, dear, are you saying you can read my thoughts in my eyes?'

'Not quite, but I think on closer acquaintance, I would very soon be able to. That is as it should be between husband and wife, don't you think?'

'My lord, you go too fast,' she said breathlessly. She must learn to control her expression, to veil her eyes so that they did not speak so readily. 'I beg you to stop looking at me like that and pay attention to your driving and the people about us, before we excite comment. Lady Graham and Constance are in a chaise coming towards us and we cannot ignore them. Nor Lady Willoughby in the following carriage. She is an inveterate gossip and I would not give her the means to feed it.'

'Very well. We will be polite to all, even Corringham, but I shall return to the subject when we are in a less public place.'

Lavinia had not seen James and found herself shaking more than ever. She was truly thankful no one had heard what Lord Wincote said, except perhaps Tom, who would never repeat it. She and Edmund acknowledged the ladies with a small bow, a smile and a few words, and then they were abreast of James. She knew her face was flaming and her hands were shaking. In an attempt to cover this she gave him one of her brightest smiles and waved a hand to him in greeting. 'Good afternoon, my lord,' she called to him.

He pulled up and doffed his riding hat as the carriage bowled past him, but his smile faded as soon as it had passed. Wincote had looked so self-satisfied, as if he had scored a point over him. And as for Vinny, she had looked startled, her colour unusually high and her greeting almost too blithe to be genuine, which left him wondering what had caused it. He cursed the agreement he had made with Sir Percy to hang back, when all he wanted to do was ride up alongside her and demand to know what had happened. But doing that would only alienate her.

'Who was that with Lady Lavinia?' Donald Greenaway asked him. Major Greenaway was a few years older than James and a friend of the Duke's. Since the war he had been on half-pay, but he supplemented his income by making himself useful in any number of ways, sometimes as a private investigator. James's meeting with him that afternoon had not been accidental.

'Lord Edmund Wincote,' he answered. 'He has an estate in Cumberland, I believe.'

'Are they going to make a match of it?'

'Not if I can help it,' James said grimly.

Donald looked sideways at him, as they continued, walking their horses so that they could converse. 'You do not like him?'

'No, I do not. Don't ask me why.'

'I won't,' Donald said. 'No need. I can see the little green god on your shoulder as plain as day.'

James laughed good-humouredly. 'It is not only that, there are other reasons. I believe he is a fortune-hunter, though so far I have been unable to find evidence.'

'In dun territory, is he?'

'I can't be sure. I know he owes his tailor, but who doesn't? He bought that equipage not three days ago, but it is far too soon to be paying for it.'

'Where does he lodge?'

'Mount Street, I believe.'

'A respectable address.' Donald paused. 'Do you want me to see what I can discover?'

'Please do. But be careful—if Vinny ever hears of it, she will never speak to me again. And say nothing to the Duke. If I am wrong, he will give me the roasting of a lifetime and if I am right, I would rather deal with Wincote myself.'

'And take pleasure in doing it, I shouldn't wonder. Why don't you just step in and stake your claim to the chit?'

'I will, when the time is right. At the moment she looks on me as a brother.'

'And whose fault is that?' Donald grinned.

'Mine, I have no doubt. Now, be a good fellow and do as I ask, will you?'

It *was* his fault. He had never been a coward where other young ladies were concerned; he was able to flirt with the best in the accepted way of Society, to pay pretty compli-

ments and declare an undying love which both knew meant
nothing at all. When it came to the real thing the words
would not come. Lavinia's rejection of everyone at her
come-out had confirmed to him she was not yet ready for
courtship and marriage, but now, two years on, Wincote
was receiving the attention he had hoped would one day
be his. Had he delayed too long?

He left the Major to set about his enquiries, rode slowly
back to Corringham House in Duke Street. He and his
sister, Augusta, had grown up in the house under the
watchful eye of his 'Little Mama', and he loved it, but it
was too big for a bachelor. It needed a woman's touch and
a young family, but even more so did Twelvetrees, his
Essex estate. That cried out for children to fill its huge,
empty rooms with running feet and laughter, as his stepmother never tired of telling him. He had promised her he
would do something about it this year.

Damn Edmund Wincote, damn the King and the Queen,
and damn everyone else who thwarted him!

Riding home in Lord Wincote's phaeton after seeing
James, Lavinia felt thoroughly confused. She had had suitors before and dispatched them with admirable prompt-
ness, but Lord Wincote was different. For a start, he was
not so easily banished, but that could be because she did
not want to banish him. She had a feeling that she was
being drawn into something she did not understand and
might very well regret. But how could she regret his lordship's obvious sincerity? He had as good as said he loved
her, had talked of husbands and wives as if she had already
given him leave to speak.

But she hadn't, had she? She had not, by look or word,
conveyed her feelings towards him. Had he read something
in her eyes, as he said he could? Had James? Surely it

didn't matter so much what James thought. So why, when she had encountered him in the park, had she felt a wave of guilt wash over her? Suddenly, she had wanted to jump down and run back to him to explain.

Explain what, for goodness' sake? That she had not wanted to ride straight past him, but short of taking the ribbons from his lordship's hands, she could not have brought the horses to a standstill? He knew that perfectly well. She sat stiffly beside Edmund as he drove her home, her mind in turmoil. They were outside the front door of Stanmore House before she realised it.

'May I have the honour of driving you to Hampstead on Friday?' Edmund asked, as he handed her down from the carriage. 'We could have grooms follow on our mounts, so that you may ride when we arrive, if you wish.'

'Thank you, I shall be de—' she began, then stopped, remembering her stepmother's words. 'But if the Duchess decides to go, I shall naturally ride with her in the family carriage.'

His look of annoyance quickly turned to a rueful smile. 'I am sorry I cannot be of service, my lady, but I understand.' He bowed and climbed back into the phaeton. 'I shall look forward to meeting you there.'

'Yes, of course.' The footman on duty had opened the front door and she turned and went inside, pulling off her gloves and hat, thinking of Friday's outing.

Almost everyone she knew would be going; there would be quite a cavalcade of carriages as well as riders. Being away from the stifling heat of London and in the fresh air with the excitement of horse racing, games of cricket and the flying of kites would be a welcome change. There was even talk of racing curricles and phaetons. She would have some fun with James, teasing him into letting her drive one of the light carriages. With James, she could relax.

She refused to analyse her feelings about him, as she climbed the stairs and changed into an afternoon gown before joining Frances in the drawing room. It was enough of a problem making up her mind how she felt about Lord Wincote.

'Did you enjoy your ride?' her stepmother asked. She had a sketch book on her knee and a piece of charcoal in her hand. Drawing was her favourite pastime and she had an unerring eye for a picture.

'Yes, though it was extremely hot. I wish we could go back to Loscoe Court.'

'That would disappoint Lord Wincote,' Frances said, with a gentle smile.

'So he told me.' And before her stepmother could ask what else he had said, she added, 'We saw Lady Graham and Lady Willoughby. They asked me to convey their good wishes and to say they hope to see you at Hampstead on Friday.' She paused. 'You will be coming?'

'I certainly hope to, though I think the Duke will have to stay in London. I wish he would come with us and forget Westminster for a few hours, he looks so drawn.'

They were interrupted by the butler announcing that dinner was ready and, as there were only two of them, they took their meal in the breakfast room. It was nearer to the kitchens and saved the servants having to walk so far. They spent their evening in quiet companionship until the Duke arrived home and claimed his wife, when Lavinia, pleading tiredness, kissed them both goodnight and went to her own room.

The arrival of the children with Miss Hastings, who looked after the younger ones, caused a flurry of excitement the next morning. The children were hugged and kissed, questions asked about their health and good behaviour and news exchanged. Jack, the adopted son of the Duke's brother, was seven years old and full of mischief, but he was a lovable child and was soon regaling everyone with what had been going on at Loscoe Court in their absence.

He had been riding his pony, as well as the cart bringing the hay to the barn, and Lavinia's menagerie, which he prided himself on looking after whenever she was absent, was thriving. 'There are seven baby rabbits,' he said. 'I liked them but Benton was not best pleased, though he would not tell me why. He took the babies away.'

Two-year-old Freddie, the only child who could truly call the Duchess his mother, was the apple of her eye and was just beginning to say a few words, mostly trying to repeat what Jack said, making everyone laugh. In the middle of it all, Augusta arrived with Andrew, now a manly seven-year old, and Beth who was blonde, blue-eyed and not quite five. All four children were very fond of each other and were soon chasing one another about the lofty rooms and screaming with delight.

It was into this pandemonium that James arrived and was immediately attacked. He fell to the floor, pretending they had bowled him over and they scrambled on top of him. He extracted himself to greet the ladies, but was soon crawling on all fours giving the children rides on his back and when Beth fell over under the greater exuberance of the boys, he picked her up and cuddled her, kissing away her tears.

'He is so good with the children,' Frances said. 'It is about time he had some of his own.'

'He has to find himself a wife first,' Augusta said. 'And though I have seen several young ladies on his arm, they have not been what you might call wife material. I do not think he is making any kind of push at all.'

'He promised me he would do so this Season, but the weeks are flying by and he has done nothing about it.' Frances sighed. 'I know what I would like him to do, but—'

'What would you like him to do?' Lavinia had escaped the game the children were playing in order to regain her breath. 'Have you someone in mind?'

'If I had, I would not be so forward as to suggest it,' the Duchess said. 'These things must take their course.'

'I cannot imagine James falling in love,' Lavinia said, watching his antics. He had taken his coat and shoes off and was now teaching the boys the rudiments of sword play, dancing back and forth in stockinged feet with the poker in his hand. 'He always seems so cool and unperturbed when in Society, though you would not think it to see him now.'

'Oh, that is just a pose, my dear,' her stepmother assured her. 'James is deeper than you think and capable of strong attachment. The trouble is his reluctance to show it.'

'I did not mean he is shallow, Mama, but is strong attachment the same as falling in love? He is, after all, strongly attached to you and Augusta and the children, even me, but that is not the same, is it?'

'No, but I live in hope,' Frances replied enigmatically.

James left the boys to their game and joined the ladies. He was breathless and laughing and Lavinia felt something inside her give a wild lurch as if she had been winded by a blow to the heart, but it quickly subsided and she was able to smile teasingly at him. 'James, you are no more grown up than they are. If your friends could see you now, they would wonder what had become of the urbane exquisite they knew.'

'My friends do not see me as an urbane exquisite, at least I hope not.'

'Not even the ladies?' she quizzed. 'All those newly come-out young misses with high hopes and fixed ideas about marriage? They must see you as highly eligible.'

'Which you are,' Augusta put in. 'Any young lady would be gratified to be noticed by you and overjoyed to have an offer.'

'I do not want any young lady. My requirements are quite specific.'

'And what are they?' his sister asked him.

'Oh, he wants to marry for love,' Lavinia put in, smiling. 'He told me so.'

He refused to smile. 'Can you not be trusted to keep a fellow's confidence at all, Vinny?'

She knew her teasing had gone too far and was mortified that she had embarrassed him. 'I am sorry, James, I did not mean to put you to the blush. I will not say another word.'

'Let us have nuncheon,' the Duchess put in quickly. 'Emily, take the children to Nurse and then come and join us. James, you will stay, won't you?'

He retrieved his coat and shoes and put them on as Miss Hastings ushered the children from the room, amid loud protests. 'Glad to, Mama, but only if the subject of my marriage is not mentioned.'

'Very well, I will say no more and neither will Vinny, will you, dear?'

'My lips are sealed,' she said, as they were rejoined by Emily and trooped into the dining room together for a family meal without formality. 'I shall talk about my play.'

'*Your* play?' James queried, as they took their places. 'I had thought it was Shakespeare's play.'

'Oh, you are abominable, James. I think I shall not speak at all.'

'Wonderful!' he said. 'Peace at last.'

They were silent for five minutes while a light dish of boiled eggs and anchovies in a cream sauce was served, but it did not last.

'What is this about a play?' Miss Hastings asked. She was a small sharp-featured woman whose looks belied her warm heart and her sentimental belief in romance, as portrayed in the novels which were the main enjoyment of her leisure hours.

'I am going to put on *A Midsummer Night's Dream*,' Lavinia said. 'I thought it would take people's minds off the coronation, but now there isn't going to be one, it will take their minds off the lack of it.'

'We have all been bullied into taking part,' James said.

'Even you, my lord?' Emily asked, eyes twinkling.

'Yes. Lavinia wants me to be Demetrius.'

'Will you take a part, Miss Hastings?' Lavinia asked. 'I need someone to play Hippolyta. She is the one who is going to marry Theseus, the Duke of Athens.'

'Yes, I do know the play,' the governess said, smiling gently. 'And who is to be the Duke?'

'Sir Percy Ponsonby.'

'Sir Percy?' She only just managed to stifle her laugh. 'I cannot imagine him as an actor.'

'No, but as he pointed out to me, he is very good at acting Sir Percy, and that will do very well.' She paused. 'You already know the play, Miss Hastings, so please say you will.'

'But I am here to look after the children, Lady Lavinia.'

'Oh, I want them to take part too, at least Jack, Andrew and Beth, if Augusta thinks she will enjoy it and not be overcome by tears. Freddie is too young, of course. Do say you agree. It is for a very good cause. The proceeds are to go to Mama's orphans.'

'It is not for me to agree or disagree, child. Your mama must say.'

Lavinia appealed to Frances. 'Mama?'

Frances smiled and turned to Augusta, who had been silently listening while she ate. 'What do you say, Gussie? Shall we humour her?'

'I think we shall have no peace unless we do,' Augusta said. 'So long as I am not expected to play a part. I most certainly could not do it. And if Beth becomes upset by it, then she must not be coerced.'

'Of course, I agree,' Lavinia said eagerly. 'Oh, I feel better about it already. And tomorrow we are going to have a day out on Hampstead Heath. James is organising horse racing and cricket for the men and the ladies can watch or wander about and pick wild flowers and have a picnic. Do say you will join us, Augusta. It will be heaven.'

'Who is going?' Augusta asked.

'Why, just about everybody. Not Papa, perhaps, because he is still worrying about the King and Queen and whether we shall have a revolution—'

'Oh, surely not,' Miss Hastings said, turning pale.

'No, of course not,' James said. 'Lavinia, as usual, is exaggerating.' He smiled gently at the old lady. 'The outing began as a friendly wager on a horse race and has developed into an exodus, but it should be enjoyable and far less hot and uncomfortable than city streets. You'll come, won't you, Gussie, and bring the children? I promised Andrew I would teach him to bat.'

'Yes, why not? I'll speak to Richard.'

'Good, that's settled,' James said. 'If you take Jack and Freddie and Miss Hastings in your carriage, Mama, I shall take Vinny. It will be too much of a squash for you otherwise.'

'Oh, but...' Lavinia began, thinking of Lord Wincote.

He turned to look at her, lifting one well-defined brow. 'Does that not meet with your approval, my lady?'

'Yes, of course it does,' she said quickly. 'But can we take Misty? I should love to ride when we get there.'

'Anything for you, my dear,' he said, with a smile she could not quite fathom. And she wondered if he knew or guessed that Lord Wincote had asked her and he was determined to prevent her accepting the offer. 'I shall be here at nine o'clock for an early start, and we can join up with Gussie on the way.'

He was as good as his word and arrived at Stanmore House at the appointed time next morning, driving his phaeton, with a groom in attendance riding his stallion. He had hardly jumped down when the Loscoe barouche was brought to the door from the mews and the children tumbled from the house, laughing and shouting in glee, followed by a flustered Miss Hastings carrying a bag full of things she thought the children would need—clean clothes and stockings, towels and cold drinks for the journey—although the servants had gone ahead in another coach to prepare the picnic.

When Lavinia emerged and saw James put the bag in the coach, she decided he had been right; there would certainly not be room for her as well. But she did not mind; she would be cooler and more comfortable in the phaeton and, with a little luck, James might even allow her to take the ribbons for a spell.

As Tom Bagshott trotted round the corner on Misty, James turned to her, smiling cheerfully. 'Ready?'

She settled herself into the seat, drawing her skirt about her feet so that he could shut the door, and by that time the Duchess had come from the house and climbed in the barouche. The two carriages set off at a sedate pace for

Upper Brook Street where the Harnham carriage joined them, and then they turned up Park Lane into Oxford Street, which reminded her of the day the mob had nearly bowled her over and she hoped the Queen would not decide to venture forth at that moment. But it was, perhaps, too early in the day for that, and Oxford Street was no busier than usual.

By this time several more coaches had joined the cavalcade, including Lord Wincote in his phaeton. His eyebrows lifted a little on seeing her with James, but he smiled and bowed and fell in behind them.

'You are quiet, Vinny,' James said after they had safely negotiated the traffic of Oxford Street and turned to skirt Regent's Park with its new, imposing villas spreading inexorably northwards.

'Am I?' She was acutely aware of Edmund behind them and knew he was watching them. Did he think she had deliberately refused his offer in order to accept James's? 'It is just that Lord Wincote offered to take me today and I told him I would ride with Mama.'

'Very wise of you, my dear,' he said, his heart lifting a little.

'But I am not with Mama, I am with you.'

'And very glad I am, too.' He turned to look at her. She was wearing a forest-green habit which emphasised her neat figure, with a full skirt that was suitable for both riding and walking. However, it was not her clothes which claimed his attention but her face. She looked concerned, her usually bright eyes clouded. 'What is it that troubles you, my love?'

She turned sharply at this endearment and then, confused by his expression, looked away again. 'Nothing is troubling me, except what he will think.'

'Do you care what he thinks?'

'Of course I do. I do not want him to think I am a dissembler and deliberately turned him down for you.'

'Shame on you,' he said, but he was smiling at the thought.

'But I didn't. You know I didn't.'

'Yes, I do know.' He sighed. 'If he cares for you at all, he will understand.'

'Oh, do you think so? Shall I tell him how it came about?'

'No, Vinny, I do not think you should. He will believe it matters to you and that might give him too much encouragement.'

'You do not think I should encourage him?'

He longed to cease talking about the man and put his own case forward, but until she was in a more receptive frame of mind, he could not. 'I do not think he needs much encouragement, do you?'

'No, I suppose not.'

'How do you feel about him, Vinny? Really feel, I mean.'

'Oh, James, I do not know. He has a way of looking at me that makes me shiver from top to toe and then I do not feel in control of my own body and he says the most flattering things—' She stopped suddenly.

He could have yelled with frustrated anger, but forced himself to sound calm. 'There is a but?'

'I suppose there must be, or I would not be so muddled.'

'Then my advice is to wait until you are no longer muddled, but sure of yourself.'

'Supposing he does not want to wait?'

'Why should he not?' he asked sharply.

'He might be impatient.'

'Good heavens! Surely he has not already declared himself?'

'Well, not directly, but he has hinted…'

'Then you must be deaf to his hints.'

'Why, James? Why?'

'I am not sure I am the right person to ask, Vinny.'

'Why not? Because you are a man?'

His smile was almost a grimace of pain, as he answered, 'That is one reason. The other is that I am too close to you. I could not be objective.'

She did not understand what he meant; if by being close, he meant he knew her very well, surely that made it easier for him to be objective? 'I collect you do not like Lord Wincote.'

'I do not know him. And neither do you, not properly. An outing or two, a compliment, a way of insinuating himself into our circle of friends and becoming popular is not enough. Marriage is for life, Vinny, it needs careful consideration, but most of all it needs certainty on the part of both and from what you say, I think you are far from certain.' He paused, then smiled. 'Now, I think I have lectured you long enough on the subject. Shall you like to drive now that we are out of town?'

She brightened at once. 'Oh, yes, please.'

As soon as the road widened enough to allow another vehicle to pass, he pulled up and handed her the reins. A minute later they were bowling along Finchley Road, all thoughts of Lord Wincote almost eradicated, even though he had refrained from passing them when they stopped and was still bringing up the rear.

They were in the country now, the houses no longer crowded together as they were in London, but spaced out, with fields and meadows about them, and here and there were farms nestling in the protection of tall elms. Once they were passed by a mail coach, its guard blowing on his yard of tin to announce its arrival at the next staging post, and once she had to pull up and wait as a herd of cows trod their sedate way to Smithfield, kept in check by a drover and his dog.

Before they turned off the main road on to a small lane which led over the Heath, James took control again and in another few minutes they found the coach in which the servants had travelled. They all tumbled out of their respective carriages and walked about to stretch their legs and greet acquaintances. They were on slightly rising ground, dotted with bushes and briars and an odd hawthorn tree here and there, but otherwise wide open grassland.

The children were highly excited and in danger of rushing off and getting lost, so Lavinia hurried to organise them, leaving James to find Donald Greenaway and Sir Percy, who had undertaken to decide on and mark out the course for the racing. 'What would you like to do first?' she asked them, as Frances scooped Freddie up to keep him safely with her.

'Fly our kite,' Jack said.

'Play cricket,' Andrew said.

'I want to play cricket, too,' Beth said.

'I believe Uncle James will arrange the cricket when he has finished talking to Major Greenaway,' Lavinia said. 'So shall we fly the kite first?'

Jack ran to fetch it from the coach and gave it to Lavinia to unravel its long tail and lay out the twine. She handed the stick with the ball of twine to Andrew, who ran as fast as his young legs could take him but was not big enough to get it airborne.

'Allow me,' Lord Wincote said, taking the kite from the boy, who looked surprised and a little resentful. 'I will have it airborne in a trice and then you may take over.' He smiled at Lavinia, who stood holding Beth by the hand.

She watched him pulling at the string and saw the kite

begin to rise until it was high above their heads, then he gave the string back. 'There, keep it into the wind, boy, and it will stay up for hours.' Then he strolled over to Lavinia. 'My lady.'

'Good morning, my lord. It is a lovely day.'

'Yes, indeed it is, but it would have been lovelier if you had been beside me on the journey.'

'I am sorry, my lord. We did not know the children were coming and there would be no room for me in Mama's coach.'

'Then perhaps you will return with me.'

'I must ask Mama.'

'Then I shall await her decision.'

'Oh, dear, the kite has come down,' she said, looking away from him to the group of children who had run some way from them. 'I must go and help.'

She set off, walking quickly, but if she thought she had dismissed him, she was mistaken, for he easily kept up with her and they reached the children together. 'Jack's turn now,' she said.

Edmund retrieved the kite and set it going again, this time giving the string to Jack. Again Lavinia stood and watched as the boy set off. He was more competent than Andrew and kept the kite airborne longer, as he ran along, whooping with glee, followed by Andrew, Lavinia and Edmund, who was carrying Beth. Because of the direction of the wind, they were going farther and farther from the main party and by the time Lavinia became aware of it, they were completely out of sight.

She stopped and looked about her. There was nothing to be seen but heath and sky with a few tiny white clouds, the only sound was her own laboured breathing and the voices of the children. Edmund stopped beside her and set Beth on her feet.

'Good,' he said, watching as Beth ran to join the boys.
'Now, at least we can talk uninterrupted.'

'Talk? What about?'

'You and me. Will you give me leave to speak to your
papa?'

She turned to face him and found herself looking into
eyes so dark they were almost black, and yet there was a
golden light in the depths of them which seemed to be
drawing her in, drowning her, taking her will and her reason. She knew she ought to fight it, but she could not. She
stood, gazing at him, her mouth slightly open.

A strand of hair had come loose and was drifting across
her face; unthinking, she lifted her hand to push it away.
He reached out and caught her wrist to stop her, then with
his other hand wound the strand about his finger. 'You do
know what I mean, don't you?'

'N…no. Yes, yes, I suppose I do.'

'Then what is your answer?'

'I don't know. I really don't…'

'Then perhaps this will help you to make up your mind.'
He pulled the strand of hair gently but insistently, so that
she leaned towards him. She knew he was going to kiss
her and she wanted it. She wanted to know if it would
make her feel any different, if the rubbery feeling she had
in her legs would intensify or lessen, whether she would
regain her breath or lose it altogether.

'Lavinia! Lavinia!' It was Jack's voice, loud and insis-
tent. 'Andrew let go of the string and the kite is stuck fast
in a tree. Come and see!'

She came out of her trance and turned towards the boy.
Edmund released her. 'Damn him!' he muttered.

Lavinia felt the world right itself. The grass and the sky
were in their appointed places; her feet were on the ground
and the man beside her was pink with anger. She ignored

him and ran towards the children. 'Look! Look at it!' Jack shouted. 'I told him to keep away from the tree. It isn't as if it wasn't the only one for miles.'

'I can't help the wind, can I?' Andrew retorted. 'Anyway, I can get it. I'll climb after it.'

'You'll do no such thing,' Lavinia said, looking upwards. 'It's too high, you'll fall.'

'Then will you get it, sir?' Jack asked Edmund. 'You can reach that bottom branch easily.'

'Certainly not!' he said brusquely. 'I don't intend to risk my neck for a yard or two of coloured cotton. It will have to stay where it is.'

'Lord Wincote is right, children,' Lavinia said but, though she agreed with him, she did not think he needed to be quite so bad-tempered about it. 'Now, I think it is time to go back to the others, they will be wondering what has become of us.'

The children left reluctantly, mourning their kite, and they all walked silently back to the main party, with Lavinia wondering what would have happened if they had not lost it at that particular moment. The first person they saw was James. He did not need to ask the children why they looked so downcast, they surrounded him all talking at once.

'We lost our kite.'

'It went into a tree and stuck.'

'I wanted to climb up and fetch it but Vinny wouldn't let me.'

'And glad I am of that,' he said, looking at Lavinia. Her cheeks were unusually pink and she would not look at him. He glanced at Wincote, whose face betrayed anger. What had happened? Would she tell him if he asked?

'Lord Wincote said he couldn't get it, either.'

'Oh, be fair, Jack,' Lavinia put in. 'It was too high to reach.'

'In that case you must consider it lost, young shaver,' James told him. 'Now, I thought you wanted to play cricket.'

'Oh, we do, we do!'

The game was soon organised with men, children and even the younger ladies taking part, becoming helpless with laughter when they dropped a catch or their bats missed the ball. The children shrieked their delight or consternation, depending on whether the unfortunate ladies were on their side or not. James had endless patience with them, teaching them how to bat and bowl, until everyone had had enough and Major Greenaway came to tell them the races were about to begin.

'If you want to take part, Wincote,' James said, turning to Edmund, 'I suggest you find your mount and make your way to the start.'

'Certainly. And I'll put a little wager on the outcome.' He turned to Lavinia. 'I will rejoin you directly, my lady.'

The two men left and Lavinia shepherded the children to a spot where they could watch the races in safety. The course was a hilly one which would test the stamina of the horses as well as their speed, especially as they were to race in a series of heats in which only the first two would compete in the next round. Lavinia was surprised at the number of entries, far more than the members of their party, but then she remembered that James had been talking about the event before she had suggested the day out.

The children became very excited as the starter dropped his flag and the race was on. They cheered themselves hoarse for James, jumping up and down in excitement when he came to the front and Lavinia found herself joining in, willing him across the finishing line first. Edmund was in the second heat and she expected the children to shout for him, but for some reason they were reticent and put their support behind Donald Greenaway.

'Are you not going to cheer Lord Wincote?' she asked.

'No,' Jack said. 'We do not like him.'

'Why ever not? He helped you fly your kite.'

'Only because he wanted to talk to you.'

'And when the kite was stuck, he would not to fetch it down,' Andrew added. 'He was angry.'

'Perhaps he is not very good at climbing and he would have spoiled his clothes. You must not blame him for that, my loves.'

'Uncle James would have got it down if he had been there.'

'Well, perhaps,' she conceded.

Edmund won his heat with Donald very close behind and both went on to the next heat. After four gruelling races there was only James, Edmund, Donald and a rider Lavinia did not know to battle out the final. She was tempted to cheer the unknown, simply because she could not bring herself to favour either Edmund or James. James won and she went over to congratulate him and commiserate with the others. Edmund, who saw her coming, quickly changed his look of disgruntlement to a smile and offered his hand to James. 'Well done, Corringham. I am in your debt for fifty guineas, I believe.'

'Yes. No hurry, though.'

'Oh, but there is. A debt of honour is a debt of honour.' He almost winced as he said it. 'Shall we say double or quits in the carriage race?'

'Done!' James said. He would not ordinarily have accepted, but Wincote had set his hackles up and he could hardly refuse without inviting some sharp rejoinder. He could easily afford to lose a hundred guineas, but could Wincote? It would be interesting to find out.

Lavinia watched with her heart in her mouth as the men raced for their phaetons, which were already being brought to the start line by grooms. James's vehicle, having such high wheels, was not as stable as Edmund's and this became evident as the race progressed since he had to use every ounce of his skill to keep it upright. Several times one wheel left the ground as it bumped over a tussock of grass but it jolted back and miraculously kept going. James's handicap enabled Edmund to draw ahead and for a moment it seemed he had the race won, but his horses were tiring and slowly James came abreast of him. Their wheels were so close several times that it looked as though they must collide; Lavinia could hardly bear to watch.

Little by little, James drew in front and won by a head. The grooms grabbed the reins to steady the horses and the riders jumped down to shake hands. Lavinia and the children raced to join them, but they were beaten by Frances, who had been frightened out of her wits. 'James, don't ever do that to me again,' she scolded him. 'My heart is beating enough to burst.'

He smiled at her. 'We were in no danger, Mama. Neither of us is foolish enough to risk our lives for a hundred guineas. Isn't that right, Wincote?'

Edmund smiled at him through gritted teeth and inclined his head as if to agree.

After that the ladies' races were tame affairs, which Lavinia won easily, there being few women prepared to take up the challenge and none in her league. She derived little pleasure from her victory. Somehow, the day had been spoiled. She did not know why. Was it because Lord Wincote had failed to kiss her? Or that he had had the temerity to try? Or was it that he could, with a little effort, have retrieved the kite? If he had not been there and there had been no one but the children to see, she might have attempted it herself. It was not so many years before she had been climbing trees at Loscoe Court dressed in her brother's breeches.

Or was it something to do with the races? James might not have been prepared to risk his life, but Lord Wincote's expression had been a strange one, as if James had won more than a hundred guineas. His had been furious and afraid. Oh, she could understand someone being frightened by that gruelling race, but not after it was over. It had taken all his self-control to smile at her when she had offered her commiserations. But in a minute he was his usual urbane self and escorted her to join everyone else in the shade of a chestnut tree to eat the picnic the servants had prepared.

Afterwards they rested in or beside the carriages, leaving their horses unharnessed to graze. Lavinia leaned against the tree trunk with her eyes shut and Beth's head in her lap, as James and Donald got up and strolled away, taking Jack and Andrew with them.

'Well?' James asked when as the boys scampered ahead. 'Did you discover anything?'

'He is in debt, no doubt of it. The Cumberland estate is mortgaged to the hilt, but the story goes that he expects a windfall, something to do with his grandfather's will.'

'Or Lavinia's dowry.'

'Possibly. At any rate, the word is strong enough to make the dunners hold back. I'll try and find out more.'

'Make it quick, if you can. I believe he has already made advances.'

'Step in yourself, then.'

'I intend to.' He paused, noticing the boys pointing up

at a tree. 'In the meantime, let's have a look at this kite and see if we can't get it down.'

Half an hour later, the peace of the heath was disturbed by the return of an excited Jack and Andrew, hauling on the string of a bravely flying kite. 'Uncle James got it down,' Andrew shouted, waking the slumberers. 'I knew he would, even though Lord Wincote said he couldn't. See, it flies as well as ever.'

'Put it away now, Jack,' the Duchess said. 'I think it is time we returned home.'

Lavinia was indifferent to the argument going on about who should ride with whom on the return journey, which was solved by James taking the two boys with him, leaving room for her to ride with the Duchess. She was glad of that; she did not want to ride with either James or Lord Wincote. James would quiz her about how she was feeling, advising caution, and Lord Wincote would go on about speaking to her papa and at that moment she did not know how she felt or what she wanted.

Chapter Five

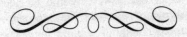

Lavinia wore yellow for Lady Graham's ball. The open-fronted gown, worn over a satin slip in pale lemon, was of a gossamer silk so fine it was almost transparent. It was shot with silver thread which seemed to ripple as she moved. It had a low square neckline and small puffed sleeves, drawn in with silver ribbon. The same silver ribbon delineated the high waist and more of it was threaded through her lustrous hair which Daisy had braided *à la Didon*.

She stood in front of the long mirror, appraising herself, turning this way and that, glad she was already out and did not have to wear white, which didn't suit her. Her figure was good, her skin clear and her eyes bright with anticipation.

'You look real lovely, my lady,' Daisy said, as Lavinia slipped her feet into yellow satin shoes with silver buckles. 'You will have all the dandies at your feet.'

The idea of being in demand was not unwelcome; it had happened two years before at her own come-out ball, and she would have to be made of stone not to enjoy it, but she had always been aware that her father was one of the richest men in the kingdom and that her dowry might have something to do with it. It was that confounded dowry that she found so bothersome. How could she possibly know a suitor wanted her for herself, because he loved her? How could she tell?

How could she know that Lord Edmund Wincote was sincere? She liked him, and might very well be falling in love with him so, if that were the case, she shouldn't even be thinking about her dowry. Would he need an answer tonight? What would she do if he approached her father and offered for her without waiting for her agreement? It would all become very complicated. James had said she must be certain. Perhaps something might happen tonight to make her sure.

She smiled as Daisy draped a lightweight taffeta cloak about her shoulders, handed her a pair of white gloves and her reticule and stood back, her job done. 'Thank you, Daisy. You do not need to wait up for me, I can undress myself and we might be very late.'

She left the maid picking up the discarded day clothes and went down to join the Duke and Duchess. For once her father was free to go with them because of further developments in the royal saga. Since the King was unable to rid himself of his wife without having his own indiscretions exposed, his government had instead created a Bill of Pains and Penalties. If passed, this would strip the Queen of her rights and privileges without the necessity for proof, and grant the King a divorce.

'It is a mockery of justice and so I have said,' declared the Duke, when he came home that afternoon.

'Then your conscience is clear, my dear,' Frances had replied. 'Put it from your mind and let us enjoy what is left of the summer. You do not have to attend.'

He sighed. 'Unfortunately, I do. Everyone entitled to sit in the House of Lords must be there, and refusal could lead to a heavy fine or even imprisonment. We are all to be in our places by ten in the morning on the seventeenth of August.'

'So much for the Season being extended for the coronation,' Lavinia put in. 'The effect will be disastrous with half the gentlemen absent. Poor Constance's ball will be quite spoiled with everyone talking about the latest developments.'

'Then we must set a good example, Vinny, my dear, and not mention it,' the Duke had replied. 'Nothing will happen for another month, so we may as well make the most of the time.'

And now here she was, about to be borne away to a ball where her own future might be decided. This business with the King and Queen had really brought home to her the terrible consequences of entering into a marriage without love. She was unusually quiet as they left their carriage at the door of the Graham house in Holles Street.

Lord Graham had done his best for his daughter on two previous occasions and was still trying, though now the flowers were those common in almost any summer garden instead of exotic ones imported from abroad, and the music was provided by a string quartet and not a full orchestra. Nor was the ballroom as crowded as on the first occasion when there had been little room to move, though one would hardly have believed it before entering it, judging by the volume of noise.

It seemed everyone was determined to air their views on the Royal marriage. There were hundreds of witnesses to the Queen's adultery, so it was said, all who were being brought over from Italy at the government's expense and probably paid to give evidence into the bargain. Lord Brougham was going to bring up the King's indiscretions whether His Majesty liked it or not, including a romp with the daughter of a tavern-keeper and his illicit marriage to Mrs Fitzherbert, which everyone knew about.

'I knew it,' Lavinia said, leaving the Duke and Duchess to find seats, while she stayed to commiserate with Constance who was standing beside her parents.

The shy, quiet Miss Graham had abandoned the dull colours she usually wore and was in a blue taffeta gown which set off a commendable figure and heightened the colour in her cheeks, while her carefully dressed hair had been brushed until it gleamed. There was a glow about her that Lavinia had not noticed before, as if she had suddenly come alive. Could there be an offer on the cards? 'You look lovely,' Lavinia said sincerely.

'Oh, Vinny, I am so glad you came,' she said, reaching out for her friend's hand. 'It is going to be a disaster.'

'No, I am sure it is not,' Lavinia soothed. 'The babble will die down when the music begins for the dancing.'

However, it was not so much the music which silenced everyone but the entrance of Sir Percy Ponsonby. His attire was certainly colourful—a buttercup-yellow breeches suit of satin, a pea-green waistcoat, red-heeled shoes, cream hose and an enormous lace cravat. But it was not his dazzling appearance that had everyone open-mouthed—it was the lady on his arm.

Although past the first blush of youth, she was extraordinarily beautiful, with oval features, rosy cheeks and hair as black as a raven's wing. Her diaphanous gown was of a pea-green spider-gauze only decent because of the silk slip she wore under it. Round her throat a heavy necklace flashed with precious stones, matched by eardrops and a thick bracelet. She was generously curved without being fat and stood beside her escort, surveying the company as if summing them all up before making the grand entrance.

'Where, oh, where did he find her?' Lavinia murmured

as the couple moved into the room and, bowing this way and that at Sir Percy's many acquaintances as though they were royalty themselves, they joined the Duke and Duchess of Loscoe.

'Sir Percy is so often the odd one out,' Lady Graham told Lavinia. 'So when he asked if he might bring a friend, I was happy to oblige. But I have never met her.'

'I must go and be introduced,' Lavinia said, unable to contain her curiosity. 'Please excuse me.'

She returned to her parents, just as Sir Percy was presenting the lady to the Duchess. 'Your Grace, may I present Lady Rattenshaw,' he was saying. 'She is but lately returned to England from India. Sir Arthur, her husband, died just over a year ago. He was serving with the East India Company, don't you know, died of one of those terrible diseases they have out there.'

'Oh, I am sorry,' Frances murmured, as the lady inclined her head in a slight bow.

'Thank you,' she said with a sad smile. 'But I have learned one must accept what cannot be helped. He left me more than adequately provided for, but lonely. We had no children, you see, so I thought I would return to the old country and visit my very dear friend, Percy.' She patted Sir Percy's hand and smiled at him.

Sir Percy smiled back, introduced her to Lavinia and then presented her to James and Lord Wincote who strolled over to join them.

While Edmund was making polite conversation to the newcomer, James seized Lavinia's dance card and, as the first dance was beginning, the two of them took the floor.

'The old dog,' he said, as they moved into the set. 'I never knew Percy had it in him.'

'He is only acting the gallant to his friend's widow, but

I think it is not very kind to upstage Constance. It is her ball, after all.'

'She is no threat to Constance, my dear. Not in the same league.'

'I hope you are right.' They parted, circled another couple and came together again. 'Do you think those diamonds are real?'

'Undoubtedly.'

'Interesting,' she said. 'I imagine every penniless gentleman in town will be showing his true colours after tonight.'

'Now, there's a thought,' he said, grinning.

She looked up at him aghast. 'James, not you. Oh, I know Mama said you should—' She stopped in confusion. 'You wouldn't, would you?'

He looked down into her upturned face and those speaking eyes of hers were telling him something that lifted his spirits. She did not like the idea at all. Oh, it was not jealousy, not yet, but it could be. He smiled, turned her about him and they promenaded the length of the set before joining it at the end. 'Why not?'

'But you do not need money, do you?'

'You can never have too much of it, Vinny dear.' He glanced over to where the lady was surrounded by sycophants, all clamouring to dance with her while Percy stood by with a knowing smile on his face. 'But she has other attributes besides money, don't you think? She has the looks of a goddess.'

'Perhaps she has feet of clay,' Lavinia said hopefully. 'Or maybe the stones are made of paste.'

He left her, bowed and did a turn with the lady opposite him and returned to Lavinia. 'Paste doesn't sparkle like that.'

They continued in silence; he was smiling, she was

thoughtful. At the end of the dance, they returned to their own group, but not before he had written his name against a waltz later in the evening. Percy was still looking pleased with himself and Lady Rattenshaw was being charming to everyone.

'I am so glad Sir Percy prevailed upon me to come tonight,' she was saying. 'I had thought that since I knew no one I would not enjoy it, but nothing could be further from the truth. Everyone has been so kind. I do hope you will all join me for a little soirée at my house in Upper Brook Street on Friday week.'

'Delighted,' they murmured, one by one, and this was followed by reciprocal invitations until it looked as though the lady would not have a minute to herself for the next month. 'It seems to me,' Lavinia whispered to James, 'you will have a few rivals to contend with.'

'Oh, I care nothing for rivals. They may be easily dispatched,' he said, making Lavinia frown at him. 'And do not wear such a disapproving expression; it spoils your looks.' And with that he turned, bowed before Lady Rattenshaw and asked her to stand up with him for the next dance. She accepted charmingly and they took to the floor.

Lavinia watched them go, until she heard Edmund's voice at her elbow. 'My lady, will you do me the honour?'

She smiled and offered him her hand and they followed James and Lady Rattenshaw into a country dance. 'They are flocking round her ladyship like bees round a honey hive,' she said. 'Never mind that she is ten years older than most of them.'

He looked across the room at the Earl, smiling down at his partner. 'By that, I collect, you mean the Earl of Corringham,' he said.

'No, not only him. All the eligibles.' She looked round

the room as they danced. 'Except Lord Haverley, who is so staid, he knows he would have no chance and so he is sticking close to Constance, which I find very touching.'

'Do you include me in your censure, my lady?' he asked, affecting to be hurt.

'Should I?' she asked in a teasing tone.

'No. My heart is already lost, it is no longer mine for disposal.'

'Oh.'

'Is that all you can say? I had hoped that you might give me leave to speak to your papa. After all, he is here tonight and apparently free of his other duties for the moment. What better time to approach him?'

'My lord, this is Miss Graham's ball and her last chance to make a match. I think it would be unkind of us to steal her limelight.'

'I think it has already been stolen by Lady Rattenshaw. Not deliberately, I believe, because she is charming, but I cannot think that my speaking to the Duke can adversely affect Miss Graham. We do not have to make the announcement tonight.'

She hesitated. He was looking at her now, holding her in a kind of mental embrace which was making her heart beat faster and her legs feel rubbery. If he had that effect in a crowded room when their only contact was her hand in his, then what would it be like in some quiet place when they were alone? What would she feel if he took her in his arms and kissed her? When at last, she forced herself to look away, the feeling slowly subsided so that she was able to breathe again. 'It is too soon,' she said.

'Why? You came out two years ago, you have met all the eligibles in that time, how can you say it is to soon?'

'You are not all the eligibles. I had no difficulty with those.'

'Then does that not prove I am different? I cannot wait much longer, my dear, I really cannot.'

'Why not?'

'I want you all to myself, to be able to say, ''This treasure is mine.'''

She looked at him sharply, alerted by the tone of his voice. Then she laughed. 'Would you love me as much if I were as poor as a church mouse?'

'Of course I would. I am affronted that you feel the need to ask.'

'Good,' she said, smiling wickedly. 'Because I am.'

'Am what?'

'Poor as a church mouse. I haven't a groat to call my own.'

'Of course you haven't. No single girl has, but you do have a wealthy father.'

'Ah, but that's just it. Papa is not inclined to pay a large dowry.'

He laughed. 'My lady, you are bamming me, but no matter, I will play your little game with you. So you are poor. I am not. Oh, I have not the wealth of the Duke of Loscoe, but I have an estate and an income from it as well as prospects.'

'Oh, good,' she said. 'I am so relieved. Papa was so concerned that I might be wanted for my money.'

'I can understand his concern.'

'Then you will not mind if he enquires into these prospects you spoke of?'

'No, but they will not materialise until my grandfather's affairs have been settled. It is why I am in London, you understand.'

'Oh, that is a pity,' she said, smiling. 'You may speak to Papa, if you wish, but I should warn you that he is determined that I shall be in receipt of no fortune until after I have been married two years so, you see, you will have to convince him that you can keep me in the manner I am accustomed to for that time.'

He looked astonished. 'I am persuaded he does not mean it. He would not see you in want.'

'No, but then…I will not be in want, will I? Not with you. You have your own fortune and prospects—have you not just told me so?'

'Yes, yes, of course,' he said hurriedly.

At the end of the dance he returned her to her stepmother and then excused himself.

'You were in very earnest conversation with Lord Wincote, Vinny,' Frances said, as Lavinia sat beside her. 'I wonder if he is not becoming a little too ardent.'

'Would you disapprove?'

'My dear, it is not my approval you should seek, but your papa's.' She paused. 'Is that what you want?'

'I don't know. When I am with him, it is. When he is pouring compliments into my ears or looking at me with those intense eyes of his, which seem to hold me in some kind of thrall, then I think there is nothing in the whole world I want but to be married to him, but when he is not present, when I am in my right senses, I am a mass of indecision, as if I must be close to him to feel anything.'

Frances smiled and put her hand on Lavinia's. 'I think you should not make a hasty decision.'

'He wants to speak to Papa.'

'Well, we cannot stop him doing that, but that is not to say the Duke will agree or that you have to accept.'

'I told him a fib.'

'Oh?' Frances raised an eyebrow and waited.

'I told him Papa would not pay any dowry until I had been married two years. It was Papa's idea to test the sincerity of anyone who offered for me.' She looked up as her stepmother laughed aloud. 'You can laugh, Mama, but what will Papa say when he hears?'

'I should think he would say how clever you are. But did his lordship believe you?'

'I do not know. We shall soon find out. If he goes to Papa, believing it, then he is sincere in wanting me for myself alone and—'

'You would accept him?'

'I do not know. I would certainly think about it.'

'And supposing he goes to the Duke, not believing it, thinking that you have been testing him and the dowry is quite safe, what then?'

'Oh, I hadn't thought of that. Do you think you could prime Papa? I hate to think my dowry is the main attraction; if it is, then I had as lief not marry at all.' She looked up as a shadow fell over them and Lord Haverley asked her to stand up with him and the conversation was brought to an abrupt halt.

His lordship was followed in subsequent dances by Martin Drew and several more young men of her acquaintance. They were all very pleasant, personable young men and she managed to listen to their compliments and tease them in response while her attention was elsewhere. Had Edmund found the Duke? And where, oh, where was James when she needed him?

James was in the small room set aside for cards, but he was not playing. He was sitting in a corner, nursing a glass of brandy and talking to Sir Percy. 'Where did you find her, Ponsonby?' he demanded.

'Who?'

'Lady Rattenshaw.'

'Old friend, me boy.'

'You never mentioned her before.'

'Long time ago. Married Sir Arthur, went out to India. Now she's back.'

'And?'

'Looked me up, like she said. Rich as Golden Ball, don't you know. Richer even.'

'You've already got more blunt than you know what to do with.'

'So I have. But he hasn't.'

'He?'

'Your rival. Lord Edmund Wincote.'

James looked at his friend, eyes wide with surprise. 'You think…?'

Percy shrugged. 'I'll lay a pony on it.'

James began to laugh and it was some moments before he could gather himself to speak again. 'Does the lady know what you have in mind?'

'Oh, yes,' he said, his eyes wide with innocence.

James stood up, still smiling. 'I am agog to see what happens. I think I shall rejoin the dancers. But not a word to Lady Lavinia, my friend.'

'Oh, no, most decidedly not.'

Lavinia was dancing with Augusta's husband, Richard, when he returned to the ballroom and he sat down beside the Duchess to wait for the dance to end.

'Vinny seems to be enjoying herself,' he said, apparently idly.

'Why should she not be?'

'Oh, no reason, but I cannot see her latest admirer.'

'If you mean Lord Wincote, I think he may have gone to find Marcus.'

'My God, he doesn't waste much time, does he?'

'No.'

'Is the Duke of a mind to allow it?'

'I really cannot say.'

'She hasn't been such a ninny as to encourage him, has she?'

'Unlike you, my dear, he does not need encouragement.'

'What do you mean, Mama?'

'Oh, I think you know.' She was smiling. 'I have never seen anyone so slow. You will lose her if you are not careful.'

'*Me?*' He affected astonishment. 'You think I—'

'James, you forget I have known you since you were in leading-strings, listened to your childish complaints, nursed you when you were ill, picked you up when you fell over. I know what is in your heart as well as you know it yourself.' She paused, smiling. 'Now, tell me I am wrong.'

'No,' he conceded. 'You haven't told Vinny this?'

'Good gracious no. I may have done almost everything else for you, but I cannot do your courting for you, James.'

'But, Mama, it was you who warned me against turning my thoughts in Lavinia's direction, don't you remember? You told me the Duke would never countenance an offer from me. I could not—' He stopped; he did not want her to know that one of the reasons he had held back in those early days was that he loved his Little Mama too much to risk spoiling her chance of happiness with the man she loved.

'Yes, but that was three years ago and a great deal has changed since then. You have become a young man any mother could be proud of and Lavinia has grown into a beautiful young woman.'

'Oh, I know that,' he said, a wry smile on his lips, watching as the dance came to an end and Lavinia came back to them.

'Then make a push.'

'What push?' Lavinia demanded, overhearing.

'Oh, nothing,' James said. 'My dance, I think.' He bowed to her and took her by the hand to lead her on to the floor. From the corner of his eye he saw Lord Wincote return to the room and begin looking around as if searching Lavinia out. When he caught sight of them, his eyes narrowed and his lips were closed in a thin line of annoyance.

'Good,' James murmured, with a smile.

'What do you mean?' she asked him.

'Oh, that you are dancing this waltz very well, my dear.'

'I like it. And the music is so—' She stopped; she had been about to say romantic, but that might make him think she thought of him in a romantic way and she didn't, did she? 'So satisfying, don't you think?'

'Delightful,' he said, holding her a little closer and whirling her round. 'You know, you are in looks tonight, Vinny. I am to be envied at this moment.'

'Thank you, kind sir.'

He had been the one to teach her the steps and she loved dancing with him. They were so much in tune with each other; she could follow him without a moment's hesitation. Feet, hands, bodies moved as one. Her gown floated round her and swirled about his black-clad legs, almost as if entrapping him. She smiled and looked up at him and found him gazing at her with an expression that made her heart turn over. His grey eyes were as soft as a dawn mist, his mouth a gentle curve. His head was bent towards her and for a second, which seemed like an eternity, it was almost as if he meant to kiss her.

There was no question that he would do so, not in such a public place, but in any case, the startled look in her eyes would have made him desist. He smiled wryly and continued dancing, reverting to holding her at the regulation arm's length. As the music came to an end, she gave him a full curtsy and he executed a sweeping bow and offered her his arm to escort her back to the Duchess.

But Lavinia knew something had changed between them. It was like suddenly growing up and finding what she had assumed would last forever had disappeared with her childhood and would never return. She was disconcerted, a little sad, knowing that the teasing, the familiarity, she had taken for granted was no longer permissible.

James was not her brother, as he was so fond of pointing out, and perhaps it meant that she ought to treat him as she did other young men of her acquaintance, with correctness, politeness and respect. She did respect him; there was no one she would sooner turn to in trouble, no one to whom she would rather confide, not even her father or stepmother. So why, at this moment, could she find not a word to say to him? Why could she not tell him how she felt, not only about him, but about Lord Wincote?

As if her thoughts had brought him to her, Lord Wincote came to claim his second dance, but instead of leading her on to the floor, he chose to promenade about its perimeter. 'You do not mind, do you?' he asked her. 'I wish to talk to you.'

'No. But what do you want to talk about?'

'I have spoken to your papa…'

'And?' she asked, holding her breath.

'He has given his consent for me to speak to you. I am overjoyed.'

'Oh.' She was thoughtful. It did not sound as if Papa knew about the untruth she had told, so perhaps the Duchess had not been able to speak to him, or perhaps she had and he had chosen not to corroborate it. On the other hand, perhaps he had and it had made no difference at all to Lord Wincote.

'You are quiet, my dear. I would have expected some

expression of gratification that his Grace has been so con-
descending as to look kindly on my suit.'

'Oh, I am,' she said, wondering if his pomposity was
his way of dealing with his feelings, or if he had been out
of society so long he was afraid of saying something
wrong and had to wrap everything up in verbosity. He did
not give her the impression of someone afraid, but he was
tense. She smiled; talking to the Duke often had that effect
on people.

'Good,' he said, noticing the smile. 'This, of course, is
not the time or the place to take the matter further, but,
with your permission, I shall call on you tomorrow afternoon.'

For a moment she felt inclined to tell him she would
not be at home, but that would not serve; she would have
to hear his proposal sooner or later and make up her mind.

The music stopped and the dancers began milling about,
making further conversation impossible, for which Lavinia
was grateful. Lady Graham was busy trying to usher everyone in to supper. 'Come along,' she was saying. 'There is
food in the dining room, I am sure you would all like some
refreshment. Lord Wincote, do take Lady Lavinia in.'

But instead of leading her into the dining room he took
her back to Frances, bowed to them both and turned on
his heel, making his way from the room. Lavinia watched
him go, wondering why he did not stay to eat. Surely nothing she had said had made him suddenly want to leave? It
was James who took her into supper, which was a noisy
affair with everyone returning to the subject of the Queen's
trial and offering their own opinion as to the outcome.

Lavinia took no part in it, she was busy mulling over
the conversation she had just had with Lord Wincote. Had
she really given him the impression that she would accept
an offer from him? He seemed to think so. Why had she

done it? Did she really want to spend the rest of her life with him? Then she thought of James sitting beside her, joining in the chatter and laughing at the jokes, and, suddenly, she knew she did not.

James did not think of her as a wife, of course, but surely somewhere in that teeming city there was a man whom she could be as comfortable with as she was with him? Or was that the only prerogative of a stepbrother, and a husband had a completely different role to play?

It was all far too much for her and, begging to be excused, she almost ran from the room. Pushing past the people still going in to supper, she made her way upstairs to the room set aside for the ladies to refresh their toilette, where she sat down on a chaise longue and covered her face with her hands. There was no doubt that her life was about to change forever.

Her come-out two years before had been meant to mark her transition from childhood to womanhood and she had always supposed that had been the turning point, the highlight of her young life, and though some things were different—the young men who flocked round her, the fact that she could go to balls and routs, take part in adult conversations and make a few decisions of her own—nothing had really altered. Simply passing her seventeenth birthday had not transformed her into a woman. That, she realised, had been still in the future.

Now it was here and she was not at all sure that she liked it, especially if it meant losing the friendship of James or having a man other than her father take over the management of her life. Marrying meant giving yourself to a man—body, soul and fortune—to do with as he pleased. It was an enormous step to take and surely love and trust were the only means of being certain that you were stepping into sunlight and not falling into a dark abyss of misery?

That had been the lot of her father and mother, and not until Papa married Frances had he been truly happy, so even he whom she revered could make a mistake. Oh, if only she could be given a sign…

She lifted her head as the sound of loud voices, and then screams, reached her from downstairs. She scrambled to her feet and ran out on to the gallery where she could see down into the hall. Judging by the number of people milling about, it seemed that almost everyone had decamped from the ballroom and was crowding round a group of people in the middle of which was Lady Graham, apparently in hysterics. She was grasping her throat as if someone had tried to throttle her.

Lavinia hurried down and joined the throng, pushing her way through to Constance who stood leaning against the wall for support. All the colour had drained from her face and she looked close to tears. She was staring at the crowd round her mother.

'What has happened?' Lavinia asked her. 'I was upstairs in the rest room when I heard the commotion.'

'Someone has stolen Mama's diamond necklace. She was wearing it before supper, but she can't be sure when it went…'

'It was taken from around her neck?' Lavinia asked in surprise. 'Didn't she feel it go?'

'Apparently not. She has been so busy all evening, making sure everyone was enjoying themselves and instructing the servants that she has hardly had time to draw breath. When she did, she put her hand to her throat and realised the necklace had gone. Papa said she must have taken it off and put it down somewhere, but she swears she did not. Lord Corringham has gone to fetch a Runner, though what he can do I have no idea.'

'Oh, Constance, I am so sorry.'

'It has ruined the whole evening. Everyone is looking at everyone else with suspicion and wondering if they might have the necklace in their pocket. It's horrible.'

'Yes, it must be. But it cannot be one of the guests, they are all known to your parents—someone must have come in from outside. The town is full of all sorts of strange people, pickpockets and footpads and the like, more this year than ever before.'

'Or it was one of the servants. Papa engaged extra ones for the evening. He has shut them all up in the morning room and intends to search every one of them.'

'And if that yields nothing?'

'Well, he can hardly search the guests, can he? Oh, Vinny, it was my last chance and now…' Her lip trembled and the tears spilled down her cheeks.

'Oh, I do think they make too much of these balls as a way of meeting a husband, Constance dear. And if anyone intended to offer tonight, this will not make any difference, he will come back.'

She sniffed and smiled. 'Lord Haverley was most attentive and I thought—'

'Lord Haverley?' Lavinia asked in surprise. 'But he has a family already.'

'That does not matter to me. It might be a point in his favour that he is already past his youth and settled. And I like him.'

'There you are, then! He will be at our rehearsal tomorrow, you will see him again then and who knows, he may yet be brought up to the mark. If that is what you want…'

'Oh, it is, it is.'

James returned accompanied by Major Greenaway, whom he quickly introduced to Lord Graham. 'As an investigator, he will do more good than a Runner, I think,' James said. 'And I can personally vouch for his credentials and his discretion.'

'Let him do what he has to do, then,' his lordship said. 'I've got all the servants locked up. You can begin by searching them.'

'Very well. I suggest everyone goes back to the dancing. There is nothing to be gained by standing about here.'

'Yes, yes.' Lord Graham turned to James. 'Corringham, will you organise things? I must go with the Major and my wife is in no fit state…' He looked across at Lady Graham, who had sunk into a chair and was being comforted by the Duchess.

But dancing was the last thing on people's minds. They allowed themselves to be ushered back into the ballroom but, despite the musicians playing, remained in groups discussing the theft. Many wondered aloud if they should leave, but James, backed by the Duke, persuaded them to stay, at least until the servants had been searched.

'It will spoil Miss Graham's evening if we disperse,' James said. 'And perhaps Major Greenaway will wish to question everybody.'

'Question everybody!' exclaimed Lady Willoughby. 'I never heard the like. Does he think we should stoop so low as to steal? And from a friend, too? I am affronted, truly I am.'

'I am sure he does not,' James soothed her. 'Nevertheless, without realising it, you might have seen or heard something which, together with other evidence, makes up the whole picture, like the pieces of a Chinese puzzle I once had as a boy.'

'Well, I am sure I saw and heard nothing or I would have said so,' the lady said.

'I think Lord Graham is right, she took it off and put it down somewhere,' Lord Wincote added. 'Ten to one she will find it tomorrow.'

'Let us hope you are right,' the Duchess put in. 'But is seems a strange thing to do to a valuable piece of jewellery.'

'Well, I intend to dance,' James said. 'Miss Graham, will you join me in the gavotte?'

Constance seemed reluctant at first, but his sympathetic smile soon persuaded her and she joined him in the middle of the floor.

'Come on,' Edmund said, seizing Lavinia by the hand and pulling her after them. 'Let us follow their example.'

'My lord,' she said in dismay. Dancing more than twice with the same man was considered as good as an engagement. 'I have already stood up with you twice tonight. You will have the tabbies talking…'

'Let them. I make no secret of my intentions.' He swung her into the dance.

'But you have not yet made an offer and I have not accepted. You go too fast.'

'I beg your pardon, my lady,' he said quickly. 'But I cannot slow down, the measure is an energetic one.'

'I did not mean your dancing, my lord.' She was breathless with exertion, making further protest impossible. In any case it was too late. It was not only the exercise that was making her cheeks flame, but knowing that everyone was watching and drawing their own conclusions. She was aware of James and Constance galloping alongside them and wished with all her heart that she could disappear into the floor.

The music came to an end and she stood, breathing

heavily, waiting for Lord Wincote to restore her to her stepmother, when she knew she would be in for a scolding. But it wasn't her fault, was it? She was disconcerted when she heard James call for an encore and the next minute he had whisked her away to begin all over again.

'My lord,' she protested. 'This is the third time tonight.'

'So it is,' he said mildly. 'But if Lord Wincote can dance with you three times, then so can I.'

'Everyone will talk.'

'I hope they may,' he said. 'They will come to the conclusion that I saw Wincote's *faux pas* and, to save you from mortification, stepped in to follow suit. I hope it will be considered the act of a gentleman.'

She pondered this as they galloped up and down the dance floor until she was exhausted and called a halt. 'Please take me back to Mama, James.'

'Certainly.' He stopped and offered her his arm.

She laid her fingers upon his sleeve and they walked decorously back to the Duchess, passing Edmund dancing with Lady Rattenshaw on the way. 'He is certainly enjoying himself,' James commented.

'He has spoken to Papa.'

'The devil he has!'

'Yes. Papa has given him leave to pay his addresses.'

'And how do you feel about that? Is that what you want?'

She looked up at him. He appeared to be gazing at something above and beyond her head, as if he were not particularly interested in her answer. A little wave of annoyance passed through her, which she did not understand, and that was followed by the need to assert herself.

'Of course,' she said brightly, and immediately wished she had held her tongue. It was simply not true and she cursed her contrary nature which so liked to tease. Not an hour before, she had been telling herself she could no longer roast him and here she was doing it.

'Then may I offer my felicitations,' he said, through gritted teeth.

It was too late now to explain, too late to say she had not made up her mind, too late to protest that she had never wanted it in the first place, too late to retract. In any case, the opportunity was lost because Donald Greenaway returned with Lord Graham and both looked grim.

Their arrival silenced the musicians as if they had been given a signal, the dancing came to an abrupt halt and everyone stood expectantly facing them. 'We found nothing,' the Major said.

'They could have hidden it,' Lady Willoughby said, loudly enough for all to hear. 'There is no other explanation.'

'If they have, then we have not uncovered it. If you would all have a little patience while I ask a few questions...'

'If you think I am going to stay here to be insulted with questions, then you are in error.' Lady Willoughby turned to her husband. 'Come, George. And you, too, Benedict.' She sailed up to the door, intending to leave.

'My lady, I would not for the world detain you,' Lord Graham said, moving aside to allow her to pass. 'Nor anyone else desirous to leave.' Then, to Donald, 'You can't go round accusing people. They are my guests, here at my express invitation, every one a member of the *haut monde*.'

'I do not intend to accuse anyone, my lord. But if you want the jewels restored to you, then some questions must be asked.'

'No. I would as lief lose the jewellery than lose my friends.'

Donald sighed. 'Very well, let them go home, if that's

what they want, but if you want me to continue the investigation, I shall require a guest list.'

The whole evening was coming to a sad conclusion. No one felt like dancing and, one by one, they took their leave of Lord Graham and Constance. Lady Graham had long ago retired distraught to her bed.

'What a to-do,' Lavinia said, as their coach took them home. 'It is Constance I feel sorry for. She told me she had almost brought Lord Haverley to the point when it happened and she was very much afraid it had put him off.'

'Why should that be?' Frances asked. 'Constance could not help it and if he is so easily deflected from his purpose, then I do not think his intentions were so fixed after all.'

'I told her she would see him again at our next rehearsal.'

'Vinny,' her stepmother said, 'you are on no account to allow them to be alone together. Her mother would never forgive me.'

'Yes, Mama.'

'Talking of making matches,' Marcus put in. 'You know Lord Wincote spoke to me earlier?'

'Yes, Papa. He told me you said he could approach me.'

'That does not mean the whole thing is cut and dried, you know, and so I told him. I mean to make enquiries.'

'Oh.' His lordship had not told her that.

'No.' She could sense her father smiling in the darkness of the coach. 'I told him the greater part of your dowry would be withheld until you had been married two years.'

She laughed. 'Oh, Papa, you never did!'

'Is that not what you wanted?' he asked, affecting surprise.

'Yes, but…' She paused. 'How did he take it?'

'Oh, he blustered a bit, said that the dowry was of no consequence at all and he was mortified that I should think it did.' He chuckled suddenly. 'But methinks he doth protest too much.'

'He said he is going to call tomorrow,' Lavinia said. 'Well, today, since it is gone midnight.'

'Oh, then I had better be at home,' Frances said. 'It is an inconvenience, but I will not have you receive him alone.'

'I do not intend to, Mama,' she said, laughing. 'He does not know it, but I have called a rehearsal for tomorrow—he will be one of many on our doorstep.'

'Vinny, you are a wicked girl,' Frances said, smiling. 'Have I not told you thousands of times, it is unkind to tease. It would have been better to have turned him down outright, if you do not intend to take him seriously.'

'Oh, I take him very seriously,' she said. 'But I mean to test his mettle.' She paused as the coach stopped outside the house and the groom jumped down to open the door. 'But please, Mama, not a word to James.'

'James?' queried the Duke, as they left carriage. 'What has it to do with him?'

'Oh, everything, I think,' Frances murmured.

Lavinia was already going up the steps to the front door, which had been opened by the late-duty footman, and did not hear them.

Chapter Six

Lavinia accompanied the Duchess on the customary courtesy call to Lady Graham the next morning, to find the house almost as full as it had been a few hours earlier. The King and Queen had been replaced as the main topic of conversation by the mysterious robbery. Lady Graham was lying on a chaise longue, looking pale and exhausted.

'I cannot imagine how I did not feel it being taken,' she moaned, dabbing at her eyes with a lace handkerchief. 'But I was so busy. Lord Graham is very angry. He believes I should have been more aware of what was happening, but I was not. I think it must have been someone very practised in the art to have undone the clasp without me feeling the slightest thing.'

'Then it could not possibly be one of your guests,' the Duchess said. 'We know everyone. Their lives are an open book.'

'We do not know Lady Rattenshaw,' one of the other ladies pointed out.

'But Sir Percy does,' Frances said. 'You might as well accuse Sir Percy himself.'

'That I never would,' Lady Graham said weakly. 'Sir Percy is so rich, he could buy my necklace a dozen times over, even though it was a family heirloom and worth thousands. And everyone knows he is as honest as the day is long, for all his strange ways.'

'Besides, Lady Rattenshaw was dripping with diamonds,' Lavinia put in. 'Lord Corringham assured me they were real. She has no need of more.'

'But there *is* Lord Edmund Wincote,' someone else said. 'He is new to town and something of a dark horse.'

'That is a dreadful thing to say,' Lavinia exclaimed, furious at the suggestion. 'He is a gentleman.'

'And you would know, of course, since you have set your cap at him.' This from Decima Rowland, a young lady of three and twenty with a long nose and protruding teeth.

Lavinia opened her mouth to make a sharp retort, but Lady Graham was there first. 'I am exhausted with all the speculation,' she said. 'Lord Graham will not allow his guests to be questioned, so that is an end of it. Mr Greenaway has said he will keep a look out for the necklace being offered for sale; it is the only way it will be recovered.'

Taking this as a dismissal, some of the visitors began drifting away and the Duchess and Lavinia were preparing to leave when James was announced. In spite of having only a few hours' sleep he looked fresh and alert. His chin was newly shaved, his hair neatly arranged and his cravat pristine. He bowed to Lady Graham and asked how she did, to which she responded wanly, and then he turned to greet everyone who remained. He smiled when he came to Lavinia. 'Why, my lady, I hardly expected to see you about so early.'

'I am not a slug-abed, my lord.'

'No, but it was such an eventful night for you, I thought you might still be recovering.'

'No more eventful for me than for anyone else.'

'You don't say,' he said, cocking one eyebrow in that teasing way he had which confused and infuriated her. 'I had thought otherwise.'

'James,' Frances reproved him, 'let us have no more of your teasing. Why are you here, anyway? Have you news of the necklace?'

'I regret to say, no, though Major Greenaway is at this moment visiting every known jeweller and angling cove in London.'

'Angling cove?' Lavinia asked.

'Receiver of stolen goods.'

'And how would Major Greenaway know who they are?'

'He has ways of finding out. It is in the nature of the work he does.'

'Then let us hope he finds the necklace soon and the mystery is solved,' the Duchess said briskly. 'Lavinia we must return home if you are to be there to receive guests this afternoon.'

'Receive guests?' James murmured in Lavinia's ear as they were leaving. 'That would not be Lord Wincote, would it?'

'Of course,' she said, then laughed at the expression which crossed his face. It was there one second and gone the next, but it was enough to tell her he did not like the idea. 'What have you against the gentleman?'

'Nothing at all,' he said airily. 'Just be careful, that's all.'

'Oh, I shall. Not that it is any of your business, my lord.'

'Then I beg your pardon.'

'So you should.' And then she relented and added, 'You are expected too, you know. Had you forgot we are to have a rehearsal?'

He laughed suddenly. 'Vixen!'

He saw them into their carriage before mounting his horse, which was being minded by a street urchin, and riding away.

'Vinny, one day you will try his patience too far,' the Duchess said as they proceeded at a brisk trot towards St James's Square. 'I cannot think why you do it.'

'I don't know, Mama, it is as if a little imp sits on my shoulder and whispers the words into my ear, and they just come out.'

'I think, my dear, you would do well to banish that imp before you do irreparable damage. Think before you speak in future.'

'Yes, Mama. But he started it.'

'Then you are as bad as one another.'

They had arrived home and no more was said as they went up to their rooms to change before settling down to eat a light nuncheon in the nursery with Miss Hastings and the children. Afterwards Lavinia went down to the ballroom to work on the scenery until the arrival of the members of the cast.

Duncan strolled in with Benedict Willoughby, both trying to ape the latest fashions with collars stiff enough to cut their cheeks and their cravats tied in complicated knots. They were closely followed by James and Edmund. Lord Haverley and his daughters came next and then Mr Drew and Sir Percy, who brought Lady Rattenshaw with him.

'Hope you don't mind, me dear,' he said to Lavinia. 'Thought her ladyship might be some help.'

'Of course,' Lavinia said brightly. 'You are welcome, my lady.'

'I doubt Miss Graham will come,' Sir Percy said. 'Too upset, don't you know, but aren't we all. It's not comfortable to know that people you are well acquainted with can do such a thing. Not comfortable at all.'

'I do not think it is anyone we know,' Edmund said. 'It was either someone who came in from outside or it was one of the servants.'

'Let us hope that is the case and the necklace will soon be recovered,' Lavinia said. 'But talking about it will not bring it back, so shall we make a start?'

She had hardly finished speaking before Constance arrived, pink and breathless. 'I am sorry I am late,' she said.

'Oh, do not think of it,' Lavinia said, as Lord Haverley hurried forward to escort the young lady to her place and sat down beside her. 'We are pleased that you felt able to come.'

'Oh I had to get away for a while. Everyone is so miserable and Papa is up in the boughs, as if Mama had lost the necklace on purpose to vex him. He's had all the servants looking through every nook and cranny for it, convinced it never left the house. But it has not been found.'

'Do you feel able to rehearse?' Lavinia asked Constance. 'Because if you find it too much, I can ask Lady Rattenshaw to read Helena's lines.'

Constance turned eagerly towards the lady. 'Oh, would you? You know I really did not want to take a part at all. I am no actress and am bound to spoil it for everyone else. Do say you will.' She turned to Lavinia. 'I can help in other ways. I could be prompter and mistress of the wardrobe.'

With this settled, they began reading through the first scene in which Egeus is furious that his daughter, Hermia, shuns the man he has promised her to and accuses Lysander of bewitching her.

Lord Haverley took the part of Egeus, Lavinia played Hermia, Edmund was Lysander and James, Demetrius.

'With cunning hast thou filch'd my daughter's heart; turned her obedience, which is due to me...' Lord Haverley proclaimed in ringing tones. And so it went on, with Hermia agreeing to meet Lysander in the woods so that they could run away together.

Lavinia was so wrapped up in the play that she did not see the looks that James and Edmund exchanged, the one accusing, the other complacent and enjoying the declarations of love he was making to Lavinia under the guise of the play. As far as James was concerned, Wincote had bewitched Lavinia, there was no other way of describing the hold he seemed to have on her. He held her with his eyes as he delivered the line, *'The course of true love never did run smooth...'* And her loving answers, albeit made to the fictional character, made him writhe.

Why, oh, why had she chosen this play? James asked himself. For two pins he would withdraw. But he knew he could not. There was a kind of sharp relish in his torment that made it beyond him to forgo.

When Lady Rattenshaw began to read Helena's lines, it became obvious they had found a treasure. She spoke with such assurance and feeling, the character came alive. Even her face and demeanour proclaimed her to be Helena, as if she had forgotten her own identity. Helena's love for Demetrius and his rejection of her in favour of Hermia was keenly felt, especially as James brought his own frustration to bear on his part as the rejected lover. Lavinia was overjoyed. 'Why, my lady, that was wonderful,' she said, when they reached the end of the scene. 'I do believe you have done this before.'

'Oh.' She seemed confused for a second, then smiled. 'We used to put on little plays out in India, you know, simply to amuse ourselves. Not very different from this.'

'Then you must help us all to aspire to your high standard, my lady,' James said.

'I, for one, will be honoured to be so instructed,' Edmund said, not to be outdone.

'I will do my best, then,' she promised.

Servants appeared with refreshments, which gave everyone a chance to relax, talk about the play or chatter about the theft of Lady Graham's necklace. Never had the guest list of a ball been so dissected and mulled over.

'Well, my lady?'

Lavinia whipped round at the sound of Lord Wincote's voice. He was standing at her elbow, clad in a light blue superfine coat with dark facings, which she had not seen before; she concluded his wardrobe must be very extensive, for she had never witnessed him in the same coat twice. 'I am well, thank you,' she said, pretending to misunderstand him.

'My lady, you know I was not enquiring after your health.'

'Were you not? Is my well being not of interest to you, my lord?'

'I think, my lady, you love to tease. But today I am not of a mind to play your little game. You must know I crave a moment or two of your time alone.'

'Lord Wincote,' she said firmly, which was difficult because he was looking at her with that dark-eyed intensity she had come to know, and she felt helpless. 'You must know that is not possible today. I cannot leave my friends. And Papa has not given me leave to see you alone.'

'I wonder why you are doing this to me, my lady. Are you testing my steadfastness?'

'If I am, then I am sure you are equal to it,' she said, moving away before he could extract any kind of promise

GET FREE BOOKS and a FREE MYSTERY GIFT WHEN YOU PLAY THE...

Just scratch off the silver box with a coin. Then check below to see the gifts you get!

SLOT MACHINE GAME!

YES! I have scratched off the silver box. Please send me the two FREE books and mystery gift for which I qualify. I understand I am under no obligation to purchase any books, as explained on the back of this card. I am over 18 years of age.

H2GI

Mrs/Miss/Ms/Mr _____ Initials _____

BLOCK CAPITALS PLEASE

Surname _____

Address _____

_____

Postcode _____

7	7	7	**Worth TWO FREE BOOKS plus a BONUS Mystery Gift!**
🍒	🍒	🍒	**Worth TWO FREE BOOKS!**
♣	♣	♣	**Worth ONE FREE BOOK!**
🔔	🔔	🍒	**TRY AGAIN!**

Visit us online at www.millsandboon.co.uk

The Reader Service™ — Here's how it works:

NO STAMP NEEDED!

THE READER SERVICE™
FREE BOOK OFFER
FREEPOST CN81
CROYDON
CR9 3WZ

NO STAMP
NECESSARY
IF POSTED IN
THE U.K. OR N.I.

from her, and went to sit with Miss Hastings, the only person she could trust not to tease, confuse or coerce her.

'He is a strange young man,' Emily Hastings said, nodding towards Edmund who had gone to sit beside Lady Rattenshaw and was engaging her in conversation. 'He has secrets, that one.'

'Secrets, what secrets?'

'My dear Vinny, if I knew that, they would not be secret, would they? But I can tell it by his looks. I recollect meeting Lord Byron once and he has that same kind of intense, brooding look.'

'Oh, is that what it is, brooding? What can he be brooding about?'

'That I do not know.'

'He is very romantical.'

'Oh, I see...'

'No, you do not see,' Lavinia said, her voice rising in order to emphasise her point. 'You do not see at all.'

'What does the excellent Miss Hastings not see?' James said, coming to sit on the other side of Lavinia.

'Why, Lady Lavinia finds Lord Wincote romantical, my lord,' Emily said, with a smile.

'Do you?' James asked Lavinia.

'Of course,' the little imp on her shoulder said.

'Then you are of a mind to accept his declarations of undying affection as nothing but the truth, are you?'

'I do not see why not. He does not deal in double talk and conundrums, like some do. I know exactly where I am with him.'

He stood up suddenly. 'Then I must congratulate you, my lady. Please excuse me.'

'Now, what have I said?' Lavinia demanded as he strolled away with every appearance of nonchalance. But she knew the answer; that little imp had been at work again. She longed to rush after him and tell him she had not meant it, that she was very far from knowing where she was. She was as lost as Lysander and Hermia in the woods.

Refreshments over, they resumed the rehearsal and Lavinia could not help noticing that Lord Wincote deferred to Lady Rattenshaw's opinion on almost every point of discussion and wondered if he was trying to make her jealous. But she decided this could not be so, when, as everyone took their leave, he contrived to be the last to go and was thus alone with her, except for Emily Hastings, who deliberately took herself off to the far side of the huge room to study the scenery Lavinia had been working on.

'My lady,' he said, in a low voice. 'You cannot go on avoiding me forever.'

'I have not been avoiding you, my lord. I have much to do.'

'So much that you cannot even spare time to hear an offer of marriage.'

'Offer of marriage,' she repeated.

'You know perfectly well that was my intention. Ever since I met you—'

'Less than a month ago,' she said.

'So be it. An hour, a day, a second, what does it matter? To me it seems like an eternity since I first beheld you, but however long ago it was, I knew, in that moment, that I wanted you.' He seized both her hands and raised them to his lips one by one, looking deeply into her eyes as he did so. 'Tell me you have felt the same, tell me I do not ask in vain.'

She gave a huge, deep sigh. 'My lord, I do not know what to say.'

'Say yes. Say you will marry me and soon too. The sooner the better...'

'Why the haste?'

'I am an impatient man.'

She laughed suddenly. 'What has Hermia just said to Lysander about patience?'

'Oh, that play. I only take part to please you, you know. And to speak Lysander's words to you.'

'Now, do you know, I rather thought you liked to strut your stuff. You asked Lady Rattenshaw enough questions about the part.'

'Only because she knows so much about it. Goodness, you are not jealous, are you?' He smiled broadly. 'I do believe you are! Oh, that is most encouraging. I never thought... Oh, Vinny, my dear!' He grasped her shoulders and would have kissed her but for a resounding voice coming from the direction of the door.

'No one calls Lady Lavinia by that name except her closest friends,' James said. 'And I do not think you qualify.'

The thunderous look Edmund gave him was benign compared to the fury in Lavinia's eyes as she turned on him. 'James!'

'Yes and in the nick of time, it seems.' He gave a curt nod to Edmund. 'On your way, Wincote.' And when Edmund hesitated, added. 'Do you want me to call you out, you blackguard?'

'No!' Lavinia cried. 'I will not have it. Lord Wincote, please leave, I wish to have a private word with my *brother*. I will talk to you again another day.'

After he had left, with great reluctance and one dark look directed at James, she turned on her tormentor. 'That was unforgivable...'

'So it was,' he said. 'Taking advantage of you when you were alone. I could cheerfully have darkened his daylights.'

'I did not mean him, I meant you. You are not my keeper. I do not need you to stand guard over me and I especially do not like you spying on me.'

'I was not spying. I came back for my gloves. I left them on the table over there.'

She turned and realised that his gloves were indeed lying on the table, along with his cane, but she would not soften. 'That does not give you the right to insult my…my friend.'

'Friend! What I saw was not the action of a friend.'

'No, it was that of a man overcome by his feelings. He had just proposed.'

'And been accepted?' he asked, unable to conceal his horror.

'He might have been but for your untimely intrusion,' said the little imp. 'And for your information, I was not alone. Miss Hastings is over there.' She turned to point her out and then they both burst into laughter simultaneously. Miss Hastings was sitting slumped in an armchair on the other side of the room, gently snoring.

'Oh, Vinny,' he said, suddenly serious. 'I do not mean to quarrel with you, but I am concerned, especially when those who should be chaperoning you neglect their duty. Please, please, I beg of you, take care.'

'Why are you concerned? Do you know something about Lord Wincote that I do not?'

He hesitated only a moment. 'No. But your happiness and well being are very important to me.' And then he spoiled it all, by adding, 'Little Mama would never forgive me if I did not watch out for you.'

'I have Papa to do that for me.'

'But he is so involved with government and is more often absent than present.'

'That does not mean he neglects me, James, nor that

you can stand in his place.' She smiled suddenly. 'He has put a stipulation on any offer of marriage to me that will test the determination of any man who offers.'

'What stipulation?'

'That he will not pay out my dowry until I have been married two years.'

'Has he, by Jove!'

'So you see, you need not worry that Lord Wincote is after my money because he knows about it and it has not put him off.'

He picked up his gloves and cane. 'Then I see you do not need my protection.' He took her hand and lifted it to his lips. 'I bid you *adieu*, my lady.' With that, he turned on his heel and left without looking back.

Lord Wincote was waiting for him in the street when he emerged. 'A word, my lord,' he said, falling into step beside him.

A confrontation with the man was the last thing James wanted, but for Lavinia's sake, he suppressed the jealous fury that engulfed him. 'What is it?'

'My lord, I can understand why you are so protective of Lady Lavinia—'

'Can you? I doubt it.'

'A brother, even a stepbrother, would be lacking in sensibility not to be concerned for one so beautiful and desirable, but you *are* only a stepbrother...'

'Not even that.'

'It is how she looks upon you, she told me so herself. And because of that, I am prepared to overlook your unwarranted intrusion, just now.'

'Unwarranted! You were about to kiss her.'

'It is usual for a gentleman to kiss a young lady when she has been so kind as to accept his offer of marriage. I had his Grace's permission to approach her and Miss

Hastings was in the room, there was nothing havey-cavey about it.'

'She accepted you?'

'Oh, yes.' It was said so complacently James felt like hitting him. Instead he bade him good afternoon and strode away.

He was bubbling with frustrated fury. The man was a mushroom, appearing overnight from nowhere. He was deep in debt and badly needed Lavinia's dowry and yet he seemed not to mind that proviso the Duke had put on it, unless, of course, he had decided to gamble that his Grace would relent after the wedding, especially if refusing meant Lavinia would suffer. But that would be almost impossible to prove.

He turned into White's, ordered a drink and sat down in a corner to think. How could he test the man's intentions even further? Had he any right to do so? He had no claim on Lavinia's affections. She had even told that cur she looked on him as a brother. And he, like a fool, perpetuated it.

'Corringham, I have been looking for you.'

He looked up to see Donald Greenaway looking down at him. 'Oh, it's you. Any news?'

'Yes, momentous.' He pulled up a nearby chair and sat down. 'Lady Graham's diamonds were paste.'

'Oh, the diamonds,' James said dismissively. 'I thought you meant about Lord Wincote.'

'I'll come back to him later.'

'It might be too late. He has already proposed.'

'The devil he has! Did she accept?'

'As good as. He was apparently not put off by the fact that the Duke said he would not hand over her dowry for two years.'

'Then he will have to find another source of money until

then. I have it on good authority he offered to give evidence on behalf of the Queen for a consideration.'

'What evidence?'

'Something in a document left by his grandfather, implicating the King and Lady Jersey.'

'That's common knowledge. And in any case, I have heard that Brougham is not of a mind to bring counter-evidence.'

'He might have to. And hearsay is very different from sworn evidence.'

'And Lavinia is engaging herself to that blackguard. Oh, poor child! Poor Mama! If he does give evidence, it will compromise the Duke's reputation for impartiality. Can he be stopped?'

'I imagine he will withdraw the offer to give evidence in exchange for Lady Lavinia's dowry being paid on the day of her marriage.'

'Good God! That's blackmail. I'll kill him. I'll run him through!'

'Calm down, James. So far, Brougham is holding fire. But it does mean Wincote has not been paid for his evidence and must be desperate for money.'

'No doubt he will let his creditors know that he is to marry Lady Lavinia and they will hold off.'

'No doubt of it, considering whose daughter she is.'

'We have to do something. I'll call the coxcomb out.'

'And what good would that do? Duelling is against the law for a start and if you killed or wounded him, what would Lady Lavinia have to say to that? On the other hand, you could come off worse and he would still marry her.'

'You are right,' he said reluctantly. 'Though it would give me the greatest pleasure to run him through.'

'Yes, I know, but I am relying on you to keep your head

and your temper. Now, listen to me. About Lady Graham's necklace…'

'What about it?' James was still thinking of Lavinia and it was a moment before he could bring his attention back to what Donald had said at the beginning of the conversation. 'Made of paste, you said. How do you know?'

'Because it was offered for sale at a certain run-down jeweller's shop in a back alley off Oxford Street.'

'By whom?'

'I don't know. The man told the proprietor he had been given it in lieu of a gaming debt. That could be true, of course.' He laughed dryly. 'He must have had a shock when he discovered it was worthless.'

'You are sure it was the same necklace?'

'Yes, it is very distinctive.'

'But why was it worthless? We were told it was a family heirloom.'

'Lord Graham is known to be very low in the stirrups. My guess is that he had it copied and sold the original to pay for that ball.'

'No wonder his lordship is so distraught and anxious to find it himself. Do you think Lady Graham knows it is paste?'

'I do not think so. She was genuinely upset when I spoke to her.'

'What was the reaction of this fellow when the proprietor told him the necklace was paste?'

'He was angry at first. Then he smiled, murmuring that it was of no consequence, and took it away with him. I'll wager he means to use it to blackmail Lord Graham.'

'Much good will it do, if his lordship is as pinched in the pocket as you say he is. Are you going to say anything to him?'

'How can I? It would mean accusing him of duplicity.

It would mortify him to know I knew the truth. And as for Lady Graham and their daughter... No, I shall have to find the culprit and restore the copy to him as if it were the real thing.'

'I suppose you are right. But do not allow that investigation to deter you from your enquiries regarding Edmund Wincote, will you? Diamonds are inanimate objects, of little importance beside a young lady's life and happiness.'

Donald grinned suddenly and lightly punched his friend's arm. 'And yours, too, I collect.'

'Yes, well...'

'Now, shall we have a bite of dinner and a hand of cards to wile away the evening? That is, if you have nothing better to do.'

'Oh, nothing, nothing at all, my friend.' He rose and led the way to the dining room.

It seemed Lady Rattenshaw had invited the whole *ton* to her soirée and most had accepted, probably because they wanted to see inside the house and make up their own minds if she was as rich as she was reputed to be. How was it furnished? Was it full of treasures? Did she employ Indian servants? And both Lavinia and Frances admitted to being as inquisitive as everyone else.

'You know, I have known Sir Percy ever since I first came out,' Frances told Lavinia as their town coach carried them to Upper Brook Street. 'And never once has he mentioned the name of Rattenshaw. I thought I knew all his friends.'

'Was he one of your suitors?' Lavinia asked mischievously. 'Why did you not marry him?'

'I married the Earl of Corringham instead and never regretted that. But why the quiz?'

'No reason. I just wondered why people married, what

makes a woman—or a man come to that—choose one person above all others. Is it a practical thing like money or is it love? And is love the meeting of minds or is there some complicated chemistry involved?'

'Oh, my dear.' Frances laughed. 'What has brought this on? Could it have anything to do with Lord Wincote?'

'Partly. You know he has asked me to marry him?'

'No. When was this?'

'The other day, after the rehearsal. He stayed behind after the others had gone. And before you say anything, Miss Hastings was there. And James, part of the time.'

'You don't mean to say he proposed in front of James?' the Duchess asked in astonishment.

'Not quite. But I did not have time to give him my answer.'

'I should hope not. That is not the way it should be done. Your papa should have arranged the meeting formally.'

'Do you think that was why James was so angry?'

'Was he?'

'Oh, yes, he threatened to call Lord Wincote out.'

'Foolish, foolish boy.'

'Mama, you love James very much, don't you?'

'Of course I do. Oh, I know he can be tiresome, but he has a heart of gold and would do anything for me.'

'Does he think he is acting on your behalf when he tries to come between me and Lord Wincote? He said you would never forgive him if he did not watch out for me.'

'And you find his watchfulness restricting?'

'Wouldn't you?'

'I will speak to him, Lavinia. But I think you should examine your own heart. If you have to ask what love is, then you are not yet ready for marriage.'

'But Lord Wincote is so sure and very anxious for my

answer. And he has not been at all discouraged by Papa's edict.'

Frances smiled and patted her hand. 'Vinny, I suggest you tell his lordship that you will give him his answer when this interminable Season is over. When are you going to put on your play?'

'Not until September. Most of the men will have to attend the trial and that will make rehearsing difficult, so I thought I'd wait until it was over. That is, if we haven't all melted in the heat by then.'

'Good. Tell him you will give him your answer after the performance of the play.' She chuckled suddenly. 'That will keep him hard at rehearsals, if nothing else.'

And so they arrived at Lady Rattenshaw's house and were shown into the crowded drawing room. Although the room was spacious, like all the others in the house, it was crowded and very noisy with everyone was talking at once. Looking about her, Lavinia was amazed at the sumptuousness of the place. The carpets and hangings were of the highest quality, the furnishings for the most part Chippendale or French. There was nothing Indian about it at all.

'I saw enough Eastern stuff while I was out there to last me a lifetime,' Lady Rattenshaw said, when someone commented on this. 'I longed for England and all things English. Now do make yourselves comfortable.' She beckoned to a waiter carrying a tray of glasses. 'Have some champagne. It is so much better for the digestion than anything else, do you not think?' And once they had been furnished with full glasses, she drifted away to talk to more guests.

They looked about them for people they knew and soon spotted Sir Percy in mulberry and pale blue with a cerise cravat tied in a huge bow. Lord and Lady Graham had evidently recovered from the loss of the necklace, for they were the centre of a little group, talking animatedly. A little way off Lord and Lady Willoughby stood with a bored-looking Benedict at their side.

'I do not see James,' Lavinia said, sipping her drink.

'No, but Lord Wincote is over there, deep in conversation with Lady Jersey.'

He looked up at that moment and excused himself from his elderly companion to come over to them. 'Your Grace, your obedient.' He bowed. 'Lady Lavinia.'

'Lord Wincote,' both murmured.

'Such a squeeze,' he said. 'And so hot even with all the windows open.' He turned to Lavinia. 'Would you like to take a turn round the garden, my lady? The terrace is well lit and it is much cooler outside.'

Lavinia looked at her stepmother, who smiled and nodded. 'You may go, my love, but stay on the terrace, won't you?'

Lavinia put her hand on his lordship's sleeve and they made their way out of the room and through the conservatory to the paved terrace where several other couples promenaded. 'It is unbearably hot,' Lavinia said, flicking open her fan and waving it in front of her face as they walked. 'If it were not for that dreadful trial, we would have been back home in the country by now.'

'Ah, but then I would not be walking and talking with you, and that would be a great loss to me.'

'My lord, you are too kind.'

'When we last met, we were interrupted—'

'Yes. I am sorry about that, my lord. The Earl of Corringham believes he has a duty to protect me.'

'You do not need protecting from me, my lady. My intentions are honourable, as his Grace was kind enough to recognise when he gave me leave to speak to you.'

'And you did. With rather more fervour than I expected.'

'My lady, I apologise if that upset you, it was brought about by my impatience and the difficulty of speaking to you alone. I saw an opportunity and seized it.' He smiled. 'Am I forgiven?'

'Yes, of course.'

'And now, may I have your answer?'

'Answer to what, my lord?' she asked mischievously.

'My offer of marriage.'

'And undying love?'

He looked startled for a moment, then smiled. 'I see you are a romantic, my lady. But if a declaration of undying love is the way to your heart, then you have it. So what do you say?'

He was so self-assured, so positive, that for a moment she wavered, but then, remembering her promise to the Duchess, smiled. 'I am sensible of the honour you do me, my lord, but I am not yet quite ready—'

'How long?' he asked impatiently. 'How long before you put me out of my torment?'

'After the performance of our play. I really cannot give you an answer before then.'

'But that is more than six weeks away. Oh, how can you be so cruel?' His face clouded over and his jaw jutted. 'It is Corringham's fault. If he had not put his nose in where it is not wanted, you would have said yes when I asked you before.'

'No, my lord, my answer would have been the same. It has nothing to do with James.' But even as she spoke, she knew that was not true. It had everything to do with James. James was James. Always there, always a presence in her life.

And as if to confirm this, she saw him come out on to

the terrace and heard Edmund mutter, 'Damn him!', which
made her smile. But James did not appear to have seen
them. He turned and strolled leisurely along the terrace to
the end, where he stopped to light a small cigar and stood
gazing up at the starlit sky, placidly smoking.

'Let us go in,' she said. 'The Duchess will be wondering
what has become of me.'

They turned and went indoors and James, seeing them
go, ground out his cigar under his foot and followed.

In the largest reception room, Lady Rattenshaw was
singing a ballad to the accompaniment of Sir Percy on the
pianoforte. She had a melodious voice, which she knew
how to project, and her audience were sitting or standing
in small groups, listening with rapt attention. Lavinia and
Lord Wincote joined them, standing just inside the door,
so as not to disturb anyone.

There was enthusiastic applause when she finished and
shouts of 'Encore!', especially from the men.

'No, I am sure there are others who sing and play, who
might be persuaded to favour us with a rendering,' she
said. 'I do not know them, so someone tell me, whom
should I ask?'

Lavinia felt someone move beside her and was surprised
to see Lord Wincote make his way to their hostess's side.
'My lady, my voice is no more than passable, but I would
deem it an honour to sing a duet with you.'

'Capital!' she said, clapping her hands. 'What shall it
be?'

They conferred with Sir Percy for a moment and chose
a song. Sir Percy played the introduction and they began
to sing a haunting love song. It was soon apparent that her
ladyship was putting her heart and soul into the words and
was singing for Lord Wincote alone. And he, astonish-
ingly, was playing up to her.

'Well, would you believe it,' said a voice at Lavinia's elbow. 'What a pretty pair to be sure.'

Lavinia knew it was James standing just behind her and must have followed them indoors. 'Yes, they do sing well together,' she said, without turning round. 'I had no idea Lord Wincote had so fine a voice.'

'If that is the only secret he has kept from you, my dear, then you have nothing to worry about,' he said, laconically. 'By the way, am I to offer felicitations?'

'Not yet. Mama advised me to defer a decision until after we have performed the play.'

'Very wise of her,' he said. 'And how did Lord Wincote react to the news?'

'Naturally he was disappointed.'

'I'll wager he was.'

She turned sharply to look at him. 'But he accepted with a good grace.'

'I am glad to hear it.'

The song ended and they both joined in the applause; afterwards Lady Rattenshaw called on others to contribute to the entertainment. Lavinia, whose talent was for drawing and painting rather than music, was content to listen as Constance and Lord Haverley were prevailed upon to play a duet, and Martin Drew gave a rendering of a popular ballad. They were warmly applauded as they moved to one side and then Lady Rattenshaw stood up and announced a special treat. Lord Wincote was going to demonstrate the art of mesmerism.

There was a gasp from everyone and looks exchanged, half-wonder, half-fear. Lavinia found herself reaching behind her and clutching James's hand. He was startled for a moment, but then smiled and allowed it to lie there, relishing the feel of the small trembling fingers in his own.

The murmuring ceased as Edmund stood and faced

everyone. 'I learned the art from a disciple of the great Dr
Mesmer himself,' he said. And though he appeared not to
raise his voice, his words reached every corner of the
room. 'I am not a medical man, of course, and would not
presume to cure people's ills as he did but, for a little light
entertainment, I am prepared to demonstrate the power of
animal magnetism.'

'Taking over people's minds,' James murmured to
Lavinia. 'Is that what he has done to you?'

'No,' she whispered back. 'Pay attention.' But she did
not let go of his hand. She liked the feel of it.

'I need volunteers,' Edmund went on. 'I give you my
word, I will do nothing to harm anyone, nor make them
insensible against their will.'

Benedict stood up and made his way to the front, followed by one or two of the other young men. Edmund
arranged a row of chairs in a semi-circle around him and
invited them to be seated which they did, grinning self-
consciously. 'What about a lady?' his lordship went on.
'A lady might take the matter a little more seriously. Lady
Lavinia?'

'No!' James hissed at her.

He should have known that forbidding Lavinia to do
something was tantamount to a challenge. She smiled and
moved forward to join the others, among whom was Lady
Rattenshaw.

'Now, ladies and gentlemen,' Edmund said softly,
speaking to the volunteers, as he withdrew the fob from
his waistcoat pocket. 'I want to you ignore everyone else
in the room and concentrate on my voice and this little
trinket.' A shiny jewel-like object dangled on the end of
the ribbon, glinting in the light of the chandeliers. 'You
see it swings like a pendulum, back and forth, back and

forth, finding its own rhythm, neither fast nor slow, like the tick of a clock, tick, tock...'

His voice was very low, very languorous, and the people sitting in the semi-circle round him had to concentrate very hard to hear it. They gazed up at him, concentrating hard. James watched, his heart in his mouth, as he saw their limbs relax, saw their eyelids flutter, saw Lavinia's chin drop a little, though her eyes remained open. Not a sound was made by the audience. Suddenly Wincote turned towards them. 'Now they are in a dreamlike state which is similar to sleep but is not, for they can hear all I say and obey my commands, but when they wake up, they will remember nothing.'

He turned to Benedict. 'Mr Willoughby, you are a donkey. Be so kind as to get down on your hands and knees and bray like a donkey.'

To everyone's amusement, Benedict did and when he was told to do so, returned to his seat. The next young man was told he was a chicken and flapped his wings and clucked, and though the audience roared with laughter it did not wake him. He made Lady Rattenshaw take off her necklace and hand it to him. He smiled and put it in his pocket, saying, 'It is a good thing I am honest, is it not?' And then he came to Lavinia. 'Lady Lavinia, now what shall I ask you to do?'

'Nothing,' James cried, striding forward, intending to rescue Lavinia. 'You will not humiliate her.'

'My lord, if you wake her abruptly, it could be dangerous for her,' Wincote said calmly, holding up his hand to stop him. 'And it is not my intention to humiliate her or anyone. I mean them no harm.' James stopped abruptly, wondering if it were true that it might be dangerous, and Lord Wincote turned back to Lavinia. 'My lady, I think I shall ask you to recite Oberon's speech in *A Midsummer*

Night's Dream, the one that begins, *"What thou seest, when thou dost wake, Do it for thy true-love take..."'*

'James,' Frances murmured. 'I think this has gone far enough.'

'So do I.' He stepped forward. 'Wake her up, Wincote. Wake them all up.'

'Why, my Lord Corringham, do you suppose I was about to put her ladyship under a spell?' he answered, unruffled. 'You surely do not believe that is possible?'

'Of course not. But it is wrong to take away a person's will and make them do things they would never otherwise do. They will all be mortified when they realise what you have done to them. I am surprised at Lady Rattenshaw allowing it.'

'Easy, old friend,' Sir Percy said. 'The lady cannot hear you and defend herself.' He turned to Edmund. 'Bring 'em round, Wincote, you have proved your point. And return her ladyship's pendant to her.'

Edmund turned and spoke to his volunteers. 'You will wake at the count of three and you will remember nothing of what has passed.' He counted to three slowly and one by one his victims stirred themselves, looked about them and then laughed uneasily, as the audience applauded. 'What happened?' they asked, almost in unison.

James took Lavinia's arm and almost dragged her back to the Duchess. 'James, you are hurting me. What is all the fuss about?'

'That sort of thing could be dangerous if done by someone unskilled,' he said. 'Heaven knows what it would do to an impressionable mind.'

'Are you implying I have a weak mind, my lord?'

'No, but you know what he wanted you to do? He wanted you to fall in love with the first person you saw on awakening, just like the characters in *A Midsummer Night's Dream*.'

'That's rubbish. He never even spoke to me.' She paused. 'He didn't, did he?'

The Duchess smiled. 'He did, my dear. He made Mr Willoughby get down on his hands and knees and bray like a donkey and he made his friend imitate a chicken…'

'And me? I do not remember who was the first person I saw when I came to my senses.'

'Me, you noddicock,' James said, grinning suddenly. 'It was me.'

She breathed a sigh of relief. 'Oh, that's all right, then.' She looked at him in consternation when he began to laugh. 'I fail to see the cause of your merriment, my lord.'

But he would not enlighten her.

Chapter Seven

James was still smiling as he and Sir Percy left together and walked in the direction of White's club.

'It is all very well for you to laugh, Corringham,' Percy said. 'But with a gift like that he could do anything, get someone to commit murder even.'

'Oh, I doubt that, but he can evidently make a lady surrender her valuables without a qualm and it occurred to me…' He paused, shaking his head as if to deny the thought. 'No, the idea is outlandish, he never would.'

'You were thinking Lady Graham's necklace?'

'So you thought of it too?'

'Yes, but he would surely not be such a jack-at-warts as to demonstrate how he did it to a room full of people.'

'I would not put anything past him. I think he wanted to prove his ascendancy over me. Or Vinny. Picking that particular rhyme for her to say, as if she would fall in love with him as soon as she opened her eyes!'

'I thought that particular situation had already come to pass.'

'By heaven, I hope not! But he was making it very plain what his expectations are. It was almost as good as an announcement. If we are not careful, Lavinia will fall into agreeing with it without even realising what is happening to her.'

'And you, I collect, have only her happiness at heart.'

'Of course,' he said, noticing the slight tone of irony in his friend's voice. 'Can you doubt it?'

'Enough to let her go?'

He hesitated only a second before answering, 'If that is her wish, but I would need to be very sure that it was, not just some sleight of hand on his part.' He did not add that it would break his heart to do it.

'Then leave it to me, m'boy.'

'So you said before. But what have you done, apart from introducing the gentleman to Lady Rattenshaw?'

'All going to plan, my friend. He is already confiding in her. He has told her his grandfather's affairs are still not concluded and the lawyers are holding up his inheritance which he insists will be considerable. He has borrowed a hundred guineas from her with some desperate tale about being called out if he does not pay some trifling debt of honour.'

'So that was how he managed to pay me,' James murmured. Wincote had sent the money to settle his wager round to Corringham House only two days earlier.

'Yes, but if he did take Lady Graham's necklace, he would not have had to borrow so paltry a sum, would he?'

'True,' James said. Percy did not know the diamonds had been fake and James was not such a tattler as to reveal the fact.

'Perhaps we are maligning the poor fellow.' Sir Percy laughed suddenly. 'He has been telling the lady all manner of fanciful tales and when he said he could mesmerise people, she prevailed upon him to demonstrate it. She thought it might make people think.'

'She was right as far as I am concerned,' James said.

But it was not so much of Edmund's strange powers he was thinking, but of Lavinia's last remark when he told her he was the first one she saw when she opened her eyes. 'So, that's all right, then.' Could he, dare he, hope?

'Mind you,' Percy went on. '"Love looks not with the eyes but with the mind, And therefore is winged Cupid painted blind."'

James laughed. 'I did not think you were paying that much attention when we rehearsed. I'll wager a yellow boy you cannot manage the next three lines.'

'"Nor hath Love's mind of any judgement taste, And therefore is Love said to be a child, because in choice he is so oft beguiled."'

'Well said.' James dug his purse from his coat pocket and handed over a guinea. 'There is no end to your talent, is there?'

'I have been schooling Mari...Lady Rattenshaw in Helena's lines.'

'It is true, though, isn't it? Love is easily beguiled,' James said gloomily. 'Especially with the help of Dr Mesmer.'

'Oh, I do not think Lady Lavinia is as foolish as that, Corringham. But if she is blind, we shall open her eyes.'

'How?'

Sir Percy smiled and tapped the side of his nose with a bony finger. 'Wait and see.'

And with that he had to be content. But he could not forget how easily Wincote had pocketed Lady Rattenshaw's jewellery. If he could do that to a mature lady, what could he do to an impressionable young girl who imagined herself in love? If the rakeshame relieved Lavinia of her valuables, it would be disagreeable and inconvenient, though not disastrous, but if he stole her heart, which was infinitely more precious, especially to him—what then?

Knowing most of the men were going to be attending the Queen's trial every day once it began, Lavinia decided to step up the frequency of rehearsals, to throw herself into directing the play and learn her own lines so that she did not have time to think. Thinking confused her. Had Lord Wincote managed to take over her mind? Was he able to manipulate her will? James had said he could not do it, if she did not wish it, so did that mean she *did* wish it? Did she want to be subject to someone else's will? Was that what being in love really meant?

Or had she had become so immersed in *A Midsummer Night's Dream*, she was beginning to believe in the magic juice which made people fall in love with the first thing they saw when they woke? It was all very silly, she chided herself, Lord Wincote had been seeking to amuse Lady Rattenshaw's guests, no more than that. Mama had disapproved and James had put a stop to it, though he had made sure he was the first person she saw when she woke. And, though she knew it was nonsensical, she was glad of that. James she could trust.

She wondered how Lord Wincote would behave towards her when they next met. Would he be angry because he had been made to feel diminished in front of all their friends? Would he refuse to attend rehearsals, withdraw from the play? It was so advanced now, the effect of anyone withdrawing would be catastrophic. She wished Lancelot Greatorex would come, but so far there had been no news of the players and she began to wonder if he had meant it when he said he would be in London at the end of the Season.

Quite apart from needing his professional help with the

direction, she needed his troupe to take the parts of the entertainers, which she had not rehearsed at all. If he did not come she would have to leave that side of the story out, as she had told the Duchess she would do. It would spoil it and the audience would think they had been cheated. And the antagonism between James and Lord Wincote did not help. If she did not know him better, she might think that James was jealous. And that was so inconceivable it was comical.

But when they congregated for the next rehearsal, Lord Wincote was as enthusiastic about the play as ever. He treated her with scrupulous courtesy, smiled a great deal and, when they had a break for refreshment, talked about his home in Cumberland and how glad he would be to be back there, riding round his estate and putting in hand the refurbishment. 'It must be fit for a queen,' he said, then laughed. 'Not Caroline, of course, but my own dear queen of my heart.'

'My lord, you presume—'

He took her hand and raised it to his lips. 'No, my lady, I presume nothing. I await your decision with patience and hope.' And though he looked deep into her eyes, making her shudder, he did not try to hold her gaze and she began to think she must have imagined the strange power he had. The trouble was inside her, in her own emotions which she did not understand.

And there was James. He had never pretended to be an actor and was taking part only to please her, but he had been good at the beginning; it was only lately he had started reciting his lines without any feeling, as if he would be glad to have it all over and done with. He seemed to be keeping his distance from her and she could not understand why. They had not quarrelled, had not even teased each other as they were wont to do.

She used a quiet moment to study him. Dressed neatly, but not flamboyantly, in a frock coat of Bath cloth, nankeen trousers and a white cravat tied in one of the less complicated knots, he was, on the surface, his usual urbane self but she knew him well, and was certain something was troubling him.

She watched as Sir Percy, who had turned out to be surprisingly good as Theseus, Duke of Athens, exhorted Hermia to obey her father and marry Demetrius. However, she spoke her lines of refusal flatly, unable to conjure up the depth of emotion they deserved. She should be putting herself in Hermia's shoes, feeling all her anguish as she declared she would rather die, but how could she, when her mind was on other things?

James, as Demetrius, begged her: *'Relent, sweet Hermia.'* And, turning to Edmund: *'And, Lysander, yield thy crazed title to my certain right.'*

Edmund, line perfect, seemed truly passionate in his response as he pleaded his case to Hermia's father, imbuing Lysander's words with an undercurrent of meaning: he was, he said, as well endowed as Demetrius, his fortunes equal and besides, he had the lady's love. It all seemed so close to real life, a tussle between two men over one woman. Lord Wincote evidently saw James as a rival, which was foolish of him.

James's interest was avuncular, more protective than lover-like, but he did not like or trust Lord Wincote. Or had she become so involved with the characters in the play that she was imagining conflict where none existed? Was James troubled about something else entirely? Perhaps he was in some scrape or other, but why had he not felt able to confide in her? He always had in the past.

When the rehearsal ended, and everyone began to disperse, she put her hand on his sleeve to detain him. 'James, a word.'

He stood obediently in the hall and waited until everyone had gone. 'What is it, Vinny, my performance not up to scratch?' He kept his voice light, though it did not deceive her for a minute.

'Since you ask, I do not believe it is. I know you are only taking part to please me, but you are so wooden it's as if you would rather be anywhere but here.'

'My dear, I would not come if that were the case. And you have no call to accuse me of being wooden. You were positively fossilised. You know you were.'

'Then it is because I am concerned about you.'

'About me? Now I would have expected you to find a more interesting subject for your concern than an old bachelor like me.'

'Old bachelor! Oh, James.' She laughed and then stopped abruptly. 'James, what is wrong?'

'Wrong, m'dear?' he said, affecting nonchalance. 'What could possibly be wrong?'

'I do not know. You are not yourself.'

'Then I do not know who else I could be.' He looked in a mirror placed near the door and studied his face, turning it this way and that and tweaking his perfectly tied cravat. 'Yes, that is James Corringham, no mistaking that physiog.'

'James, don't be such a gudgeon. I am serious. Do you think I do not know when all is not well with you?'

'You, my dear Lavinia, are burdened with an overactive imagination. I am perfectly well.'

'You are not still brooding over Lord Wincote's demonstration of animal magnetism, are you?'

'Now, why should I do that?' The effort to appear unaffected was taking its toll; it was all he could do not to take her in his arms, shake some sense into her and then kiss her soundly and thoroughly.

'You were afraid of what he could do to me.'

'Did I say that?' he asked mildly.

'You implied it.'

'Heat of the moment, my dear. I know you are far too sensible to allow yourself to be used in that way.' He saw her eyes widen in surprise and smiled. 'But it is a powerful weapon, you must admit. You saw what he did to Benedict Willoughby and his friend.'

'No. You forget, I was asleep and saw nothing, but it has done no lasting harm. They are laughing about it now. And Lord Wincote knows you and Mama disapproved so he will not attempt anything like it again. Do give him the benefit of the doubt, James.'

'That is exactly what I am doing.' He retrieved his hat from the table below the mirror and clamped it on his head, tilting it at a rakish angle. 'And enough rope to hang himself.' Then he added quickly, 'Will you be going to the fireworks on Tuesday?'

The fireworks had been arranged to take place in Vauxhall Gardens on the first of August to celebrate the coronation of George IV. It had been billed as the event of the year, when the ordinary people of London who would not be in the Abbey to witness the coronation, could have their own festivities. The organisers, having expended a great deal of money on the pyrotechnics, had decided to set them off, notwithstanding there was to be no coronation.

'Yes, I expect so,' she said, knowing he had changed the subject because he did not like being interrogated. He was a grown man and well able to take care of himself, she had no right to quiz him. 'All our friends are going.'

'Do you have an escort? Silly question. Of course you have.'

There was most decidedly something wrong with him; he was almost distracted. 'As it happens, I am going with Mama and Papa. Jack is going to be allowed to accompany us as a special treat and I have promised to help look after him.'

'Then I shall look forward to seeing you there.' He took her hand and raised it to his lips. 'Until then.' And he was gone before she had a chance to ask him what he meant by 'enough rope to hang himself'.

Tuesday evening was still warm after another hot day and she chose a muslin dress, light as thistledown in a pale jonquil colour. It had small puffed sleeves, a wide boat-shaped neck and a deep frill at the hem which was just high enough to show off the tops of her kid shoes. A silk fringed shawl was draped over her shoulders in case it turned cool when darkness fell.

Lavinia travelled in the Loscoe carriage with the Duke and Duchess and Jack. It should not have been a long journey; however, the crowds on Westminster Bridge held the traffic up for at least an hour before the coachman dare push the horses forward, and then only at a walk. They arrived at last and, having paid the entrance fee, were soon strolling along the footpaths, admiring the clipped hedges, shady groves of trees, the rose arbours and the statuary which stood in green arbours. Somewhere, in the background, an orchestra played.

The Duke and Duchess walked arm in arm, their heads slightly inclined towards each other, enjoying the rare treat of being able to relax together. They were joined by the Grahams and Willoughbys amongst others until they became quite an animated party, revelling in the feeling of being in the countryside, with the river gently lapping its banks close at hand.

Lavinia turned to find Lord Wincote had fallen into step beside her. He was superbly clad in a dark grey coat and matching pantaloons in a fine grey wool, tucked into highly polished hessians. He was wearing a tall curly-brimmed hat with a silver buckle on the band, which he took off as he bowed to her. 'Your servant, my lady.'

Lavinia's heart began to beat a little faster, though she spoke calmly enough. 'Lord Wincote, I did not know you had arrived. How are you?'

'In excellent fettle, my lady. And you?'

'I am well.' It was a silly conversation considering they had seen each other at rehearsal only two days before and as neither could find anything else to say, they fell silent as they made their way towards the open space which had been set aside for the firework display. They were soon joined by James and Sir Percy with Lady Rattenshaw. Jack skipped along ahead of them, chanting, 'Queenie, Queenie Caroline, washed her hair in turpentine…'

'Jack, stop that at once,' the Duke snapped. 'Is it not enough we are bombarded on all sides with placards and broadsheets without teaching the children to be disrespect-ful?' he said. 'Where did he learn it?'

'Duncan taught it to me,' the boy said.

'Then I must have words with that young man. Jack, whatever anyone says about her, Caroline is our Queen and as such deserves our respect.'

'Hear, hear, your Grace!' Lord Wincote said.

'That is not to say we should not also respect our King,' the Duke added. 'Whatever his faults.'

'Oh, I concur entirely,' agreed Edmund diplomatically.

'I thought we had agreed to set that matter aside for the evening,' the Duchess put in. 'How can one enjoy oneself if one is beset on every hand by arguments and people taking one side or the other?'

'I take no sides,' murmured her husband. 'And if Jack had not—'

'Oh, Marcus, he is only a child. He doesn't understand,' Frances said.

'It is still very warm, even though the sun has almost disappeared,' Lady Willoughby commented, changing the subject abruptly. Lavinia was not surprised her ladyship was warm; she was dressed in a dark cerise round gown with a very full skirt and long sleeves, a cape and a satin turban with two sweeping feathers each fastened with a huge silver clip set with diamonds.

Almost as if she had been heard, the gardens were suddenly alight with lamps, hundreds of them, blinking on one after the other, lit by dozens of workmen, running from one to the other with tapers. The paths and trees beside them were soon illuminated, casting the rest deeper into shadow. Jack stopped skipping and stood gazing about him in wonder. 'Magic,' he said, spellbound.

'How easily we are pleased as children,' Lord Wincote said. 'A few lanterns hanging in trees and we are in fairyland.'

The sky was blue-black, brilliantly pinpointed with stars. 'Such a beautiful night,' Lavinia said to no one in particular.

'A night for lovers,' Lady Rattenshaw said. 'We could almost be in the woods of *A Midsummer Night's Dream* with magic in the air. I feel the romance all about us. Don't you feel it too, Lord Wincote?'

'Indeed,' his lordship said, looking at Lavinia.

Unabashed she went on. 'What about you, Lord Corringham? Are you feeling romantical?'

'Goodness, James's idea of romance is the feel of a good

horse between his knees and a high fence to jump,' Lavinia said and they all laughed. She was glad it was dark and they could not see the colour flare into her face. 'Oh, I didn't mean—'

'It is all right, Vinny, we understand,' James murmured. He lengthened his stride to walk at her side so that, apart from her father, she was flanked by the two most important men in her life.

The path they were following ended in a wide open space in the middle of which was a roped-off area where the fireworks were being prepared. The crush as everyone tried to reach the front in order to have the best view was enough to take their breath away and James found himself putting his arm about Lavinia's shoulders to protect her as everyone began pushing from behind. He half-expected some protest from Lord Wincote over this, but his lordship had become separated from them and he could see no sign of him.

Jack had been hoisted on the Duke's shoulders where he had the best view of all. 'I never saw so many people,' he said, wriggling excitedly. 'Oh! Oh!' This last because the first of the fireworks had hissed up into the night sky and exploded in a myriad of brightly coloured stars.

Everyone watched spellbound as new explosions followed one upon the other until it seemed the whole sky was lit up, bang after bang, cascade after cascade, each followed by cheers. The display ended with the set piece, a giant throne upon which a model of the King could clearly be seen dressed in his coronation robes and with his crown upon his head, the whole vision illuminated by fireworks sparkling like precious jewels. 'Where's the Queen?' someone shouted. 'What have you done with Caroline?' And though those who heard it laughed and cheered, no answer was forthcoming.

When the last firework fizzled out, they were left in total darkness. Everyone applauded, Jack most all, and then began to disperse. The crush, as everyone started to move at once, was frightening.

'I think we should wait until the crowd thins out,' James said. He still had his hand on Lavinia's shoulder. It appeared casual, but both were intensely aware of it. He savoured their nearness, wishing he dare say what was in his heart, but knowing that while she was still enamoured of Edmund Wincote, he could not. And Lavinia liked the feel of him so close to her, protecting her, but she had to remind herself it was only brotherly protection.

Still in the dark, they turned towards the illuminated walkways, James holding out his arm for her to take and together they followed Frances and the Duke, who had retained Jack on his shoulder.

Suddenly the shriek of a woman filled the air. It went on and on and everyone started running towards it, thinking murder was being done. James left Lavinia with Frances and dashed off to lend what assistance he could. He found Lady Willoughby, without her turban, hair all awry, clutching her bosom, surrounded by people all talking at once.

James pushed his way through, telling the curious bystanders the lady was known to him. 'My lady, what has happened?'

'My diamond clips,' she sobbed. 'They have been snatched away. Taken from my cloak.' She grabbed a handful of that garment and thrust it at him. 'See. The pin has been ripped through the material.'

'Did you see who it was?'

'No. It was a man in black and he wore a hood.' She shuddered. 'He grabbed me from behind, pulled the clasp from my cape and snatched my hat from my head. Oh, what am I to do?'

James looked about him. There were people everywhere and it was dark. There was no hope that a thief would be apprehended. 'Did you see which way he went?'

'That way, I think.' She pointed to a group of trees, dense enough to give cover.

Before he could go and investigate, Lord Wincote emerged from the wood, carrying her ladyship's turban. 'He got away,' he said, fingering a cut on his cheek. 'I nearly had him, but he pushed me over and kicked me viciously while I lay on the ground and by the time I was on my feet again he had gone, melted into the crowd. I am sorry, my lady.' He handed back the turban, now without its diamond clip.

James looked curiously at him. He did look rather bedraggled and the cut was genuine enough, and so was her ladyship's gratitude though the chase had been fruitless. 'Did you see the man, Wincote?' he asked.

'Not clearly. It was dark and he was dressed entirely in black, but he was tall and thin. I could tell that when I tried to hold on to him before he threw me down, but as to his face, I do not know. He was masked.' He paused and looked at James. 'We could make a search but...' He shrugged his shoulders to indicate how useless he thought that idea was.

The onlookers drifted away now the excitement was over, leaving James and Lord Wincote to look after Lady Willoughby. They were guiding her to a seat, set in an arbour, when they were joined by the rest of their party from whom they had become separated in the crush. Benedict went to his mother and she sobbed her story into his sympathetic ear. Everyone began talking at once, praising Lord Wincote for attempting to tackle the man and calling him a hero. James was not so sure but, despite his suspicions, he held his tongue.

The evening had been spoilt by this episode so no one felt like staying and, as the Duchess vouchsafed that it was time Jack was in his bed, they made their way to the gate. The Duke sent the gatekeeper to call up their carriages, which had been left at a nearby inn, and while they waited for them to arrive they stood in small groups, talking about the robbery and speculating on the thief.

'At least you were not injured,' Frances told her ladyship. 'He could have knocked you down.'

'Perhaps he saw Lord Wincote coming to my rescue, though I did not see him myself, but when I heard him asking me if I were all right, I was never more thankful.'

'It was foolish of her ladyship to wear her diamonds tonight,' Lord Wincote said. 'There are always footpads and pickpockets about on such occasions as this and having valuables on display for all the world to see is asking for trouble. I am only sorry I was not able to apprehend the villain.'

'No, but you did your best.' Lavinia bestowed a warm smile on him. 'And you have suffered as a consequence. I think as soon as you arrive home, you should ask someone to tend that cut. It looks quite painful.'

'Oh, it is nothing of consequence my lady,' he said, fingering it.

'Look at him,' James murmured to Percy. 'Preening himself in Vinny's adulation like the coxcomb he is. I begin to think this night's work has elevated him in her eyes and countered any plans we might have to discredit him.'

'Oh, I do not know,' Percy said, tapping his chin thoughtfully with the knob of his cane. 'He did not, after all, recover the stolen goods...'

'No, but he tried and that is enough for Vinny and Lady Willoughby too, by the sound of it.'

Lady Willoughby had ceased to wail about her loss, and was fulsomely praising Lord Wincote for coming to her rescue. 'Such a gallant gentleman,' she was saying. 'He could have been set upon, killed even…'

'Do not upset yourself, Mama,' Benedict said. 'Lord Wincote is unharmed and so are you, except for the shock of it. I will report the theft to a magistrate first thing tomorrow.'

'What good would that do?' the lady said sharply. 'The man is long gone.'

'I wonder,' James murmured to Sir Percy. He had seen nothing of Wincote throughout the display; he could have been anywhere. He could have been hiding in the trees, waiting for an opportunity to spring out on his unsuspecting victim and then pretend to chase the non-existent robber.

'What do you wonder?'

'Whether he *is* long gone. Perhaps we should be looking closer to home for the culprit. Is it simply coincidence that Lady Graham and Lady Willoughby should both lose valuables when in the same company?'

'Whatever do you mean?' Lavinia had returned to James's side in time to hear the last part of their conversation.

'Nothing, my dear,' Percy said, when it became evident James was not going to answer her. 'We were simply comparing the theft at Lady Graham's ball with tonight's crime.'

'Why do that? There is no similarity at all. The first one took place in Lady Graham's own home, the second in a dark garden packed with all manner of people. That is hardly the same company, unless you were referring to our own group.' She stopped speaking to look enquiringly into James's face. 'You weren't, were you?'

'Vinny—'

'Who?' she demanded. 'Who, among our friends, do you think capable of such a dastardly act? Tell me that.'

'Oh, none,' he said quickly. 'None among our friends, I am sure.'

'In any case,' she went on, 'Lord Wincote caught a glimpse of the man and said he was tall and thin and dressed in black. There is no one of our company fitting that description.'

'At night all cats are black,' he said. 'I am wearing black and Wincote's coat is dark and we are both tall.'

'Don't be so absurd, James. You were with me when we heard Lady Willoughby scream and Lord Wincote was with her ladyship. How else could he have set off in pursuit so quickly? And neither of you is thin.'

'You are quite right, my lady,' he said, bowing to her and casting a rueful glance in Percy's direction. 'We are not thin. I am afraid I have not been so often to Gentleman Jackson's as I ought these last few weeks. We must blame the rehearsals for that.'

She did not answer as Jack rushed over to them, his eyes bright with excitement. 'I saw it all from Uncle's shoulders,' he said, hopping from one foot to the other. 'Everything, even the men hiding in the darkness, running from one display to the other, setting them all up and lighting them. They all wore black hoods so their faces wouldn't show up white and spoil everything. I bet you didn't see them, Vinny.'

'No, I was too busy watching the fireworks going off.' Men in black clothes and wearing hoods, running about all over the place! How easy it would have been for one of them to slip away and rob Lady Willoughby. So much for James and his theory that it was one of their company.

'What else did you see?' James demanded sharply.

'Why, the fireworks. They were grand! All those colours and the noise. Bang, bang, like guns going off.'

'Did you see any of the men leave?' James asked.

'What men?'

'The ones who were lighting the fireworks. Did they leave their posts?'

'No, the fireworks wouldn't have gone off if they had, would they?'

James ruffled the boy's hair and smiled. 'No, of course not.'

'It might be an idea to have the display people questioned,' Sir Percy put in.

'Yes. I'll put Major Greenaway on to it.'

'I do not see what good he can do,' Lavinia said. 'He has done little to resolve the riddle of Lady Graham's necklace.'

'Do not be so sure,' James said. 'I believe he is making great strides in that direction.'

'Is he?' she asked in surprise. 'I never knew. What has he discovered?'

'Oh, that would be telling, my dear.'

'Then do tell.'

'Certainly not, it might jeopardise the outcome.'

'You mean you do not trust me.' She felt aggrieved. James and Sir Percy too, by the looks they were exchanging, knew something she did not and it was excessively mean of them not to say.

'Oh, I trust you, my dear,' James said with a wry smile. 'I trust you implicitly. Now here come the carriages.'

The carriages were drawing up beside them and there was a flurry of activity as the doors were opened, steps let down and people clambered in, calling goodnight to each other. In a few minutes the street was empty, except for James and Sir Percy who were sharing James's phaeton, and Lord Wincote who had arrived on horseback and was waiting for an ostler to bring his mount forward.

'What about following him?' James suggested.

'He would smell a rat right away. You can't hide in a phaeton. Besides, it was probably one of the men setting up the display, don't you think? We should not be in too much of a hurry to condemn a man, just because that is what we would like to do.'

'No, you are right.'

They climbed into the phaeton and James gave the horses the office and they bowled away, leaving Lord Wincote to make his own way home.

Lavinia was furious with James. He was taking his dislike of Lord Wincote too far. Whatever else he was, Lord Wincote was a gentleman and to suggest that he might know something about the loss of Lady Willoughby's diamond clips and Lady Graham's necklace was the outside of enough. That was what he had been implying, wasn't it? It was dreadful. If Lord Wincote ever heard of it, he would be justified in demanding satisfaction and there would be the most prodigious scandal. And Sir Percy was as bad; he should have stopped James, not encouraged him.

She dreaded the next rehearsal and began to wonder if she should not abandon the whole project. But what excuse could she give for doing so? Everyone had worked so hard and the orphanage needed the money and, besides, there was Lord Wincote's proposal. She had promised to give him an answer at the end of the first performance and if she cancelled, he might think... She did not know what he might think. Had he any idea of what people were saying about him being a fortune-hunter, if nothing worse? If he had, he would surely have no more to do with her or the play.

But in the event it was not Lord Wincote who did not turn up, but James, which only added to her annoyance with him. Was he too ashamed? Or was there another attraction? Her stepmother had extracted a promise from him to find a wife during the Season, though she had seen no evidence that he was seriously looking. But he was not one to wear his heart on his sleeve and, instead, viewed life with a studied nonchalance which she had often thought was a cover for deeper feelings.

Was he in love? If he married it would be the end of their closeness; a married man could not put his arm about a lady who wasn't his wife, could not laugh with her and tease her and take her out riding, could not listen to her woes and give her good advice. The idea was not one she could contemplate with detachment and so she pushed the thought from her and concentrated on the rehearsal, asking Benedict to take the part of Demetrius.

The afternoon sped by and if it had not been for James's absence they would have made great strides. When two servants brought in refreshments a couple of hours later, they were able to relax and enjoy the break, feeling that, at last, they were making progress.

Lavinia took the opportunity to study Lord Wincote surreptitiously. There was nothing about his behaviour to arouse suspicion. When he was not concentrating on his role, he was considerate and charming; there was no hint that he might have a guilty secret. How could James have imagined he knew anything at all about the loss of Lady Willoughby's clips? It was unthinkable.

As if to make up for the calumny, she went out of her

way to be attentive to him and he responded with every
appearance of pleasure, though he was careful not to force
himself on her as he had before, nor did he mention his
proposal of marriage, but as they were in mixed company
there was little opportunity to do so. She concluded he was
waiting, as he said he would, until she was ready to give
him her answer. Or was he so sure of himself and her that
he thought he no longer needed to press his suit as ardently
as before?

When everyone had gone, she tidied up the props they
had been using and then decided to work on the scenery.
The Duke was at the House of Lords and the Duchess
attending a committee of one of her charities and would
not be back until supper time. She put on an apron,
dragged out the piece of scenery she was working on and
propped it against a table. Then she fetched paint and
brushes from their storage place and set to work.

She was completely absorbed and murmuring Hermia's
lines beneath her breath when James wandered into the
room without waiting to be announced, and threw his tall
hat on to a chair.

She turned to look at him. He was dressed for riding, in
a buff coat with a huge collar, which she would have considered too heavy for town wear, and nankeen breeches
tucked into polished riding boots. 'Oh, it's you, James.
Where have you been? We finished rehearsing over an
hour ago.'

'Sorry. I had business that could not wait.' He advanced
into the room, his eyes feasting on her. She looked heart-
stoppingly attractive, wearing a voluminous cook's apron
over a spotted cambric day dress. There was still so much
of the child about her, innocence and wisdom combined.
He hoped she would never change and that if she was so
foolish as to insist on marrying Wincote, he would not

spoil that. The thought of that possibility made him grit his teeth, but the grimace turned into a crooked smile.

'What business? And what are you laughing at?'

He touched her cheek with the back of his finger. 'I am not laughing, my dear, simply smiling because you look so…' He paused, wondering how to describe what he saw, the child-woman, the cheeks pink from exertion and hair coming adrift from its pins, the rising and falling of her breasts, the sparkle in her eyes, which might just as easily be caused by anger as merriment. She was not at all pleased with him and when he had told her what he meant to do, she would be even less pleased. He tipped his head on one side, trying to make her smile. 'So workmanlike. And you have paint on your face.'

She scrubbed at it with the back of her hand and made it worse. He took his handkerchief from his pocket and bunched it up. 'Spit.' She did so and he carefully wiped her face.

It was such a familiar, loving gesture, one she was sure James made without even thinking about it and one, a few short weeks ago, she would have accepted as nothing out of the ordinary. But now, with a heightened awareness of her confused emotions, she found it both uncomfortably disturbing and achingly touching.

'That's better,' he said, replacing the handkerchief in his pocket.

She looked up at him, her eyes wide, searching his face. Yet she saw nothing but a kind of melancholy and decided not to press him on his reasons for abstaining himself from the rehearsal. Instead she managed a smile. 'Thank you. Now help me shift this scenery over to that wall. It needs to be left to dry.'

It could not go on, this strange intimacy, it was tearing him apart. He reverted to the dandy in self-defence.

'Vinny, I am wearing a new riding coat. You do not expect me to risk getting it dirty, do you?' He flicked imaginary fluff off the sleeve. 'I will not tell you how much it cost, but my tailor grows rich and I grow poorer.'

'Take it off, then.'

'My waistcoat is also new, the latest thing in striped marcella.'

'Then you had better remove that too and roll up your sleeves.'

'Vinny, I cannot do that! It would be highly improper.' He paused, then added, 'You are, after all, no longer a child but a genteelly brought-up young lady about to enter wedlock.'

'Am I?'

'Are you not?'

'James, you are only being obtuse to annoy me. Now, are you going to help me or shall I ring for a servant?'

He did not want a servant interrupting their tête-à-tête and so he took off his splendidly tailored coat and hung it carefully over the back of a chair, then he pushed his shirt sleeves up to the elbows and took hold of one side of the painted scenery. Lavinia took the other and they carried it over to the wall, where they propped it at an angle.

'Thank you,' she said.

'My pleasure. But you have not answered my question.'

'What question?'

'Are you about to marry?'

'Not today, not this week, I am far too busy.'

'With the play?'

'Yes, of course. What else?' She paused. 'James, why have you come so late? You surely did not think we would still be rehearsing?'

'No. I came to tell you that I am going into the country

for a few days to visit a friend. I have been making the arrangements.'

'Into the country? But, James, you can't,' she wailed. 'We have rehearsals next week. Everyone will be here…'

'Then you will not miss me.'

'I missed you today. Benedict had to read your lines.'

'Then he can continue to do so. I will not be gone any longer than I can help.'

'I knew you were in trouble!'

'In trouble? What makes you say that?'

'You must be. Why else would you be taking a repairing lease if not to escape your creditors?'

He laughed. 'I am not in debt, Vinny, not in trouble at all, though I am disappointed that you have such a low opinion of me.'

Not being in a mood to discuss her opinion of him, she did not pick him up on that. 'If you are not in trouble, why must you go?'

'Because I must.'

'James, how could you?' She turned to face him, her eyes glittering more green than brown as they always did when she was upset. 'How could you be so heartless when you know how hard everyone has worked and what with persuading Papa to let us have the ballroom and—?' She stopped, blinking hard. 'I am seriously displeased with you, James Corringham.'

'I am sorry but it is important.'

'More important than me?'

'That is a hit below the belt, Vinny, and one I hope you do not expect me to answer.'

'No, for I know the answer. You are deserting me. Just when I need you most.'

'Do you?' he asked softly, coming to stand in front of

her, taking both her hands in his, hardly daring to ask. 'Now, why would you need me, especially?'

She found that unusually difficult to answer. 'Oh, you know why. I need your support. There is so much to do and Lord Wincote...' She could not go on, could not explain that she was half-afraid of the future, her feelings and thinking so muddled she could make no sense of them. And now she could not even talk to him about it.

'Oh, it always comes back to Lord Wincote, doesn't it?' he said, somewhat acerbically as he dropped her hands. 'I do not see how I can help you there. You must make up your own mind about him.'

'At least he has never missed a rehearsal.'

'He has good reason not to.'

'Oh, James, what is the matter with you? It is not Lord Wincote who has been behaving strangely but you. I thought I could rely on you...'

'So you can. A man may go about his business without being accused of strangeness, surely?' How he wished she had not overheard his comment to Sir Percy after that incident at Vauxhall Gardens. It was indiscreet of him to have made it and it had given her a disgust of him, which he was afraid could not be reversed. But perhaps when he came back, he might have some answers.

Emotions she could not control took over, love and anger in equal measure and, because she could not cope with love, she allowed her anger to have the ascendancy. 'Oh, you are the outside of enough. Go, if you must, but do not be surprised if Mr Greatorex has taken your part when you come back.'

'Oh, has he arrived, then?'

'No, but I am sure he will very soon. He is not a man to break a promise, unlike some I know. We cannot hold up the play just because you take it into your head to go travelling. Who is this friend, who is so important to you?'

'No one you know.'

'No, I'll wager I do not. A light o' love, I shouldn't wonder. Well, off you go. Enjoy her favours. Do not give me a second thought.'

'Vinny—'

'Go!'

He shrugged and strode out, slamming the door behind him. He did not see her sink on to a chair, nor hear her sobs, for they were silent ones.

Chapter Eight

There were two rehearsals in the following week with everyone frantically trying to commit their lines to memory while attending fittings for their costumes. It was all becoming very fraught and she had to admit that without Lady Rattenshaw and Lord Wincote, who knew their lines and delivered them with great sensitivity, the play would almost certainly be a failure. Her ladyship's helpfulness always managed to keep everybody concentrating on what they had to do.

Lavinia missed James dreadfully. She told herself she missed his good humour, his steadfastness, the way he protected her, even his constant teasing; he was her rock. Without him she felt she had no one to lean on, which was too foolish for words; she had her father, her stepmama, Miss Hastings and a whole host of other friends. Where had he gone? It was so unlike him to disappear without saying where he was going. But the date of the play's performance was only a month away and there was that infamous trial to be attended. He would have to come back for that.

The whole country, rich and poor alike, could talk of nothing else. The satirists, cartoonists and versifiers were having a field day. Hundreds of broadsheets were being distributed ridiculing either the King or the Queen, depending on the particular allegiance of the writer. And Caroline did nothing to help herself. She could have stayed quietly at home and kept her dignity; instead a stream of callers went in procession to Brandenburg House, where each received a shilling medal with her likeness to commemorate the visit.

'She is being used and degraded for political ambition,' the Duke said, for once spending an evening at home. 'And the Monarchy has been dealt a blow from which I doubt it will recover.'

'Yes, but surely they were forced into a marriage neither of them wanted?' Lavinia said. 'That is what is so tragic about it. I am sure I could never marry for expediency. I would rather die.'

Marcus laughed. 'Then let us be thankful you will never be put to the test.' He paused. 'I have not heard you mention Lord Wincote's name recently. Is he still waiting for your answer?'

She hesitated momentarily before answering. 'Yes, Papa, he is.'

'Vinny,' Frances put in, looking up from a sketch of Freddie she'd begun the week before. 'If you are not sure…'

'If I am not sure, Mama, I shall turn him down, you may rely on that.'

'Good. I should hate to think any undue influence had been brought to bear.'

'What undue influence?'

'That distasteful display of animal magnetism. It quite changed my mind about him.'

'Oh, Mama, it was only harmless fun.' She felt obliged

to defend her suitor. 'And you know Lady Rattenshaw encouraged him. I doubt he would have done it otherwise.'

'Perhaps.' She paused. 'How is the play coming along?'

'Very well, I think. Everyone knows their entrances and exits, though I am not sure about James. He could not have gone away at a worse time.'

'Did he say when he would be back?'

'No, but I expect he will return for the trial. He will not want to pay a fine for his absence, will he?'

'Another week, then.'

'Yes.'

Two days later, she was sitting in the drawing room, trying to learn Hermia's lines, when the Duchess came into the room, ready to go out in the carriage. 'You are looking tired, Lavinia,' she commented. 'I think perhaps you have been putting too much into that play. If you are not careful you will make yourself ill.'

'I am perfectly well, Mama.'

'So you say, but my eyes tell me differently.' She began pulling on her gloves. 'I am going to the orphanage,' she added. 'Why not come too? It will do you good.'

It was the perfect excuse to lay aside her self-imposed task and she readily agreed. She had enjoyed going to the orphanage ever since her stepmother, then the Countess of Corringham, had raised the money in a dozen different ways to set it up. Sometimes she helped serve the children with their food, sometimes she gave them reading and writing lessons, sometimes she sat and sketched them. Lavinia invariably departed feeling humble and thankful for her own good fortune. She had parents who loved her, enough to eat, good clothes on her back, a soft bed with clean sheets and warm blankets. Oh, she had so much for which to give thanks. And if she never married, that would always be the case.

The morning flew by and by the time Tom Bagshott brought the carriage back to take them home, she was feeling far more cheerful. 'Mama, do you think we could stop at the Pantheon Bazaar to buy some ribbon for the costumes?' she said as they made their way along Oxford Street. 'I told Constance I would try and have them for the next fittings.'

They were descending from the carriage, when they saw two people dressed as Harlequin and Columbine walking towards them, handing out leaflets to everyone they met.

'Oh, it's a playbill,' Lavinia said eagerly, taking one. 'Lancelot Greatorex and Lydia Gosport in Mr Sheridan's *The Rivals*. You remember Lancelot Greatorex, Mama? He is the manager of the Thespian Players, who came to Risley at the beginning of the year. I heard he was to come to London. Oh, do let us go and see it.' Somehow she had to remind the actor of his promise and inveigle the Duchess into inviting him to a rehearsal without her realising it had all been planned. 'Watching professionals like Mr Greatorex, I might learn something about putting on a play.'

Frances smiled. 'Is it not a little late for that? You have been hard at work for weeks now and must be nearly ready.'

'It is never too late to learn. And I must admit, I am a little worried...'

'Worried, dearest? How so?'

'Oh, everyone knows their lines, but they are so wooden and I am the worst culprit of all, I know it.' She knew why her own performance lacked fire. It was all due to playing opposite Lord Wincote, saying Hermia's lines to him and hearing him say Lysander's to her; before long she would not be able to tell Shakespeare from real life, or distinguish between Lysander and Edmund Wincote.

She hoped by the time the first performance was over, some flash of insight would tell her how to answer him. 'So, do you think you could persuade Papa to take us? Once the trial starts, he will have little time for entertainment…'

In the event Mr Greatorex sent three complimentary tickets to Stanmore House, delivered by special messenger, with a note saying he would be honoured if they would attend as his guests on the first night.

Lancelot Greatorex was renowned for his lifelike performances; the way he managed to convey great emotion without overacting. On the other hand, he could play farce with great dexterity until his audience were almost falling out of their seats with laughter. He always gave of his best whether he was playing to Royalty in London or entertaining a couple of hundred inhabitants in a tent on a village green.

If it had not been for the trial, the King himself might have attended one of the performances, but His Majesty, knowing how unpopular he had become, was staying out of sight at Windsor, seeing no one but his latest mistress, Lady Conyngham, until the wretched affair of his divorce was settled. Between them Frances and Lavinia persuaded the Duke that this did not mean his ministers could not enjoy themselves, especially as there was nothing they could do until the trial began. A few hours' entertainment was exactly what he needed.

The great actor did not disappoint and Lavinia watched enthralled from the first word to the last. After the curtain descended at the end and everyone prepared to leave, chatting animatedly about the play, Lavinia moved closer to her father. 'Papa, do let us go backstage and congratulate

Mr Greatorex. I am sure he would appreciate a word from you.'

'Oh, he has enough adulation as it is.'

'Yes, but he did send us tickets, so what you think must be important to him.'

'Very well, for a few minutes.' They left their box and Marcus called an usher to conduct them to the actor.

And so it was that Lavinia found herself in the great man's dressing room, breathing in the atmosphere of greasepaint and powder, wigs and costumes. Greatorex, however, had divested himself of all of these and was sharing a drink with the cast and members of the audience to celebrate the successful conclusion of the play.

He was a handsome man with dark eyes and a mass of curly black hair and was wearing, over a pair of pantaloon trousers, a kind of Russian tunic in pink satin with very full sleeves gathered at the wrist and caught about the waist with a leather belt. Seeing the newcomers, he left the adoring sycophants who surrounded him and made his way over to them.

'Your Grace,' he said, executing a flourishing bow to the Duchess. 'Your very obedient servant. So glad you could join our little gathering.' Having given the Duke the same greeting, he turned to Lavinia. 'Lady Lavinia, I hope I find you well?'

'Yes, thank you.' She was suddenly tongue-tied. How pretentious she had been to think she could put on a play! How had she had the temerity to aspire to be an actress? The great Lancelot Greatorex would have nothing to do with her poor effort.

'We enjoyed the play very much,' Frances said.

He bowed. 'Then I am content.'

'Lady Lavinia is putting on a play,' she went on.

'Oh, it is only for friends and family, not for public

display,' Lavinia put in quickly. 'But I have learned a great deal watching you tonight.'

He turned to look at Lavinia, his eyes telling her he remembered his promise. 'Then I am honoured to have been of assistance, my lady. If there is any other way I may help, you have only to say the word.'

'Oh, would you? If only you could find the time to attend one of our rehearsals, I am sure you would offer good advice and improve the performance of every one of us.'

'I would be delighted, my lady. We have no performance on Monday and, if the Duke and Duchess agree, I could give you an hour or two then.'

The Duke hesitated, but consented in the face of Lavinia's imploring looks. However, he declined an invitation to join the party and the three of them left to find their carriage had been drawn up at the stage door ready to take them home. It was astonishing how easy it had been and Lavinia went home in a glow of euphoria.

Now, if only James would come back, they could really make great strides. She pushed all other thoughts from her, determined that when he returned from wherever he had been, they would make up their quarrel and regain the easy relationship they had once enjoyed. She could not understand why she had been so angry with him, why it mattered so much that he should not go to his *chère amie*. Thinking about it made her want to burst into tears all over again.

James galloped his horse into the suburbs of London where he reluctantly slowed it to a walk on account of the heavy traffic. The whole country seemed to be descending on the capital for the trial which was due to begin the following Thursday. He wished he did not have to attend as he had no interest in the antics of the Royal family. His concern was solely for Lavinia. He fervently hoped that she had not been such a goose as to accept Lord Wincote's offer of marriage while he had been away. She had been angry enough to do something foolish, but surely not enough to agree to a marriage that would undoubtedly make her miserable.

He would have liked to have gone direct to Stanmore House but he was tired, dusty and dishevelled from riding on hard-baked roads and so he turned his horse towards home. Tomorrow morning he would seek out Donald Greenaway and tell him what he had discovered. After that he would call at Stanmore House. He was impatient to see Lavinia, though he was unsure how much he should tell her, if anything at all. She might not believe him and would flare up in defence of Wincote as she had done after the fireworks. He must be very sure of his ground before shattering her hopes and dreams.

It took him some time to find Major Greenaway the next day, but he tracked him down at last at the boxing emporium in Bond Street where he was sparring with one of Gentleman Jackson's assistants.

'James, you are just in time,' the Major greeted him. 'I was about to leave and find some breakfast. Unless you would like to strip off and go a round or two?'

'No, thank you, I am still saddle sore. Breakfast will do me very well.'

They left discussing the issues which had brought them together until they were sitting in a local hostelry with ham, eggs, meat pies and coffee in front of them, and then it was Donald who spoke first. 'I've questioned all the men who were helping with the fireworks,' he said. 'They are all accounted for. Not that I didn't expect it.'

'What about the diamond clips, any sign of them?'

'No. Our man is cunning enough not to use the same

receiver twice. And I have been instructed by Lord
Graham not to proceed with the enquiry on his behalf, so
I think he must have found the money to pay the black-
mailer. It appears we are getting nowhere.'

'Not quite nowhere, my friend. I went up to Cumberland
to see for myself.'

'And?'

'I discovered the Wincote estate is not only mortgaged,
it is almost derelict. The people I spoke to, tenants of the
estate for the most part, have not seen Wincote since his
grandfather died. The rents are collected by an agent and
nothing has been done about the upkeep and repair of their
property, though the agent has promised them the trouble
is only temporary and everything will be set to rights in a
few weeks. As for the mining rights, they have been taken
over in lieu of debts.'

'Whose debts?'

'The grandfather's; lost in foolhardy investments. I
found a one-time servant who was prepared to talk. He
might have had an axe to grind and we should not rely
too much on his evidence, but he told me the old man
went to pieces after the death of the older grandson, Henry,
and he hated Edmund. After the tragedy, they lived together in the same house in a state of dreadful enmity. It
was so bad none of the servants would stay.'

'Why?'

'My informant, a Nathaniel Birch, was somewhat havey-
cavey about it, but hinted there was something strange
about Henry's death.'

'You mean he was murdered?'

James shrugged. 'Who's to say? He fell down the stairs
and was impaled on an old pike which was kept on the
wall in the hall. According to Birch it was not possible,
even if he had dislodged the pike in his fall. I tried to get

into the house to see for myself, but it was locked and barred and all the windows boarded up.'

'Were there any witnesses?'

'Only the old man.'

'Where was Edmund at the time?'

'It was late at night and he was in his room, so he said in evidence. He came out when he heard the commotion and this was corroborated by his grandfather.'

'And thereafter they were enemies?'

'That's the way it was told to me.'

'Do you believe it?'

'I don't know what to believe. As I said, my informant might have had an ulterior motive, but if it is true and Edmund is capable of murdering his brother, a strong healthy man, in order to inherit the estate, then ridding himself of a wife, especially a young and trusting one, would not be difficult. I fear for Lavinia if she accepts him.'

'James, this is all conjecture, and without proof, it would be most unwise to speak of it to anyone else. But Lady Lavinia will surely not accept him if you tell her the condition of the estate; you need say nothing of your other suspicions.'

'She will fly into the boughs. She thinks I have an aversion to Lord Wincote for no reason and telling her his house needs repairing would not put her off. It might very well drive her into his arms.' He smiled grimly. 'Wealth or lack of it would not count with her if her affections were genuinely engaged.'

'I can't see how you are going to prove criminal intent. The old man is dead and Wincote is not going to confess.'

'No. But we can try to prove he took those jewels.'

'Not an easy task, my friend, when there are hundreds

of angling coves in the capital and the clips could well be broken up by now.'

'True, but it is our only hope.'

'I will do my best.'

'Thank you. I knew I could rely on you, but time is not on our side. Vinny may shackle herself to him at any moment, even though the Duchess did prevail upon her to wait until after the play has been performed.'

'And if he should be innocent?'

'I'll wager he is not.' He smiled crookedly. 'Sir Percy has another ploy, but I am not sure it will work, and if it does Lady Rattenshaw is also in danger. I shall have to warn them.' He finished the dregs of his coffee, now grown cold, and stood up. 'I must be off. Contact me if you discover anything.' He threw some coins onto the table to pay for the breakfast and left. But when he went to Brook Street, he was told that Sir Percy was not at home and was not expected back until late afternoon.

While James was talking to Major Greenaway, Lavinia was in Hatchard's in Piccadilly with Daisy, browsing among the shelves for a book her stepmama had asked for when suddenly she saw Lord Wincote and Lady Rattenshaw enter the shop together. They had their heads together, laughing in an intimate kind of way, and did not see her. Instead of coming forward to greet them, as she should have done, she stepped back behind the shelf, pulling the astonished Daisy after her. 'Shh, not a word,' she hissed.

They stayed out of sight, while her ladyship chose and paid for two books and then she and Lord Wincote left. Lavinia emerged from her hiding place to see them climb into her ladyship's carriage and drive away. But she had heard Lady Rattenshaw address Lord Wincote as 'Edmund dear' and he had called her Emma. It had been said so easily, as if they were used to the intimacy and it left Lavinia shaken to the core.

'Well, I never did!' Daisy said, as she joined Lavinia. 'Nice and cosy, weren't they?'

'Oh, it is of no consequence,' Lavinia said airily. 'I believe they are old friends.' That was not true, at least she did not think it was, but she could not allow Daisy to see how much it had affected her. Edmund had not been so attentive in the last two weeks, but she had supposed he was only doing as she asked and was waiting until after the trial and the performance of the play; now it was clear he had tired of her.

She found the book she was looking for and, having purchased it, hurried home without doing the rest of the shopping she had planned. This new development needed some thought and she could not think properly surrounded by people and with Daisy chattering beside her. As soon as she had taken off her outdoor clothes, she went into the ballroom and began adding to the scene she was painting of a room in Theseus's palace. The outline had already been done and it was simply a matter of adding depth, light and shadow.

The first question she asked herself was how much did she care? The answer was she cared a great deal, but honesty made her admit that it was her pride that was hurt more than her heart. The whole *haut monde* knew Lord Wincote had spoken to her father and proposed marriage so, even though she had deferred giving him an answer, the offer was binding on him.

She took her mind back to when she had first met Lord Wincote and how he had flattered her and after that how he had used every opportunity to make his intentions known, especially at that demonstration of mesmerism. He had been intent on capturing her heart then, everyone knew it. And since then, at rehearsals, he had said he was waiting patiently for her answer. Had he changed? Had Lady Rattenshaw drawn him away with sweet words and compliments and her vulgar display of wealth? Could it possibly mean that he was a fortune-hunter, after all, and, having found he must wait for her dowry, had decided that Lady Rattenshaw's wealth was more immediately available?

Only two days before, they had been doing the scene where Lysander wakes up after his eyes are anointed with the magic juice to find himself in love with Helena. Lord Wincote had imbued the scene with deep emotion, schooled, no doubt, by Lady Rattenshaw. 'Content with Hermia,' he had declared. 'No; I do repent the tedious minutes I with her have spent. Not Hermia, but Helena now I love.'

Thinking about it, she recalled the looks that passed between them, the way he contrived to touch the lady's hand when he thought no one was looking, the smiles they exchanged, the tone of their voices when they acted the love scenes. Would she have given that a second thought if it had not been for seeing them together in the bookshop?

The memory of it made her seethe with anger and she daubed great splashes of pink paint on the canvas, so furious she did not care where it went. If he thought... Her eyes suddenly filled with tears and brushed at them with the back of her hand, smudging her face with paint. Hurt pride, she was bound to admit, was almost as painful as a broken heart. Hearing footsteps approaching, she pulled herself together and quickly scrubbed at her eyes, ready to smile at whoever it was.

'James!' Her eyes lit up with pleasure, but quickly became clouded again. 'You decided to come back, then.'

'As you see.' He smiled and walked forward, flinging his hat nonchalantly on a chair as he passed it. She was obviously unhappy and, though he was tempted to rush forward and comfort her, he did not want her to frighten her with a show of affection she would not welcome. 'You know, that backcloth was coming along nicely, and now you have spoiled it.'

'I do not care,' she said angrily, throwing another brushful of paint at it. 'I wish I had never thought of doing the silly play. I wish I had stayed at Risley all summer…'

'My dear, what has brought this on? I thought rehearsals were going very well, especially since Lady Rattenshaw joined the company.'

'Lady Rattenshaw! Not you, too.'

'What do you mean, not me, too?'

'Toadying to her as if she were the answer to everything. Who is she anyway? Coming here and—'

'Vinny, Vinny,' he said, taking her wrists in his hands to stop her flinging paint all over the room. 'What has she done?' He took the paintbrush from her and put it down on the table beside the paint pot, then took her shoulders in his hands so that she was obliged to face him. Her distress hurt him so much that he began to wonder if she really did love Wincote. He should never have colluded with Sir Percy in introducing Lady Rattenshaw into Society. 'Could it have something to do with Lord Wincote?'

'You know?' She stared up at him, her huge green eyes wide and bright with unshed tears. Had she somehow discovered the truth?

'Know what, my dear?' he asked, endeavouring to keep his voice light.

'That he and…and Lady Rattenshaw are…are becoming very close?'

'Are they?' he queried, relieved that it was not the worst he had feared. 'I can't say I noticed.'

'No, you wouldn't have, considering you have spent the last ten days in the country, instead of here attending rehearsals. He used to be so attentive. I thought he was sincere…'

'Perhaps he is and his attention to Lady Rattenshaw is all very innocent.'

'Then why did he call her "Emma dear"? I heard him say it. And she is driving him around in her carriage for all the world as if… He is making a laughing stock of me.'

'How can that be? One visit to a book shop together means nothing and you may be sure if he had been seen in the lady's company more than once, you would have heard of it. There is nothing the *haut monde* likes better than a good gossip.' How he hated playing the devil's advocate, but until Donald found some evidence, he could say nothing.

'That is just what I mean.'

'But you have not accepted his offer, have you? There is nothing official.'

'No, but everyone knows he made it.' That was what she found so humiliating, that others might have noticed. 'I may have told him I want time to consider his offer, but that does not mean he can go off and pay court to someone else. He should at least have waited until I turned him down.'

'Are you going to turn him down?' he asked casually, though inside he felt like singing.

'I have not made up my mind and I would certainly not tell anyone before I had communicated my decision to him,' she said sharply. 'So you must wait and see, like everyone else.'

Wait and see, those were the words Percy had used.

Now their chickens were coming home to roost and he was not at all sure they had done the right thing if it meant his darling Vinny was going to be hurt. And could he be sure his own motives had been altruistic? After all, he hoped to gain the lady himself in the end. And there was no guarantee she would turn to him, simply because Lord Wincote had let her down. 'Very well, my dear,' he said. 'But if you think he is not sincere, why wait to give him his *congé*?'

'Because, if I do that, he will surely walk out on the play and where will I find another Lysander so late in the day?'

'Oh, the play,' he said, dismissively.

'Yes, the play,' she said, her determination returning. Now James was here, she could face them all. 'If Edmund Wincote thinks I am going into a decline because he sees fit to play fast and loose, then he may think again.'

He laughed and touched her cheek with the back of his finger. 'Good for you, my love.'

His touch and the endearment were so unexpected that they set her pulses racing and made her breathless. He was so gentle and yet so firm; there were not many men who would put up with her tantrums. She took a huge gulp of air to steady herself. 'Now you are here, I presume you are going to stay for the rehearsal. It is the last one before the trial starts. It is no use having any while that is on, no one will be able to concentrate and you and all the other peers will have to attend the House of Lords.'

He gave her an exaggerated bow accompanied by a wide smile. 'I am at your service, as always.'

'Good. I trust you have not been enjoying yourself so much you have forgotten your lines.'

If she had hoped he would deny he had been enjoying

himself and tell her what he had really been doing, she was disappointed. He smiled.

He was tempted to tell her what was in his heart, but perhaps she was not in a mood to listen. Her whole mind was on Lord Wincote and Lady Rattenshaw.

'Oh, Vinny, I wish…' he began and then stopped as Sir Percy arrived, followed by Duncan, Benedict and Constance who were in turn followed by Lord Haverley with Sophia and Eliza. Whatever wish James had been going to voice was left unsaid.

In the general hubbub, Lavinia became aware that Lord Wincote and Lady Rattenshaw had not arrived. 'They have never failed to attend before,' she said. 'I hope nothing untoward has happened.'

No one answered her. It may have been that they were as puzzled as she was, or perhaps too embarrassed to say what they thought. James glanced at Sir Percy, who shrugged his shoulders.

'Perhaps they have been held up,' Benedict said. 'I heard the Queen is moving back to town for the trial and is to stay in St James's Square. There was a huge crowd outside number eighteen when I came past.'

'It did not stop everyone else arriving,' Lavinia put in, as they all began discussing the Queen moving into the square and the disruption it would cause to the residents of the area. 'Oh, this would have to happen today of all days. Mr Lancelot Greatorex is coming to see how we do.'

'Lancelot Greatorex?' queried Martin Drew. 'You mean the actor-manager?'

'Yes. He will be here soon.'

This news was greeted with mixed feelings. The actor was bound to be dismissive of their amateurish efforts and if he took a part would certainly make them look ridiculous. Others, who did not mind making fools of themselves, realised it would certainly mean they would raise more money for the orphanage if his name was on the bill.

The missing two had still not arrived by the time Lancelot Greatorex had been announced and advanced into the room as if he were making an entrance on stage. He had a commanding presence that made everyone stop whatever they were doing and look at him. Dressed as he was in a green frock coat, pale green pantaloons and a yellow shirt, he outdid Sir Percy in the colourfulness of his attire. He stopped in the middle of the room, swept off his hat which had a peacock's feather curling about its brim, and bowed right and left.

'Mr Greatorex, how good of you to come,' Lavinia said, hurrying forward to greet him while James hid his smile.

'The pleasure is mine, dear lady.' He looked about him as if summing up the cast. 'Are you ready to begin?'

'We would be, but I am afraid we are missing Helena and Lysander.'

'Dear me, *A Midsummer Night's Dream* without two of its main characters cannot be done. Actors, if they are to be true actors, are always reliable. They appear for rehearsals as assiduously as they appear for the performance.'

'They have never let us down before,' she said. 'I fear something must have happened to them. Perhaps you would do us the honour of reading Lysander's part and Miss Graham will stand in for Lady Rattenshaw. This is Miss Graham.' She held out her hand to draw Constance forward.

'Oh, Lavinia, I could not,' the young lady protested, looking nervously from Lavinia to Lancelot.

'Of course you can, my dear,' Lord Haverley said. 'You have been prompting us all along. You know everyone's part.'

Lavinia, surprised by his familiar address, looked sharply at Constance, who blushed scarlet. So, her friend might be going to have her wish after all.

'Then let us begin,' Mr Greatorex said.

Lancelot was a master, not only of his craft, but in dealing with people. He seemed to know exactly how much censure each could take, those who would improve by being berated and those who needed sympathetic encouragement to give their best. His own performance as Lysander was a model of how to play Shakespeare. At the end of the session, the hostility that had been evident at the beginning was gone and everyone's enthusiasm had been renewed, not least Lavinia's, but there was still the problem of the play within the play.

'Mr Greatorex,' she said, almost timidly, 'you have seen what we can do, and have been kind enough to praise our efforts. I wonder if I can prevail upon you to allow some of your players to take the part of the entertainers? It would ensure the success of our venture and Mama's orphans will reap the benefit.'

'I would be delighted, my lady, but when would you need them? I am committed to *The Rivals* for the next two weeks and then we are to do *Romeo and Juliet*, though that need not be an obstacle. We have performed *A Midsummer Night's Dream* many times and would need only one rehearsal with your friends.'

'So many of the cast are peers and are obliged to attend Westminster for the trial,' she explained. 'And we would have no players and certainly no audience while everyone is in such a ferment over it so, if everyone is agreeable, I think we should aim for Friday, the twenty-eighth of September. It should all be over by then.'

'I do hope so,' Lord Haverley said. 'Eliza should be back in the schoolroom, you know. And Sophia has been promised a visit to her aunt in Hertfordshire. I had no idea when we began that it would go on so long. I have affairs of my own which I am anxious to pursue.' He looked across at Constance as he spoke, making Lavinia wonder if Lord Wincote was not the only one who was waiting for the answer to a certain question.

'The prosecution case is so damning, I cannot believe the defence will have anything to say in rebuttal,' Sir Percy put in. 'It will all be over in a week.'

Duncan, standing just behind Lavinia, bent to murmur in her ear, 'I heard that Lord Wincote has evidence, but it is so shocking no one dare use it.'

She twisted round to face him with her back to his lordship. 'Where did you hear that?'

'Oh, it is the latest *on-dit*.'

'It is nonsense.' She kept her voice low. 'What can Lord Wincote know of it? He has been living in seclusion in Cumberland for years.'

'I am only telling you what I heard, Sis. But I tell you this, if his name is being bandied about in connection with the Queen, then you would do well to think twice before accepting his offer.'

'And I thank you to keep to your own business, brother,' she hissed. Aloud, she said, 'Mr Greatorex, is the twenty-eighth convenient to you?'

'Quite convenient,' he said. 'But what of the missing members of your cast? Are you sure you can rely on them?'

'I am sure they will be at the next rehearsal.' Although she spoke firmly, she was not at all sure. If it had been either one, she might have been able to dismiss it as of little importance, but both at once was more than a coincidence, surely?

'James, are you positive you know nothing about their

whereabouts?' she asked him, after Mr Greatorex had gone and everyone was leaving.

'Vinny, I have no idea, I promise you.'

'What about you, Sir Percy, do you know why they were not here? Lady Rattenshaw is your friend, after all.'

'She is, my dear, but I am not her keeper. She is free to come and go as she pleases.'

'But she has always been so reliable. And so has Lord Wincote. I cannot think why he should decide not to come today.' But she had a horrible feeling she did know.

'No doubt his lordship will explain,' Sir Percy said, discounting the lady's absence. 'It is nothing to worry about. He will be here next time.' He smiled and patted her hand. 'Now, I must be off. You coming, Corringham?'

James looked at Lavinia, wondering if he could resume the conversation they had been having before everyone else arrived. 'Go on, I will catch you up,' he said, then turned to Lavinia and took her hands in both of his, cupping them as if he were holding a wounded bird. 'Don't worry, Vinny, everything will turn out for the best, you'll see.' He raised her hands and turned them over, kissing the palms one by one.

His lips, softly caressing her skin, sent a current racing through her, until her whole body was a quivering mass of desire. Even her legs were shaking and deep in the pit of her stomach something stirred, something so strong, she found herself reaching out towards him, wanting to be enfolded, not only in his arms, but by every part of him. It was a shocking revelation.

Suddenly she realised it was more than loneliness which had made her miss him. She had always loved him, but now it was more than that; she had fallen in love with him. Head over heels. How could it have happened? When had a sister's love changed into the love of a woman for a man?

It must have been before he went away, which was why she had been so miserable when he left. But it had taken until now to realise it. Had he realised it before she had and been so appalled at the idea that he had to get away? She felt hot with shame. Sisters did not become lovers.

He looked up and saw her gazing at him, her mouth half-open, her eyes wide in shock, and realised he had overstepped the mark. Disgusted with himself, he dropped her hand and smiled crookedly. 'Sorry, Vinny, didn't mean to startle you. Forgot myself.'

She did not understand. He was apologising; he was sorry he had done it. The bright hope in her breast died; he still thought of her as his little sister, to be teased and pulled out of scrapes, to laugh with but not to love as a man loves a woman. And she would rather die than allow him to see how she felt. 'Oh, go on, James, go after Sir Percy and stop playing the fool, will you?'

He gave her a sardonic smile, turned on his heel and left her.

She sank into a chair, too weary to do anything, but it was a weariness of the heart, not the body. She had not imagined that sudden surge of desire which filled her whole being, the wild pounding of her heart, the tingling in her limbs, the longing to be kissed properly by him, mouth on mouth, as if that would prove what she already knew: that she loved him.

Never in her wildest dreams had she imagined falling in love would be like this; elation and despair, fury at his blindness, for it was obvious he did not feel the same way about her, and impatience with herself. He was a light-weight, or affected to be, no doubt so that he could remain heart whole. On the other hand, Lord Wincote had made no secret of his serious intentions and was waiting in the wings with every appearance of patience for the answer to his offer. He took her very seriously indeed. Or he had done, until a few days ago. But he was second best.

She really ought not to let him go on thinking she might accept him, but she could hardly expect him to come to rehearsals if she turned him down. The play had become an obsession. Everything took second place to that, even the ordering of her life. She knew it was a kind of defence, a bulwark against having to think about her future.

She shook herself and left the ballroom with its half-constructed stage and its unfinished scenery and made her way across the wide hall to the stairs. Halfway up them was a small landing and a long window which gave a view of the street. James and Sir Percy were walking side by side in animated conversation, towards the crowds gathered about number eighteen where the Queen was staying. What did they have to say to each other that was so absorbing?

'You know why they didn't turn up?' James asked.

'No, but I am heartily glad they did not. I had no idea Lady Lavinia was going to bring Lancelot Greatorex into it.'

'What difference does that make?'

'Everything, dear boy. He cannot be allowed to come face to face with Marianne.'

'Marianne?'

'Lady Rattenshaw.'

'I thought her name was Emma.'

'No, her name is Marianne Doubleday. I believe she has trod the boards with Greatorex in the past. He is almost certain to recognise her.'

An actress! He might have known it. The woman was

too good in her part of Helena to be an amateur. 'What do you propose we should do?'

'Abort the whole scheme. Have to.'

'And what do we tell Lavinia? And the rest of the cast, come to that? And perhaps it is too late. They may have gone off together.'

'No, she would not do that without telling me.'

'I hope you are right because, if what I have learned is true, she might be in danger.'

'How so? The man is not violent, is he?'

'He could be.' He went on to explain what he had learned and ended, 'If he is prepared to kill for money…'

'I had better go and see her.'

'And if Wincote is with her?' He paused. 'Better to send her a note. Tell her to come to Corringham House, no chance of anyone else listening in there.'

'Very well. What time shall I suggest?'

'As soon as possible. Tonight. Seven o'clock.'

Marianne Doubleday answered the summons promptly and was offered refreshment, which she accepted gracefully, still every inch the lady. On being told by Sir Percy that Lord Corringham knew who she really was, she suddenly dropped her pose and laughed. 'What do you think of my little performance, Lord Corringham?'

'Very good, though I am not convinced it will achieve anything, except to make Lady Lavinia very unhappy.'

'Oh, so I am brought here to be rung a peel over, am I? Then you should know it was not my idea. If you want someone to blame, then I suggest you talk to Percy.'

'Oh, I have. I do not question his motives or yours, only the outcome. However, that is not why we have asked you here. We have hit a stumbling block. Lady Lavinia has prevailed upon Lancelot Greatorex to help with rehearsals of *A Midsummer Night's Dream*.'

'Really? That is a coup. It would be fun to meet the old poseur again, but I can see the difficulty. He will know me at once. We were once like that.' She laughed and held up two crossed fingers.

'Is that so?' Percy asked in surprise. 'You never said.'

'You never asked.' She turned back to James. 'So, what do you propose to do?'

'You must drop out of the rehearsals, of course. It is a pity because Lady Lavinia has worked so hard and she will feel terribly let down.'

'But she is going to feel that anyway, is she not? I thought that was the whole point.'

'Yes, let down by Lord Wincote, not by anyone else.'

'We have gone too far to back out now. It is only a matter of bringing it forward.'

'Bringing what forward?'

'Lord Wincote and I will run away together, cause such a scandal that he will never be received in Society again, certainly not at Stanmore House.'

'Nor will you.'

She laughed. 'No, but then I do not aspire to be anything more than a good actress and, once it becomes known how I bamboozled his lordship, you may be sure it will do my reputation nothing but good. I thought if he was prepared to let Lady Lavinia down over the rehearsal, it would give me some idea of how far he was prepared to go, so I invited him to come for a drive into the country with me.'

'And called at Hatchard's on the way,' James put in.

'Yes, how do you know?'

'Lady Lavinia saw you.'

'Oh.' She paused. 'I bought him a book of love poems. I wanted to set the scene, to make him think I loved him, assure him I had money enough to keep both of us in luxury.'

'And how did he react?'

'How do you think? Eagerly, of course. I am an actress and a good one.'

'And then what? You are not wealthy, are you?'

'No, what I appear to have is almost all down to Sir Percy. The rent of the house, clothes, jewellery, the lot.' She sighed. 'I shall miss it dreadfully when it is all gone.'

'Oh, I think I can allow you to keep a knick-knack or two,' Sir Percy said. 'For services rendered, don't you know.'

'But that still doesn't explain what you intend to do with Lord Wincote when you have him,' James said, impatient with them.

'Oh, I shall take him somewhere nice and quiet and tell him the truth. It will be fun to watch his face.'

'I doubt it will be fun at all,' James said. 'I believe he could be dangerous.'

'Why?'

James told her. She was silent for a few moments. 'As I understand it, if you cannot prove him a murderer, then you want him discredited?'

'Yes, but—'

'Then we have to go on. If I suddenly grow cold towards him, he will smell a rat and who knows what he might do?'

'That is exactly my point, Miss Doubleday.'

'I have his confidence; we must work on that.'

'I forbid it!' Sir Percy put in. 'I am as fond of Lady Lavinia as anyone, but I cannot permit you to put yourself in such danger.'

'There is no danger so long as he does not suspect I know the truth,' she said.

'No,' James said. 'It is too risky.'

'Have you a better plan?'

'Only to prove he took Lady Willoughby's diamond clips.'

'But perhaps he did not; I have seen no evidence to suggest he did. If he is innocent of that, then you have nothing. Oh, do let me do it. I am very fond of Lady Lavinia. She is so talented and plucky and I should hate to think of those virtues being ruined by an evil man.'

James felt exactly the same; the thought of Lavinia being incarcerated in that mausoleum of a house in Cumberland, being made miserable, the chattel of a man who wanted her only for the wealth she could bring, was more than he could stomach. And once the marriage settlement had been paid over, he might even dispose of her, as he had his brother.

'I will agree,' he said. 'But only if you do nothing without informing either Sir Percy or me first.' He went to a drawer in his desk and extracted a tiny pistol. 'Do you know how to use one of these?'

'I have used one on stage, with blanks in it, of course. Is it any different?'

'Only in its effect.' He took her reticule from her, loosened its tie and dropped the weapon inside, before drawing the cord up again and handing it back. 'Just in case. But I shall have Major Greenaway watching you. Come back here tomorrow so I can introduce you to him and he will tell you what to do.'

'I hope you know what you are doing, Corringham,'' Sir Percy said, as he prepared to escort Marianne home.

'So do I,' James murmured, sinking into a chair as soon as they had gone. He was drained of all energy, full of apprehension mixed with rage; rage at Wincote, rage at fate which denied him the love he wished for more than anything. Whatever the outcome, Lavinia was going to be hurt and angry and he would have to tread very carefully indeed not to be seen as the villain.

Chapter Nine

'Your Grace, Lord Wincote is here. Will you receive him?'

Frances turned towards Lavinia, who was sitting by the withdrawing-room window with a copy of *A Midsummer Night's Dream* on her lap, murmuring her lines. She looked startled, as if his lordship was the last person she expected to see. 'Vinny, do you wish me to receive him?'

'I do not see why not, Mama.'

The Duchess nodded to the footman, who went off to conduct the visitor to them. Full of confidence, he strode into the room, carrying an enormous bunch of flowers, which he offered to Lavinia, before making a flourishing leg to them both. 'Your Grace. My lady.'

Both women smiled, though Lavinia's was a little fixed, as she thanked him for the bouquet.

'My lord, good afternoon,' Frances said, indicating a chair. 'Do sit down.' Then to the hovering footman, 'Dobson, please put the flowers in water and bring in the tea tray.'

Edmund flung up the skirts of his dark green frock coat and seated himself, before addressing himself to Lavinia.

'My lady, I owe you an abject apology. I should have been at the rehearsal yesterday.'

'Yes, my lord, so you should.' She was surprised how cool she sounded. 'You missed the excitement. Lancelot Greatorex, the actor-manager, joined us. He was most helpful. I am sure everyone gained from having him with us.'

'I am most sincerely sorry. I should have liked to meet the great man, but I was called away on urgent business just as I was preparing to come and I was unable to let you know. I pray you will forgive me.'

She was reminded of Duncan's comment that he had evidence concerning the trial and wondered if that was the business which had prevented him from appearing. She was intrigued, but not enough to question him; she did not want him to think she was troubled by it. 'As it happens, you were not the only absentee. Lady Rattenshaw did not come either.'

'Really?' he queried. 'Her ladyship has always been most conscientious. Do you know why?'

'No. I thought you might.'

'Me?' He appeared startled. 'I do not understand.'

'Oh, it is of no consequence,' she said airily, aware that her stepmama was looking at her questioningly. 'I saw you leaving Hatchard's together and wondered if she might have told you then that she would not be coming.'

'No, she gave no hint of it. But then we only met by chance. Her carriage pulled up beside me as I was walking along Piccadilly. She wanted my opinion about a book she was thinking of buying and, as I was also going to the bookshop, she took me up and drove me home afterwards. We parted at my door. I had no idea she would not be coming to the rehearsal and am doubly sorry that you should have been incommoded.'

It was all very plausible, so why did she not believe him? Maybe because she had heard the familiar way they addressed each other, but they had been rehearsing together for weeks, so perhaps she was being unduly sensitive about it. In any case, it did not matter, did it? She was not going to marry him. How would he react when she told him? Would he be hurt, or angry, or would he simply shrug his shoulders and turn immediately to Lady Rattenshaw for consolation?

'You are forgiven, my lord.' She smiled, as a servant brought in the tray and the Duchess busied herself pouring tea. 'We have decided to postpone rehearsals for a week or two while the trial is on.'

'I think that is a very sensible decision,' he said. 'I, like my peers, will be obliged to attend, but I hope it will be over and done with quickly. There is a great deal of counter-evidence and, if Brougham uses it, the King will not dare proceed.'

'I am afraid I find the whole matter distasteful, my lord,' Frances said, handing him a cup of tea.

'I beg your pardon, your Grace, I shall not mention it again.' He turned to Lavinia. 'Tell me what happened at the rehearsal, my lady. What did Mr Greatorex have to say?'

Lavinia was happy to oblige him and the rest of the visit passed in pleasant conversation, at the end of which he took his leave, lifting the back of her hand to his lips, while raising his eyes to look into hers. 'I bid you *au revoir*, my dear lady.'

She was reminded of the sensation she had felt when James had turned her hands over to kiss the palms. Edmund Wincote could never stir her like that. And now that she knew where her heart really lay, even his dark eyes seemed to have lost the power to make her feel anything other than rigidly uncomfortable. 'My lord.'

'Good day, your Grace.' He turned and bowed to the Duchess and left, still as confident as ever.

'What was all that about Hatchard's?' Frances asked, as soon as the door had closed on him.

'Nothing, Mama. I saw him there with Lady Rattenshaw, but as he has explained what happened, it is of no consequence.'

'Of no consequence! Lavinia, if he is playing with your affections…'

'Mama, he is not. If anything, it is the other way about.'

'Does that mean you have made up your mind about him?'

'I think so, Mama.'

'And?'

'I shall turn him down.' She heard her stepmother's sigh of relief and smiled. 'But I do not intend to tell him until after the play and you must not say anything either. Not to anyone, especially not to James.'

'Why not James, in particular?'

She felt the colour flare into her face and got up to look out of the window. Lord Wincote's phaeton could be seen making its way through the crowds. 'No reason. He loves to torment me and… Oh, he will find some way of giving me a roasting over it.'

'Oh, Lavinia, you do him an injustice. I am sure he has only your happiness at heart and would do anything for you.'

James, who had stood buff for her on so many other occasions, could do nothing about this problem; she had to find a way out for herself. And it was nothing to do with Lord Wincote. It was James himself. Pulling herself together, she returned to her seat. 'I know, but it would be discourteous to tell anyone before I have told Lord Wincote himself, do you not think?'

'Of course it would, but if you have made up your mind, is it not equally discourteous to refrain from telling his lordship so?'

'Yes, but if I say anything before the play is performed, he will not take part and I cannot find another Lysander at short notice.'

The Duchess smiled. 'Oh, Vinny, how could you! It is unfair of you to keep him waiting, especially if he believes you will accept him in the end. I really do think you should tell him. I am sure he is not such a rakeshame as to let everyone down.'

Lavinia sighed, knowing her stepmother was right. 'I suppose I must. I will do so the next time we meet, I promise.'

The subject of the trial would not go away; the closer it came, the more people talked and speculated. The crowds that crammed themselves into London for it led the constabulary to expect a huge crush around Parliament on the day it began and there was some talk of riots and armed insurrection.

As a result, the whole area had been enclosed by a strong timber fence which, by seven o'clock on the morning of the trial, was being patrolled by the law. A whole regiment of guards surrounded Westminster Hall, the Law Courts and the approaches to the Houses of Parliament, while mounted cavalry and the Horse Police patrolled the streets.

'The whole place is under siege,' Miss Hastings said, returning from a reconnaissance before breakfast that morning. 'You would think they were going to fight a battle. And what with the Queen staying only a few houses away, one cannot move.'

'Then I, for one, will remain indoors today,' Frances said. 'And you must keep the children in the garden.'

The Duke, of course, was obliged to attend as was every peer who was neither sick, bereaved, or too old and infirm. They had to be in their places by ten o'clock so, in order to do that, began assembling hours before. They were greeted by cheers or hisses, according to which way the crowd thought they would vote. Marcus and his son, the Marquis of Risley, left Stanmore House at eight, using the family coach with the blinds drawn.

'I think today will only be preliminaries,' Marcus told them before he left. 'And perhaps common sense will prevail and the Bill will be dismissed, though I am not optimistic.'

'We must find something useful to occupy us,' Frances said as she and Lavinia sat over their breakfast, listening to the tumult of the crowds gathering outside the Queen's temporary residence. 'I have some household accounts to do and a report to write for the orphanage committee. What will you do, Vinny?'

'I have scenery to paint,' Lavinia said, remembering the dreadful mess she had made of the palace scene, on the day of the last rehearsal. She had put off going back to it, knowing it would remind her of how she had made a fool of herself in front of James. She had flown into a jealous rage over Lord Wincote and Lady Rattenshaw, as if she cared two pins what they did! James must think she did, James must think she was breaking her heart over his lordship. It was not Lord Wincote who was breaking her heart, but the Earl of Corringham. He filled her thoughts night and day. He was there in her head, accompanying her wherever she went, jumping out of the page at her when she was reading, smiling and teasing her when she silently murmured Hermia's lines to herself. She saw his handsome face reflected behind hers when she gazed in the mirror. He invaded her sleep.

She went to the ballroom and fetched the piece of scenery out from behind the curtain she had draped over it and was shocked at what she had done. Had she really thrown paint with such ferocity? It was not as if she had anything to be angry about. She did not want Edmund Wincote and looking back now, she realised she never had. She had been flattered by his attention and mesmerised by his dark, brooding eyes, but that was all.

The man she wanted was James. But he thought of her as a mischievous child and who could blame him? She had flown into the boughs and flung paint everywhere. Now she must repair the damage, not only to the scenery, but to her good standing with James.

She worked all morning; by the time she stopped for nuncheon, she had covered the board with new background paint. It had to be left to dry before she could begin painting the scene again and she joined the Duchess for a light repast.

In the middle of the afternoon, cheers in the street told them the Queen was returning and that must mean the day's session was over. 'I wonder what happened,' Frances murmured, going to the window to look out on the street. 'My goodness, just look at that.'

Lavinia joined her at the window. The Queen's carriage had just drawn up at the door of number eighteen, but instead of descending and going inside, she sat for a moment enjoying the adulation of the crowd, bowing from the waist and waving to right and left. She was wearing a gypsy hat with a huge bow on the front from which sprouted a plume of ostrich feathers. And to crown it she had a large white veil, which she had flung back to reveal heavily rouged features, painted eyebrows and a curly black wig.

'Straight from one of Mr Greatorex's farces,' Lavinia said. 'But she seems to have captured the hearts of the populace, though it may be that they hate the King so much, they will support anyone who is against him.'

It was another hour before the Duke and Duncan returned, accompanied by James. All three looked tired. 'We could not get through the crush,' Marcus said, kissing his wife's cheek. 'It was frightening.'

'Then I am glad we did not go out today,' Frances said, then, to James, 'Will you stay and dine with us? The crowd might have thinned by evening.'

'Delighted,' he said, but he was looking at Lavinia, as he spoke.

She tried to give him a bright smile in return, but she was sure her eyes gave her away and dropped her gaze. He noticed it and wondered why she would not look at him. She was pale too, as if she had not been sleeping well. Was she still shocked and mortified by the way he had kissed her hands? He cursed himself for his clumsiness. Had he damned himself forever in her eyes?

'Come on, tell us what happened,' Frances said. 'Is it all over?'

'No, far from it. We were still finding our seats when a great roar went up and the Queen arrived. You would think she'd come in quietly with a little dignity, wouldn't you? But no, she rode in a magnificent coach and six surrounded by her retinue. The crowd was so excited it broke down the barriers and cheered her all the way to the doors.'

'I was afraid they would engulf the hall itself,' James

put in, still watching Lavinia. 'But thankfully they desisted when she was met by Black Rod. She took her place in the chamber, as calm as you please, to listen to the debate.'

'It will go ahead then?' the Duchess queried.

'Yes, I am afraid so,' Marcus said. 'I spoke for the motion being rescinded, but unfortunately I was in the minority.'

'Have you any idea how long it will take?' Lavinia asked, thinking of the play. She did not want to postpone it, but if they had to do it in the middle of the furore, it would be a disaster.

The Duke smiled. 'No, my dear, but judging by the fuss made today, no one in London will think of anything else until it is all over.'

They were interrupted by the arrival of the butler to say that dinner was served and they made their way to the dining room, the Duke and Duchess followed by Duncan, with James and Lavinia bringing up the the rear. Usually on such occasions, they conversed easily about almost every topic under the sun, but there was now a barrier between them which could not be breached and they were silent. They were each aware of the proximity of the other, but walked a little apart as if afraid that they might inadvertently brush against each other.

Once seated, they waited until the first course was served, and then both started to speak at once. They laughed awkwardly. 'I beg your pardon,' he said. 'What were you about to say?'

'Oh, nothing. I was going to ask if the streets were safe and could we venture out tomorrow.'

'You have something in mind?'

'I find being confined to the house irksome in the extreme and I thought a ride...'

'It would have to be very early, before the crowds begin to gather.'

'Tomorrow will be the same as today?'

'Yes and every day while the trial lasts.'

'Then let us hope it is soon over,' the Duchess put in.

'Amen to that,' Marcus said. 'Now, let us eat our dinner in peace. What have you been doing with yourself today, Vinny?'

'Painting scenery, Papa,' she said, avoiding looking at James. 'The interior of Theseus's palace. Most of it is done now. Constance still has some of the costumes to finish, but we are almost ready. There will be no more rehearsals while everyone is rushing off to Westminster every day.'

'And when can we expect to see the finished production?'

'On the twenty-eighth of September, Papa, all being well.'

'And Lord Wincote? Has he not pressed you for an earlier answer?'

'No, Papa.'

'Then don't give him one,' James said so emphatically that Lavinia turned to him in surprise. Seeing Wincote in his place at Westminster that morning had given him a start. He had expected him to have gone off with Miss Doubleday but there he was, large as life and apparently intending to take his part in the debate. 'He knows when he can expect his answer. He must be prepared for the wait.'

'And if he is not?' she asked him.

'Then I must think there must be a reason for his haste.'

'Of course there is. He is eager to make me his wife.' Why, oh, why, did that little imp choose now, of all times, to sit on her shoulder and put words like that into her mouth? She did not care how eager he was. If only it were

James who was impatiently awaiting her answer, she would not keep him waiting a single minute.

'Still?' he queried, lifting one eyebrow.

She knew exactly what he meant. 'He called the next day and apologised,' she said. 'I was quite mistaken.'

'What is this?' Marcus asked, unaware of the tension between James and Lavinia. 'Has there been some dissent?'

'No, Papa,' Lavinia put in quickly, casting a sideways glance at James. 'I was disappointed Lord Wincote did not come to our last rehearsal, but it appears he had to attend to urgent business. He was most apologetic and I have forgiven him.'

'And have you not even hinted to him what your answer will be?' the Duke asked, while James fumed silently. How could she be so blind! Miss Doubleday was not nearly as clever as she thought she was and Edmund Wincote was even cleverer.

'No, Papa, there would be no point in telling him he must wait for an answer if I also told him what that answer was going to be, would there?'

'But you can tell me—us—surely?'

'Is it important that you should know?'

'Not immediately, but I would like to know before you communicate your decision to him. There are arrangements to be made. Your dowry—'

'But, Papa, I thought that was not to be paid until we had been married for two years.'

The Duke laughed. 'That was meant to put him off, if he was not sincere. You did not think I meant it, did you?'

She was alarmed. 'You have not intimated as much to Lord Wincote, have you?'

'Lavinia, the man has been most faithfully patient and not deviated from his intention, so we may assume that he is genuine in his regard for you. It is not fair to deceive him.'

'So you have let him off the hook, your Grace,' James said. His voice carried an edge of bitterness he could not disguise. No wonder the man had decided not to run away with Lady Rattenshaw, after all. Lavinia was the greater prize.

The Duke looked searchingly at him and then at his wife, who slowly shook her head, so he refrained from comment and smiled at Lavinia. 'I had a short conversation with him while we were waiting for proceedings to begin but I made it clear the decision is yours. The important thing is that you know what you want. There is nothing more terrible than being married to the wrong person, believe me. I want you to be very sure.'

In the last three years she had learned a little about the life he had led with her mother, that they had been pushed into a marriage by their parents, a marriage that had been a disaster from the beginning, which was why they had led almost separate lives and why she had seen so little of him as a child. Family life as James and Augusta had experienced it was unknown to her. It was only since her father had married Frances that she was beginning to understand how happy it could be. With James. Only with James...

She shook herself and smiled. 'I have no doubts, Papa.' And before he could question her further, she turned to James. 'What about it, James? A ride in the park tomorrow?'

'I must be at Westminster before ten.'

'Seven o'clock, then. If you can rouse yourself from your bed, that is.'

'I will call for you at seven.'

* * *

He kept his word and was lifting the door knocker at precisely seven, but Lavinia was waiting for him, dressed in her most becoming habit, her eyes bright with nervous anticipation. If she told him she had refused Lord Wincote, then he would understand, wouldn't he? And if he understood, he could not fail to see that she was not the child-sister she had once been and would say something, anything to give her hope. He would explain why his lips in the palm of her hand had wrought such a change and why he had done it.

'Good morning, Vinny.' He sounded inordinately cheerful, considering the early hour.

'Good morning, my lord.'

He escorted her to the gate where her horse, already saddled, was being walked up and down by Tom, who helped her mount and then stood back as she set off along the almost deserted street.

'No chaperon?' James queried, as they rode side by side.

'Why should I need a chaperon to ride with my brother?' Her answer was instant, almost defiant.

'Why indeed?' he said. 'Where shall we go?'

'Green Park and you shall buy me some fresh milk. I have had no breakfast.'

The milkmaids in charge of the herd of cows which grazed in the park sold their milk by the beaker to anyone who fancied a drink. Foaming and still warm from the cow, it was very refreshing. Her thirst slaked, Lavinia trotted her horse along the path for a little way and then cut off across the grass, before putting her mare to the gallop. James followed.

For a few minutes she was able to forget everything else in the pleasure of riding. She enjoyed the feel of wind on her face, the horse beneath her, the strength of the mare's muscles, the way her mane flew out and the way her ears pricked as if she, too, was enjoying herself. James, staying a little behind her, was filled with admiration and a terrible longing. He wanted her, needed her, could think of nothing but her, day and night, and they were not the thoughts of a brother.

Should he tell her so and risk losing the friendship they had? He was sure it would be lost, because once he had put his feelings into words, everything must inevitably change. Perhaps it already had after the *faux pas* he had committed after that last rehearsal. They could never recapture what they had once and, if it were not replaced by something stronger and deeper from which they could move on to marriage, he would be neither brother nor lover. It was a quandary which tormented him night and day.

She pulled up and dismounted, patting her horse's neck and leaning her head against the animal's neck. James reined in and jumped easily to the ground to stand beside her.

'Well?' she said.

'Well, what?'

'Admit I give you a fair run for your money.'

'Oh, there is no doubt you always give me a run for my money,' he said with a twisted smile. 'The pity is I am no match for you.'

'Don't be a ninnyhammer, James. Of course you are. You are a man.'

'So perspicacious of you to notice,' he said wryly.

'Now you are being silly.'

'Am I? Never mind. Did you mean it when you said you had no doubts?'

'Doubts about what?'

'Lord Wincote.'

'Of course I meant it. One should not marry unless one

is very, very sure, do you not agree?' She looked into his face, as she spoke. Now was his opportunity to speak, but his face was a mask of indifference.

'Oh, you are right, my dear,' he said blandly. 'As long as you are certain, I will say no more. Let us forget the gentleman.'

Bitterly disappointed, she endeavoured to change tack. 'Is that why you have done nothing about finding yourself a wife, because you are unsure yourself?'

'Oh, I am sure.' He could not keep the bitterness from his voice. 'The trouble is—the lady is not.'

'Oh, James I cannot imagine that. You are one of the most eligible men in town.' She paused. 'Why didn't you tell me?'

'Is that surprising? You would roast me alive.'

'James, how can you think that of me? Oh, I know I like to tease, but no more than you do.' She gulped and went on, her need to know so overwhelming that she was not aware of the effect her words might have on him. 'If your heart were truly engaged, then you would find me wholly sympathetic.'

'Vinny,' he said, suddenly serious, 'it is not your sympathy I want. Do you not understand that?'

'Yes, yes, I do. It would be too much like condescension, like patting a child on the head and saying, "There, there, never mind." So stupid and unfeeling. I should hate it myself.' She smiled brightly to cover her misery. If he were suffering, now was not the time to add to his burden. 'Let us make a pact: no sympathy and no recrimination and definitely no quizzing.' And with that she caught the reins of her horse and put her foot in the stirrup, mounting without help. 'Come, let us go home or you will be late at the House of Lords.'

'Damn the House,' he muttered, as he trotted behind her

out of the park and back to St James's Square. He was no further forward except in the realisation that she intended to accept Wincote's offer. How could he prevent it? Ought he even to try? If he loved her, truly loved her, he ought to be prepared to let her go. He told himself, not altogether honestly, that if the object of her regard had been anyone else but Edmund Wincote, he would stand back and wish her happy, but to see her married to that charlatan was more than he could stomach.

He saw her safely through the gathering crowds to her door and then went home to change from his riding clothes into a dark blue frock coat and matching trouser panta-loons—more fitting garb for trying a Queen for 'a most unbecoming and degrading intimacy with a foreigner of low station', as the motion had worded it. Lancelot Greatorex could not have invented a greater farce.

Lavinia went indoors, feeling so low she was on the point of tears. She was certainly in no mood for callers, but the footman who opened the door for her told her Lord Wincote was in the withdrawing room. 'Her Grace has gone out, my lady,' he said. 'Miss Hastings received him.'

Putting her riding hat and crop on a side table, she took a deep breath to steady herself and went up to the first-floor drawing room, where she found Emily Hastings and Lord Wincote sitting facing each other either side of the hearth, each with a copy of *A Midsummer Night's Dream* in their hands.

He jumped up when Lavinia entered and bowed towards her. 'My lady, good morning. Miss Hastings has been so good as to entertain me while I waited for you. We have been hearing each other's lines.'

'His lordship is word perfect,' Miss Hastings said. 'If you will excuse me. I must see to my charges.' And with a knowing smile towards Edmund, she left the room.

Lavinia did not doubt he had asked her to leave them alone together, but if he thought she would entertain any intimacy, he would find himself mistaken. 'My lord, are you not due at Westminster?'

'I was on my way there, my lady, but I decided to call on the chance I might see you. Miss Hastings told me you had gone riding, but vouchsafed you would not be long.'

'Yes, I went early to avoid the crowds. Did you have a special reason for calling?'

He smiled. 'Aside from seeing you and being blessed by your lovely smile, you mean? Why, yes, I did. As I missed meeting Lancelot Greatorex, it occurred to me we might go to the theatre. I would be able to take the opportunity to see the great man at work and perhaps make up for my absence. And we could get to know each other a little better too.' He took a step towards her and it was all she could do to stop herself from backing away. 'So what do you say, my dear?'

She did not like the endearment, it was almost proprietorial, as if he had anticipated her answer. She supposed his talk with her father had given him extra confidence. 'I have already been to see his production of *The Rivals*, my lord.'

'Then you will not wish to see it again. But I believe he is doing *Romeo and Juliet* next. May I look forward to taking you to see that?'

He was so confident, almost as if she had had already accepted him and that, she realised, was her fault. She should not have kept him dangling and now she knew exactly where her heart lay, she could not put off telling him any longer.

'My lord,' she began, 'there is something I must tell you.'

'Oh?'

'Yes.' She took a deep breath. 'You have been so good as to make me an offer of marriage—'

'Yes, there is nothing I wish for more than to have you as my wife.'

'Oh, dear.' It was far more difficult than she had expected to dash a man's hopes. 'I cannot find an easy way of saying this, so I must be blunt. My lord, I cannot marry you.'

'Cannot?' he echoed. 'You are bamming me.'

'No, my lord. I am sensible of the honour you have done me, but I cannot become your wife.'

He stared at her unbelievingly. 'I don't believe you are saying this. It is some trite phrase you have been taught. Someone has told you that it is customary for a young lady not to accept on the first time of asking—'

'No. No one has said that to me, and if they had, I would not play with your affections in that shabby way.'

'Then why?'

'I do not have that regard for you, that love, which I think is necessary.'

'You will come to love me, I am sure. That is why I asked if we might continue to meet though there are no rehearsals, so that we may learn more about each other.'

'It would make no difference.'

'Lady Lavinia,' he said, picking up her hand from her lap and looking into her eyes. 'You said I was to wait until after the performance—'

'Yes, but it is not fair of me to hold you to that, when I have already made up my mind.' She felt uncomfortable under his gaze and wrenched her hand away from his.

He appeared not to notice. 'No, I am persuaded your mind is far from made up. I will continue to be patient until the day we have already settled upon.'

She raised her eyes to his in surprise. 'You mean you will go on with the play?'

He smiled. 'Of course.'

'Even though, at the end, you know I will turn you down.'

'You won't turn me down.' He stood up, seized her hand again and for one awful minute his face was so close to hers she thought he was going to attempt to kiss her, but he must have thought better of it, because all he did was smile and raise the back of her hand to his lips. 'Until then we will forget we ever had this conversation, my dear.'

He made his way from the room and she breathed a huge sigh of relief, though the fact that he had refused to take no for an answer was an added worry. But she had made her own position plain enough and, if her father or stepmother asked about it, she could say truthfully that she had given his lordship her answer.

Going up to her bedroom, she was met on the landing by Emily Hastings. 'Well?' she prompted. 'Is he not the most refined and romantic of gentlemen? And so kind. I am so pleased that you and he are to make a match of it.'

'Is that what he said?'

'Well, not in so many words, but he made it clear that there was no reason at all why you should not be left alone together for a few minutes. So romantic…'

'Miss Hastings, I had not responded to his offer, you should not have—'

'Oh, I know you have not formally answered him, but he says it is only some fancy you have to test his fervour and keep him up to the mark, but he has no intention of failing you. He loves you very much.'

'Did he say that?' she asked in surprise.

'He said nothing could equal his regard for you, that

without you he could not survive. Of course, I cautioned
him against doing anything so foolish as to take his own
life. It is a sin in the eyes of God, and he said he would
try and remember that… Lavinia, why are you laughing?'

Lavinia straightened her face, but it was no good, the
spluttering began again and she was forced to flee.

She went into her bedroom and sat down on the bed
until the paroxysm of laughing faded and was replaced,
just as suddenly, by a flood of tears. She cried until her
eyes were red and her cheeks puffy, but tears did not help
her. Edmund Wincote wanted to marry her, James did not.
James had said he was no match for her and though they
had been out riding at the time and he had been referring
to her horsemanship, perhaps he had been trying to tell
her, in that considerate way of his, that *she* was no match
for *him*. But if he were in love with someone else, why
would he even think of her in that context? Who was the
lady? Was it someone she knew? Whoever it was, she must
learn to live with it.

She must bear it, see him frequently and speak to him
as if he were the brother she had always thought him to
be, watch him married. How could she endure it? But she
would never marry anyone else, she could not. Lord
Wincote would learn that she meant what she said.

She rose from the bed, stripped off her habit, washed
her face and dressed again in a pale blue spotted gingham
dress. She brushed out her hair and tied it back with a
ribbon before putting on a determined smile and going
downstairs again to face the remainder of the day and all
the days afterwards, for the rest of her life.

It was her own private trial that filled her head and heart,
while the travesty of a public examination proceeded in
Westminster. Opinion and speculation raged and the coun-

try was almost in a state of emergency. Once the preliminaries were over, the opening speech for the prosecution
was begun by the Attorney General. According to Marcus,
who relayed the proceedings over supper, he had begun
by detailing Caroline's wanderings on the continent, without mentioning the reason why she had become an exile
in the first place.

'I doubt any court of law has ever heard anything so
detailed and explicit,' he told them. 'It is far worse than
ever I expected and not fit for the ears of ladies, so we
shall not talk of it.'

But the fact that he said no more did not mean that his
wife and daughter were left in ignorance. There was no
escape from it; reports of the trial filled every newspaper.
They relayed the prosecution evidence in great detail, of
intimacies in hotels, on Royal naval frigates and an Italian
pollacca when Caroline and Bergami were supposed to
have slept in a tent on deck. The names of the witnesses,
cooks, gardeners, chamber maids, the captains of the ships
the Queen had sailed in, the landlords of the inns in which
she stayed, were household words. Lewd songs were sung
about them, rhymes repeated. Never had the populace enjoyed such entertainment.

None of it could not keep Lavinia's thoughts from her
own misery for long. And the worst of it was, she could
not tell anyone about it. It was not Edmund's refusal to
believe her that was the problem, it was her desperate love
for James. It was like a pain deep inside her which would
not go away.

It was exquisite torture when James came back with her
father and brother after the day's business at Westminster
was concluded and stayed to dine. Like every other peer
he was looking jaded. There were fine lines around his
mouth and his eyes were dull, which might have been the

strain of listening to the trial, or could have been down to unrequited love. But she would not speak of it to him; no quizzing and no sympathy they had agreed and she would stick to that.

On September the ninth, three weeks after it all began, the prosecution concluded its case and the House was adjourned until the third of October when Lord Brougham was to begin the defence, though how he could do that without discrediting the King no one but he knew.

Some of London's summer residents set off for their country estates, but most stayed in the capital. There was still a great deal of gossip to be relayed while soirées were being hurriedly arranged. The *haut monde* began making calls again and Lavinia decided to resume rehearsals. She sent notes to all the cast, calling them together and was preparing the ballroom for their arrival, when James arrived.

He appeared a little less strained and smiled pleasantly as he looked about him. 'Others not here yet?'

'No, you are the first.' She forced herself to sound calm, though inside she was shaking with nerves, half-afraid she would give herself away and then not only James but the whole cast would learn how she felt about him. The next two hours were going to take all her self-control.

The dress she was wearing was severely plain and her hair was pulled back into a simple Grecian knot, but whatever she wore, he decided, she was always beautiful and desirable. But she was looking pale and tired; her eyes seemed to have lost some of their lustre and the spring had gone from her step, as if she had the cares of the world upon her shoulders. 'Vinny, are you sure this is not all too much for you?'

'What do you mean?' It was almost a snap. 'I am perfectly capable of putting on a little play.'

'I shall be glad when it is over,' he said.

'Yes, and so shall I.'

He looked at her sharply. It was not the answer he had expected unless, of course, she was looking forward to announcing her betrothal. He forced a smile. 'And Lord Wincote?'

'What about him?'

'Is he still patiently waiting?'

'I have seen little of him.' Why she did not tell him the truth, she did not know, unless it was pride which prevented her. Or some perverse notion that he ought to be able to see what was underneath his nose without her having to tell him. 'Like you, he has had to attend Westminster each day. No doubt he will be here soon with everyone else.'

He wished it were otherwise. He wished Edmund to kingdom come. He wished a way could be found to make Lavinia look at him as a man in love and not a brother. He was wondering whether to force the issue when Lord Wincote arrived.

If he was disappointed to find James had beaten him to it, he managed to hide it, as he greeted them both. 'My lady, I hope I find you well?'

'Perfectly well, my lord,' she replied. 'And you?'

'I am quite well, my dear.'

She ignored James's sharp intake of breath. 'Good, I am glad you were able to come today. You missed so much the last time…'

'Yes, Wincote, where were you?' James demanded.

'I had urgent business to attend to,' he said primly. 'I have apologised to Lady Lavinia—'

'I trust whatever it was has not taxed your strength,' James put in. 'You look a trifle fagged.'

'I have been attending Westminster, just as you have, Corringham.'

'I am surprised that should tire you. I had not thought you so interested in the debate, considering you have vouchsafed no opinion on the matter.'

'Oh, but I have. If you are going to try the Queen, then you should also try the King. It is only justice, after all.'

'And you, I comprehend, are a stickler for justice.'

'Of course.'

'Then I hope you never live to regret that conviction.'

Lavinia looked from one to the other. They seemed to be talking in riddles which instinct told her had nothing to do with what was going on at Westminster. Did James still think Lord Wincote knew something about Lady Willoughby's missing diamonds? He had certainly been wrong about Lady Graham's necklace because Constance had told her it had been recovered, though she did not know the details.

'My lords,' she said, determined to stop them quarrelling openly, 'will you help me with the scenery? I want to have it in place for the rehearsal.'

They had no choice but to obey and by the time the scenery was in place, the others of the cast began arriving. First was Sir Percy, clad in yellow and pink, bringing with him Lady Rattenshaw's apologies. 'Not well,' he said vaguely. 'Said she would be right as ninepence in a day or two.' Lavinia was disappointed that the lady was going to miss a second rehearsal, but there was nothing for it but to ask Constance to stand in for her again.

'It is too bad of her,' Constance said. 'I never did want to take a part, as you know. It is easy enough to learn lines, but that is not all there is to it, is it? I have such a little voice.'

'But a very pleasing one,' Lord Haverley said, gently. 'And Mr Greatorex found no fault, did he?'

'He knew I was only a stand-in. I cannot portray emotion in the way he does.'

'But he is a professional actor,' Emily Hastings said. 'We are amateurs.'

'That does not mean we cannot learn from him, as I have said to Lady Lavinia,' Lord Wincote put in, smiling urbanely. 'I have invited her ladyship to come to a performance of *Romeo and Juliet* with me to see how the professionals do it.'

Lavinia gasped. He was forcing her into a corner, and now James would think she had agreed and that must, in his eyes, indicate that she meant to accept Lord Wincote's proposal of marriage as well. It was time she told him the truth. But when and how could she introduce the subject without making a great drama of it? On no account must he know that her decision was anything to do with him. It would be too mortifying.

It was then she hit on the notion of making an evening at the theatre a party for all the cast, a way of thanking them for all the hard work they had put in and to encourage them to continue to rehearse. Lord Wincote could not expect her undivided attention and she might find an opportunity to speak privately to James and tell him she had turned Lord Wincote down. 'We could have supper at Reid's in St Martin's Lane afterwards,' she said. 'Shall we say next Wednesday? It will set us up for the twenty-eighth.'

She dressed with more than usual care for the visit to the theatre, in a gown of pale blue *mousseline de soie* which had tiny puffed sleeves and an oval neckline edged with pearls. Her hair was piled up and braided with strings of pearls *à la Didon*, but apart from those she wore no jewellery. The skirt of her gown was short enough to reveal silk stocking-clad ankles and dainty velvet slippers. A blue velvet cape, long gloves, a silk fan and a brocade reticule completed her ensemble.

'Lovely,' Daisy said. 'You will have Lord Wincote swooning with love for you.'

It was not Lord Wincote she needed to impress, though how to convey that to James without making a complete ninny of herself, she did not know. She could not come right out with it, could she? She could not say to him, 'I love you, not as a sister, but as a woman.' It would appall him. He would be particularly alarmed if he really was contemplating marriage to someone else. Was he? That would be the ultimate irony.

But she could not give up; it was too important. Somehow, a way must be found to make him see she was no longer the schoolgirl she had been when he first met her, that since then she had grown up, become a woman. A desirable, vibrant woman who needed him and, given the chance, could make him happy.

The Duke and Duchess, both of whom were also joining the party, were waiting for her when she went downstairs, the Duke in a black evening suit and the Duchess in a soft dove grey. Seeing her descending the staircase, both smiled. 'I suppose, I should say you are worth waiting for,' her father said. 'You look very beautiful, my dear.'

'Thank you.' She smiled and dropped him a brief curtsy.

'Now we must be off,' Frances said, as Duncan joined them. 'Or we will have everyone there before us and that will not do at all. We are, after all, the hosts.'

The auditorium was already filling with noisy theatre-goers when they arrived. Some were speculating whether

Lancelot Greatorex might follow some of the other theatre managers and change the performance to a specially written farce, lampooning the Royal family. Lavinia hoped he would not; her father would disapprove and he might not agree to Mr Greatorex taking part in the play at Stanmore House.

But that was not the only thing on her mind. She was thinking of James, who had not yet arrived. Everyone began taking seats and she found herself sitting between her stepmother and Lord Wincote, while the others of the party took the chairs on either side of them, spilling over into the next box, which the Duke had taken in order to accommodate everyone. It was not at all what she had intended and her disappointment was so great she could hardly concentrate on the stage as the curtain went up for the first act.

She had set such store on this evening, as though it was the key to her whole future, and the man in the forefront of her mind had not even deigned to put in an appearance. She heard the opening words of the tragedy in a numb fog of misery which enveloped her like a cocoon. It was over before it had begun, this love of hers.

Chapter Ten

James had been delayed by a visit from Donald Greenaway, who arrived only minutes before he was due to leave. The major informed him that he had been unable to trace Lady Willoughby's diamond clips to any of the receivers he knew. 'I am bound to say, James,' he told him, 'that the chances of nailing the man now are fast fading. There is not a shred of evidence so you must consider the possibility that Wincote is innocent. That is the law of the land, innocent until proved guilty, and that goes for the death of his brother as well as the theft of the jewels.'

'Damn his hide! He has everyone wrapped about his thumb, even the Duke of Loscoe, who has told him he is prepared to pay Lady Lavinia's dowry as soon as they are married.'

'James, I am sorry, but are you sure you are not letting your dislike of the man cloud your judgement? Without evidence to the contrary, we must assume Wincote is genuine in his affection for Lady Lavinia and it is customary to pay the dowry upon marriage.'

'And what about his plans to run away with Lady Rattenshaw?'

'Run away with Lady Rattenshaw?' Donald echoed in surprise. 'What makes you think he was contemplating doing that?'

'She told me so. Now it appears it is all off and he is back pressing his suit on Lavinia and toadying to the Duke and Duchess.'

'Have you told Lady Lavinia of this?'

'Of course not. In any case, she saw them together, but he convinced her it was all very innocent and so she has forgiven him.'

'Then there is nothing you can do but wait and see what happens. Unless, of course, you offer for her yourself.'

'Do you think I have not thought of that?' he demanded irritably. 'She would be mortified. I am her dear brother, the scapegrace who amuses her and makes her laugh.'

'The ability to laugh together is a plus, my friend, and one many couples lack.'

'But it is not enough.'

'No, I suppose not, but you will never know, if you do not make the venture.' He paused. 'Do you wish me to continue my enquiries?'

'Yes. Do whatever is necessary. Now, you must excuse me. I am late for the theatre.'

They shook hands and parted. It seemed to James that Edmund Wincote had got the better of him and the knowledge stuck in his throat. Now he had missed the first act and the last thing he wanted was a quarrel with Lavinia over his tardiness.

When the curtain came down for the intermission, everyone began talking about the production and how Mr Greatorex, though no longer a youth, had brought such reality to the part of Romeo that his age did not matter.

Edmund, on Lavinia's right, leaned towards her. 'A master at work,' he said. 'I can never hope to emulate that.'

'No, we none of us can, but then we are not professional actors, my lord.' She turned and smiled at Lady Rattenshaw, who had arrived very late on the arm of Sir Percy and had apparently recovered from her indisposition. 'Though between them, Mr Greatorex and Lady Rattenshaw have brought out the best in all of us.'

She meant her ladyship to know that she was not in the least put out by her absences from rehearsal or the fact that she had seen her in the company of the man who was supposed to be her suitor. Soon everyone would know that was not the case. And then it would all be over, the Queen's trial and her own. If she could not pierce James's armour, she would go home to Risley and live quietly in seclusion.

'Oh, no, my lady, that is you,' Edmund protested. 'Your enthusiasm and commitment are the virtues which have brought us to the pitch we are. I am persuaded we shall make a great deal of money for the Duchess's good cause.'

'It is very kind of you to say so.'

He seized her hand and conveyed it to his lips. 'My lady, I shall look forward eagerly to that day and contain myself with as much patience as I can muster.'

She squirmed almost visibly. He was still hoping. 'My lord,' she murmured, afraid that everyone round them had heard the remark and would put quite the wrong interpretation on it. 'I am not going to marry you. Why can't you accept that? There are other young ladies—'

'But only one Lady Lavinia Stanmore.'

'Please, my lord, I beg of you. Do not press me. My mind is quite made up.' If only James would come. She longed for him with every nerve and sinew, even though he would probably do no more than roast her. At least she could have some bantering exchange with him which, despite it breaking her heart, would nevertheless save her from having to listen to the intensely earnest man at her side, who refused to believe she meant what she said.

As if on cue, the door of the box opened and he was there, dressed in a magnificent evening suit of black brocade. His shirt-collar points, stiff as soldiers on parade, and his cravat, a froth of pristine white lace, made her wonder if he had dressed to meet a lover. He came forward, spoke briefly to the Duke and Duchess and then slid into an empty seat just behind Lavinia. 'My lady, my apologies, I was unavoidably delayed.'

'Was she beautiful?' asked the imp on Lavinia's shoulder.

'She *is* beautiful,' he said, solemnly. 'Beyond compare.'

'And are felicitations in order?'

'Not yet.'

She managed an over-bright smile. 'I have just been telling Lord Wincote that I have come to a decision...' She paused, watching his face, but though his grey eyes momentarily darkened and a frown creased his brow that he was smiling again so quickly, she thought she must have imagined it.

'Oh? What is that?'

'What do you think?' Wincote put in before she could reply.

'I have no idea,' James said, affecting indifference, though Wincote was clearly very pleased about it, judging by the oily smile on his face. Lavinia had accepted him! Why could the fellow not have gone off with Miss Doubleday and saved him the heartache? He looked across at the lady sitting beside Sir Percy. Had she decided she could not go through with their plan? Had Wincote guessed who she really was?

He did not hear Lavinia's sharp intake of breath and her whispered words, saying she had something to tell him later. His mind was numb and he heard and saw little of what was happening on the stage. When the play ended and everyone was making their way out of the theatre to their carriages for the short ride to St Martin's Lane, he contrived to fall into step beside Sir Percy and Lady Rattenshaw. 'Percy, I have my carriage, may I offer you both a lift?'

'I would be very glad if you would take Marianne,' Percy said. 'My gut has been out of sorts all day and I would prefer not to go on to supper. Make my excuses, will you?'

'Of course. But will you be all right?'

'Oh, yes, it's nothing but a little colic. My housekeeper will make me up a powder. Go and enjoy yourselves.' He turned and hailed a passing cab.

Once they had seen him safely inside, James took Lady Rattenshaw's elbow and guided her along the road to where his coachman had the carriage waiting.

Lavinia saw them go and stood staring after them as if she could not believe her eyes. They looked so absorbed in each other, their heads close together as they walked, completely unaware of anyone around them. Was this James's mysterious lady? She was certainly not spurning him. Even then she might have dismissed the whole notion, but she was so keyed up with her own emotions, so sensitive to everything James did, she found herself looking for other signs and of course she found them.

Both had arrived at the theatre very late and James had not denied he had been with a lady. And thinking back to Lady Rattenshaw's first appearance and Constance's ball, she remembered James had been very taken with her and she had teased him about it. Later, when Lavinia had been upset about seeing her ladyship with Lord Wincote, James had as good as laughed at her suspicions. No wonder, when it was not *Edmund* who had designs on the lady, but *James*. Beyond compare, he had called her. Oh, what a gudgeon she had been!

James helped Lady Rattenshaw into the carriage and climbed in beside her, saying nothing until they were on the move. 'Now, Miss Doubleday, I need to know what happened. You were supposed to elope with Wincote.'

'Not elope my lord, that suggests a wedding and that I never intended.'

'Call it what you will, it did not happen.'

'No. It was all arranged, but then he suddenly changed his mind. Oh, he was very apologetic. He told me he could not disappoint Lady Lavinia, that he was honour bound to go through with the wedding, if he were not to be ostracised by the *haut monde*. It seems, my lord, he is more chivalrous than you gave him credit for.'

'No, his mind was altered by a short conversation with the Duke of Loscoe.'

'The Duke threatened him?'

'No such luck. He promised him Lady Lavinia's dowry immediately on their marriage.'

'Oh, there is little I can do to counter that.'

'No, but I thank you for your trouble.' He paused. 'But you could do something else. Ask him about his family and his childhood, how well he dealt with his grandfather. Ask him in a casual way, but note his answers. He might give himself away.'

'And the play? If I do not go to rehearsals there will be little opportunity to meet him, but with Lancelot becoming involved, I thought it best to stay away.'

'Can you trust him? Mr Greatorex, I mean.'

'Yes, I think so.'

'Then tell him you are impersonating Lady Rattenshaw to win a wager. That way you can also continue with the play. I am sure it would break Lavinia's heart if you should withdraw at this late stage. Where would she find another Helena half so good?'

'Flatterer.' She was laughing at his compliment as they left the carriage outside Reid's, where the rest of the party was also arriving. James, handing Lady Rattenshaw down, glanced at Lavinia, who had just descended from the Loscoe carriage and was standing on the road, staring at them. She looked away immediately but not before he had seen the bleak look in her eyes and the tight set to her lips. What could she be thinking?

But he had no time to dwell upon it because everyone was making their way into the hotel dining room where a long table had been booked for them. It was not until they were all seated, that James noticed Lancelot Greatorex, sitting alone not ten feet away. It was a hotel frequented by stage people and they often came straight there from a performance, but it was too late now, Lavinia had seen him too.

'Why, Mr Greatorex, I did not know you would be here, or I would have invited you,' she said. 'Please join us.' She indicated an empty place next to Lady Rattenshaw, the one Sir Percy should have occupied.

James held his breath as the actor looked round the company and his gaze rested on Marianne Doubleday. He opened his mouth to speak to her, but at an imperceptible shake of her head stopped him. Instead he smiled affably and said he would be delighted. James breathed again, though he could not relax.

'You know everyone, I believe,' Lavinia said. 'Except Lord Wincote, who is our Lysander.' She indicated

Edmund and the two men acknowledged each other. 'And Lady Rattenshaw. She is lately from India and has been a true find for us. You will see, when we resume rehearsals, what a good Helena she is.'

'Oh, I am sure she is, if you say it.' A smile flitted across his face and his eyes lit with amusement as he gave Marianne an exaggerated bow. 'How do you do, my lady.'

'Very well, sir, I thank you.'

Lavinia noticed the look that passed between them and for the second time that evening she was startled. Did Lady Rattenshaw have that strange effect on all men? There was Sir Percy, Lord Wincote, James and now Mr Greatorex, all exchanging knowing glances and smiles. What was it the woman had that attracted men to her like bees round a honeypot? If the lady were not so amiable, she could almost hate her.

'We have just been to see tonight's performance of *Romeo and Juliet*,' Lavinia explained, as half a dozen waiters arrived with the dishes of food.

'If I had known you wished to see it, my lady, I would have sent tickets.'

'It was a spur-of-the-moment thing. Everyone is so sick and tired of that performance in Westminster, we thought we would like to see something more enlightening.'

'And was it? More enlightening, I mean.'

'I cannot begin to describe how edifying I found it. I am sure we all feel the same. It will put new heart into us.' She glanced at Lady Rattenshaw as she spoke. 'My lady, I hope you will be able to continue.' It was a direct reference to her absence from the last rehearsal.

'Yes, I am looking forward to it.'

'And you, Mr Greatorex, may I count on you and your players to join us?'

'I would not miss it for the world,' he said and laughed lightly.

'Do you think we will be ready by the twenty-eighth?'

'I do not see why not. You have all memorised your parts, it is only a question of saying them with feeling, knowing your cues and moving about the stage confidently.' He turned to Lady Rattenshaw. 'Do you not think so, my lady?'

Lavinia looked from one to the other. Why did she think something was going on which she was not supposed to know about? Everyone was behaving strangely. It was not what they said, which was innocuous enough, but the emphasis they put on their words, the looks they exchanged, the studied nonchalance on the part of the men and Lady Rattenshaw's unease. She was tense; her laugh a little too brittle, her expressive hands more than usually active. She had almost knocked a dish out of a waiter's hand. 'Me?' she said. 'I know no more about it than everyone else.'

'Then I must be mistaken. From what I have been told, I deduced you had acted in India.'

'Only in an amateur capacity, sir.'

'Of course. I was not suggesting you were a professional.'

She shot him a withering look which was not lost on Lavinia. There *was* something havey-cavey going on and James knew about it; she could tell by his studied unconcern. She would have it out of him at the first opportunity.

As far as the rest of the company was concerned the evening was an unqualified success. The food was good, the wine flowed freely and everyone joined in the conversation, making for a noisy and rather jovial party. Lavinia, steeped in misery, laughed and joked with everyone, prattling on about anything that came into her head, teasing

James unmercifully and being extra pleasant to Lord Wincote. It was the only way she could cope.

She made no move to speak to James privately. What did it matter now? It was no longer important that he should know she had rejected Lord Wincote. He would find out along with everyone else. Nor did it matter that Edmund was looking inordinately pleased with himself. It was gone two in the morning when the party broke up and everyone made their way home, promising not to be late for the next meeting, which was to be a dress rehearsal.

Lavinia, glad to be busy, spent the intervening time drawing up an advertisement for the society publications, writing to everyone whom she thought might attend, finishing the scenery, scouring the attics for furniture to use in the indoor scenes and arranging for them to be taken down to the ballroom. She had just brought down a pile of curtains which she meant to ask Emily Hastings to help her alter, when Constance arrived accompanied by two footmen carrying a large trunk.

'I've brought the costumes,' she said, as the footmen set the trunk down. 'There might be one or two alterations still to be done.'

'Thank you, Constance, you are an angel.' She dropped her bundle on the floor and set up a cloud of dust. 'We could never have managed without you.'

'I was delighted to do the costumes, though I am glad Lady Rattenshaw is coming back, I did not like playing her part.'

Lavinia smiled. 'Not even with Lord Haverley's encouragement?'

Constance blushed scarlet. 'He has been kindness itself.'

'Kind? Is that all?'

'No, but you are not to tell a soul. Nothing has been decided.'

'But he has offered?'

'Yes, but I have deferred answering him until this play is over and done with. We have had so little time for other social occasions when we might have had the opportunity to learn whether we should suit...'

So she had been right; there was more riding on the performance than making money for the orphans and her own future. 'But you think you might say yes?'

'I think so. The girls and I deal very well together; the rehearsals have helped there. He is so attentive and he does not mind a bit that I will have no dowry.'

Lavinia hugged her, pushing away the thought that his lordship was perhaps more interested in a mother for his girls than a dowry. 'Then I am very happy for you.'

'And am I to be happy for you?'

Lavinia hesitated and then smiled. 'You will be the first to know. Apart from the gentleman in question, that is.'

She was not thinking of Edmund, but of James. The object of her thoughts arrived at that moment. She turned away to give herself time to compose herself and picked up the dusty curtains again. He came forward to take them from here. 'Here, let me.'

She refused to part with them, as if they gave her a kind of protection, though from what she did not know: his intent gaze, or perhaps her own unconquerable longing. There was a slight tussle which ended in them both coughing with the dust they set flying and being forced to drop them. He was the first to recover.

'Vinny, you cannot possibly use those.' He reached out and brushed a cobweb from her hair which set her limbs trembling. Being near him was torment enough, but to be touched by him, was both exquisite pleasure and unbearable pain. 'You will choke everyone to death.'

'They will be good as new after a good shaking.'

He looked at Constance, who was busy delving into the trunk and laying out the costumes on a long table, unconcerned with what they were doing or saying. 'And will you be good as new after a good shaking?'

She looked at him wide-eyed. 'Whatever do you mean?'

'I mean I should like to shake some sense into you.' He took her hand and led her forcefully away from the pile of curtains to a corner of the room. 'Do you really know what you are doing?'

'Putting on *A Midsummer's Night's Dream*.'

'Oh, there is a dream, I grant you, but it is a dream from which you must awake to find your love is not what you thought he would be.'

'What do you know about my love?' she snapped. 'You do not know me. Oh, you think you do, but you don't. You only know the child I once was—'

'You are no longer a child,' he said.

'So glad you noticed,' she said tartly. 'I am old enough to marry.'

'True, but I do not think you love Edmund Wincote. And I do not think he loves you. Please, Lavinia, think carefully before you accept him.'

'Oh, you are not back to accusing him of taking Lady Willoughby's clips, are you?' she said, angry that he was so blind. 'Because if you are, I think it is shameful of you.'

He sighed. She had put him on the defensive and that was not where he liked to be. 'I did not accuse him.'

'It sounded like it to me.'

'You misunderstood.'

'Then what have you against him?'

'I believe he is not what he seems.'

'But you have no grounds for saying that. And I truly do not care whether he is after my money or not. I have made up my mind—'

'Oh, Vinny, no.'

'If I did not know you better, James Corringham, I would say you were jealous. You do not like the idea of someone having me, but you do not want me yourself.'

'Vinny, you are wrong, so very, very wrong. I—' He stopped suddenly as the door was flung open and Miss Hastings came in with Augusta, Jack, Andrew and little Beth. The children were noisy and excited about rehearsing with the adults and almost threw themselves at James. He stooped to hug them all and ruffle their hair before greeting his sister, and the moment he had been waiting for was gone.

Lavinia, choking back tears and looking for a way to retreat, took the bundle of curtains out of the room to ask a servant to hang them on a line and beat them. She stayed away a few minutes in order to compose herself before returning but when she did, she found the whole cast there, including Lancelot Greatorex and five members of his company. With the exception of James, who stood stroking his chin thoughtfully, they were all talking at once. Some were muttering their lines while others were indulging in gossip which did not seem to have died since Parliament went into recess.

She stood in the middle of the room and clapped her hands for order. 'We are here to rehearse,' she said. 'And if we are to be ready on time, we must concentrate on that. Mr Greatorex, will you take charge, please?'

They began apprehensively, as if they had never rehearsed a word of it before, stumbling over their lines and being more wooden than usual. Only James was not overawed and delivered his lines word perfect and with rather more verve than he had hitherto, which made Lavinia look sharply at him and wonder, not for the first time, what went on inside his head. Was it his newfound love making him so cheerful?

At the end of two hours' intensive coaching, Lancelot told them it was no use, they were acting like tin soldiers on an imaginary battlefield. 'Good God, it is a love story,' he said in exasperation. 'Have you never been in love, never felt the depths and the heights to which love can take you? Use it, use what you know. And if you do not know, then imagine it.' He thumped his chest. 'Play it from here. From the heart.'

He turned to Lavinia, who was endeavouring to control emotions that threatened to overwhelm her. 'Hermia, your father is forcing you to marry a man you do not love and has threatened you with death if you do not obey. Does that not fill you with dread? Can you not imagine your unhappy life with Demetrius, if you should obey? You are desperate, desperate enough to run away with your lover, desperate enough to venture into the darkest part of the woods where you are lost.'

'I'll try again,' she said meekly, though lost was exactly what she was. It was all the wrong way round. James should have been Lysander and Lord Wincote Demetrius. Then she might have been able to put some sincerity into her performance. Pretending to be in love with Edmund Wincote and to hate James was more difficult that she could ever have imagined.

'Not now, my lady, you may take a break and watch the others. We will go on to the second act. Puck, Oberon, Titania and the fairies. Then Demetrius and Helena.'

Lavinia sank into a chair to watch the first two scenes, knowing that in the third, she and Lord Wincote were to act the scene when they lie down in the woods to sleep.

Determined not to disappoint Mr Greatorex and for her own pride's sake, she steeled herself to do it justice.

The two scenes passed with no more than a few terse comments and then Lysander led Hermia on to the stage, *'One turf shall serve as pillow for us both,'* Edmund intoned, drawing her down to the green cloth-covered floor of the stage. He moved closer as he spoke and reached out his hand to touch her face. *'One heart, one bed, two bosoms and one troth.'*

She shuddered and forced herself to reply. *'Nay, good Lysander; for my sake, my dear, lie further off yet, do not lie so near...'*

'No! No! No!' Lancelot shouted. 'You are in love with him. You are only telling him to lie further off because you are afraid to be so close or you will be lost to all propriety. It is your love which is asking him to keep his distance. You are making it sound as if you are repelled by him.'

It was all too much and she scrambled to her feet and fled before anyone could see her tears. She ran into the bookroom which was on the other side of the hall and flung herself into the deep leather armchair beloved of her father. Almost hidden, she allowed herself the luxury of tears.

Everyone left behind in the ballroom stared after her, transfixed. Edmund was the first to move, intending to go after her.

'Leave her, man,' James commanded. 'Can't you see, she has worn herself out and importuning her will only make things worse. Miss Hastings will go to her.'

'Sound advice,' Sir Percy said, as Emily slipped from the room. 'Best thing we can do is carry on until she recovers.'

* * *

'Oh, there you are!' Emily Hastings found Lavinia curled up in her father's chair. She was no longer weeping, but sitting immobile, staring across the room at the portrait of James which hung in the alcove beside the hearth. Her stepmother had painted it several years before and was, in the Duke's opinion, one of the best things she had ever done. She had captured not only his likeness but his youth, his slightly mocking expression, his grey eyes alight with mischief, his relaxed pose as he sat on a bench under the shade of a tree.

He was, to the casual viewer, a typical young aristocrat of his time, but to those who looked deeper, there was more to be seen. The mischievous look in his eye cloaked thoughtfulness, and the hand lying lightly on the dog at his feet showed a caring attitude; the animal itself was looking up at him in adoration. And his smile was both open and enigmatic, as though he were guarding a secret; eternal youth perhaps, or a joyful love of life.

Lavinia had always liked the picture, but now she was in love with its subject, she felt drawn towards it. It was as if, looking down at her from the canvas, he could listen to her heart, hear the unspoken words which tumbled through her brain, could ease her unrest. In the middle of mentally explaining to paint and canvas how she felt, she hardly heard Emily's voice.

'Lavinia, what is wrong? It is not like you to fall into the dismals. Are you unhappy about the play?'

'The play,' she repeated vaguely.

'Yes. You know, Mr Greatorex did not mean to be so hard on you. Indeed, it is a compliment that he thinks you are capable of doing better.'

'Oh, I know that. I am not afraid of criticism.'

'Then what is it?'

'Nothing.'

'Are you afraid Lord Wincote is cooling towards you? I must confess it would hardly be surprising, you have kept him waiting so long for his answer.'

'It has nothing to do with Lord Wincote, Miss Hastings, nothing at all. I am simply a little tired, that is all.' She stood up and shook out her skirts. 'I am quite myself again, so let us return to the others.' And with that, she marched from the room, shoulders back, head held high.

When they entered the ballroom, the Thespians were going through their comedy routine as the players, with Puck, Bottom and the fairies. Everyone concentrated on what they were doing and pretended not to notice she had returned, but James, waiting in the wings to go on, was aware of her, pale but composed, watching them. He longed to go to her, but he knew she would hate that and the best thing he could do was go on as though she had never been away. They moved onto the stage together.

'Oh, why rebuke him that loves you so?' he said, with great feeling.

She managed to answer him, to accuse him of killing Lysander. *'What's this to my Lysander? Where is he? Ah, good Demetrius, wilt thou give him me?'*

It took no acting on his part to deliver the line, *'I had rather give his carcass to my hounds.'*

'I think we have all had enough for now,' Lancelot said, when it became apparent Lavinia was still not herself. 'We will meet again the day after tomorrow. Perhaps, by then, her ladyship will have recovered.' He gathered up his cloak and hat and turned to leave. 'Lady Rattenshaw, I will escort you home. There are points in your performance I can make as we go.'

It was an order, not a request, but instead of rebuffing him, she meekly followed him out of the door, watched by James and Sir Percy.

'We have put the cat among the pigeons now, me boy,' Percy murmured after they left. 'He has recognised her.'

'He already knew. He joined us at Reid's the other night and was introduced to her.'

'And said nothing?'

'No, he was quick to take in the situation, though once or twice during the evening I thought one or other of them would let the cat out of the bag.'

'And among the pigeons,' Sir Percy said wryly.

'As you say. But she is going to tell him she is playing Lady Rattenshaw for a wager and will reveal her true identity after the play is finished. We must assume he will say nothing and in the meantime, she will work on Wincote.'

'And Lady Lavinia? It is so unlike her to be so downpin. She has always seemed so strong, so enthusiastic, the one who holds us all together, our inspiration. Without her, we are simply a group of diverse people saying Shakespeare's words to the empty air.'

'I know, Percy. I begin to wonder if we did wrong to play such a trick on her.'

'You think she has found out?'

'No. Knowing Lavinia, I am sure she could not have kept silent about it. She would have rung such a peal over me you would have heard it in the next county.'

'Then it must be the play. The weight of responsibility is too much for her.'

'So I suggested, but she denied it.'

'Then it has to be Wincote's offer. I believe young ladies do become very emotional on such occasions—' He stopped and turned towards his friend. 'Are you sure she means to accept him?'

'She has not said so in as many words, but Wincote is jaunty enough for two of them, behaving as if it is *fait accompli*.'

'I'll wager you have not told her the truth, have you?'

'I have told her that the man is a fortune-hunter and will not make her happy.'

'Dear me, that is not what I meant at all. I may know nothing of matrimony, but I do know about ladies. And pointing out the faults of one's rival never did serve.'

'I know that,' James said impatiently. 'But without proof that he is a rakeshame of the worst order, it is the only weapon I have.'

Percy, striding along beside his young friend, smiled. 'For a grown man of the world, you have no idea about women, have you?'

'Yes, I have. It is just that I have never been in love before.'

'Not ever?'

'No. Oh, there have been little bits of muslin, a mild dalliance here and there, which I had no difficulty in managing, but nothing like this.'

'You, my friend, are a mutton-head. You have the best weapon of all. Yourself. Show her your true self. Tell her—'

'That would be easier if we were not doing that damned play. Why, oh, why did she give me the part of Demetrius? She has to spurn me throughout and in the end I turn to Helena. It is indicative of how she feels towards me. We have even come to quarrelling and that is something that never happened before. I wish I could withdraw. I would, if it would not blacken me forever in her eyes.'

'Then you must bear it.'

'No. Come what may, I will speak to her, but the moment must be chosen with care or I will frighten her out of her wits and she will need all those about her on the night of the performance.'

'There is a great deal riding on that play, my friend.'
'Do you think I do not know that?'

Lavinia knew it too, and by an immense effort of will, pulled herself together to continue rehearsals, as if nothing was wrong. When she was not rehearsing, she made calls with the Duchess and attended other social engagements. If the Duchess was at home, she stayed to entertain their callers, among whom were Lord Wincote and James. Sometimes they were there at the same time when they treated each other with studious politeness, but more often than not, one would be arriving as the other left. Neither mentioned the performance; it was as if they had tacitly agreed that discussion of the play should be left to rehearsals when the whole cast was present and it could be handled impersonally.

She was beginning to count the days and told herself that when it was all over, she would go back to Loscoe Court and find some absorbing project. There was always her painting, her menagerie and riding in the countryside, so much better than riding in London, which was so strictly encompassed by protocol. And James might visit her there…

She could not quite stop herself from hoping and knew she would continue to do so as long as she had breath in her body, or until he married someone else. She did her best, but she could not prevent her thoughts straying to the man who held her heart. It did not matter what she did, sooner or later, she would find herself gazing into space, dreaming of him, wanting him.

'Mama, has James done anything about finding a wife?' she asked the Duchess one day. They were in the Duchess's studio where she was finishing her picture of Freddie, who was sitting at a table by the window, engrossed in his own efforts with paint, making a dreadful mess, daubing brilliant colour all over the sheet of paper his mama had given him. Lavinia took the brush from him to show how it should be done, but he simply laughed and continued to splash paint everywhere.

'I do not know, dear. Why do you ask?'

'No reason. You told him weeks ago you thought he should find a wife and settle down but I see no signs of it.'

'Marriage is not something to be undertaken lightly, Lavinia. And beneath his light-hearted way of dealing with things, I believe he is very deep. He wants to marry for love. I collect he told you so himself.'

'And is he in love?'

'I believe he is.'

'Who is she? Not Lady Rattenshaw—please tell me it is not Lady Rattenshaw.'

The Duchess smiled. 'Would that be so very terrible?'

'It would be a catastrophe. She is older than he is by goodness knows how many years and she has been married before. I cannot think they would be happy.'

'I am inclined to agree with you, but he is twenty-seven and must know his own mind. I cannot interfere. Why is it so important to you?'

'I should hate him to be unhappy,' she said lamely.

'Have you told him so?'

'No, of course not.'

'Why not? You used to be able to talk to him about everything. Very outspoken, the pair of you, as I recall.'

'That was before…'

'Before what?'

She hesitated before answering. 'Before Lord Wincote offered for me. James is convinced he is a fortune-hunter. He even dared to suggest his lordship knew something of the disappearance of Lady Willoughby's diamond clips.'

'Good gracious, how did he come by that idea?'

'I don't know. I was very angry with him. He does not like Lord Wincote and will do anything to discredit him in my eyes.'

'But you have refused Lord Wincote.' She paused. 'Oh, child, do not say you have not told James.'

She had told her stepmother about her interview with Lord Wincote, which had evinced a sigh which might have been one of relief, but little other comment. 'I meant to, but somehow the opportunity didn't arise.'

'Then tell him at once, Lavinia.' She paused and looked closely at her stepdaughter's troubled face. 'Tell him. And tell him why. Tell him the truth.'

'The truth?' Lavinia looked up, startled. Frances was smiling. 'You know?'

'Of course I know. Do you think I go round with my eyes shut?'

'How can I tell him? If he has set his heart on Lady Rattenshaw—'

'Lavinia, you are a fighter, you have always fought for what you want. Look how you managed to persuade all those people to act in your play and turned your papa round your thumb to allow Mr Greatorex and his company to take part. Everyone I have spoken to has praised you for your dedication. And yet you seem to have given up on James…'

'He has given up on me.'

'Nonsense! A more stubborn, prideful and contrary couple I have yet to meet. If he were here now, I would knock your heads together.'

Lavinia smiled wanly at the image her stepmother's words presented to her. She knew very well that knocking heads together would not serve. But was the Duchess right? Should she tell James what was in her heart? What had she to lose? Nothing except her pride.

It was pride which was sustained her through the last of the rehearsals as September drew to a close. It was pride which enabled her to say Hermia's lines and take Lancelot's criticisms in the spirit in which they were given. It was pride which kept her smiling as everyone's temper became more and more frayed.

There was thunder in the air presaging a storm and it was difficult to tell which would be the more severe when it broke, the one at Westminster or the one at Stanmore House. They were as ready as they would ever be. The scenery was finished, the costumes made and tickets had been sold, though not as many as Lavinia had hoped.

'It is this wretched trial,' the Duchess said, as the crowds began to gather again for its resumption. 'But perhaps more will come than you think. Those people who went home after the adjournment might return.'

It certainly looked as though they had. While the defence prepared its case and rebellion, like the thunder, hung in the air, the Queen continued to receive deputations of loyal supporters. They came in droves, choking the streets, though there was a very strong rumour that her Majesty was ill and receiving them in bed.

'I wish she would go back where she came from,' Lavinia said, one day when the crowds had kept them indoors. They were dining *à la famille*, which included James. He did not know why he continued to accept his stepmother's invitations; it was almost unbearable to be so close to Lavinia and yet so far from the place in her heart where he wanted to be.

Percy had advocated telling her how he felt about her and he fully intended to, but the right moment had not arrived. If they were not busy rehearsing, they were talking about the play, or the trial, or some other titbit of gossip and, in any case, they were never alone. He was more than half-convinced she was doing it on purpose. And at the back of it all was the fear that she had already accepted Wincote. He put all his hopes on the promise she had made not to do anything before the performance of that play. And it was getting very near now.

'If she did, London would empty overnight,' he said. 'And we would have no audience.'

'Yes, we should, for we would have performed the play during the proper Season.'

'I am afraid the Queen will not depart these shores until the trial is over,' the Duke said. 'And not then if she is found innocent.'

'She will never reign as Queen, surely?' the Duchess put in. 'The King won't stand for it.'

'Even a king can find nothing to say against a determined woman,' James said, watching Lavinia. She was concentrating on the food, pushing it around her plate, but eating very little. She had been looking very pale of late and her eyes had lost their sparkle. If she really was looking forward to being married to Wincote, would she be so listless? 'They are capable of wreaking havoc.'

'I heard Wincote had evidence against the King,' Duncan put in. 'Is it true, sir?'

Marcus sighed. 'I really do not know how these rumours start.'

'It is just a rumour, then?' Lavinia asked him and James, watching and listening, thought he detected a note of anxiety in her voice.

'He approached Brougham with a letter written on behalf of the King to his grandfather many years ago, but

Brougham would not entertain it. He has no intention of blackening the King's character.'

'So, what did this letter say?' Duncan asked.

'Nothing we were not aware of already. Wincote's grandfather had an alliance with Lady Jersey, before she caught the King's eye. The Prince of Wales, as he was then, offered him a baronetcy and the estate in Cumberland if he made himself scarce and left the field clear. And that is what he did.'

'Is that all?' Duncan was obviously disappointed.

'Yes, so you see how rumours muddy the waters. And Wincote himself has agreed that it is of little value…'

'I'll wager he has,' James murmured. He would not wish to oppose his prospective father-in-law.

The last dress rehearsal was a disaster which did not seem to bother Mr Greatorex at all. 'It is a good sign,' he said, when it was all over and everyone gathered for last-minute instructions. 'It means it will go well on the night. Have faith, my lady.'

'Faith can move mountains, so I am told,' James whispered to her. 'But if you need help moving mountains, then I am at your service. Shall I come early?'

'Yes, please.'

She could not sleep that night; everything was whirring round in her head: the play; things she had to remember; things she had forgotten to do; Lord Wincote's refusal to accept her rejection of him before her like the mountain James spoke of; and James himself, apparently restored to good humour. How could he laugh and joke when her churning insides made her feel so sick.

And when she did fall asleep at last, she had nightmares. Someone, a dark shadow she could not identify, was chasing her through the streets and she was continually falling over the long robe she wore and becoming entangled in the branches of trees, which should never have been there at all. The shape, whatever it was, had her by the throat and was trying to throttle her. She struggled and screamed, waking herself up, and then sat up in bed, panting and terrified. It was several minutes before she could bring herself to lie down again.

She had been mad to contemplate putting on a play, mad to encourage Lord Wincote and even more foolish to fall in love with James Corringham. If only she could go back to the beginning of the summer, back to the carefree days of June when she had no idea what trials were in store for her. But, for better or worse, her trial would be over tomorrow. She lifted her head to glance at the ormolu clock ticking on the mantelpiece. No, it was today. And then, in spite of her conviction she would not shut her eyes again, she fell asleep.

Daisy shook her awake when the morning was well advanced and she sprang out of bed and dressed hurriedly. There was so much to do: scenery, costumes, properties and lights to check and double-check, chairs to arrange, and musicians to accommodate. She allowed herself a cup of hot chocolate and a piece of bread and butter, before dashing to the ballroom to begin. She had no time to be nervous.

It was late afternoon and she was supervising the servants who were putting out the rows of chairs they had hired when James, true to his promise, arrived to help. Her day gown was covered with an enormous white apron which she must have borrowed from the cook and her lovely hair was pushed under a mob cap, such as her chambermaid wore. She looked so adorable, he could not help smiling.

'I am here,' he said, quietly. 'The mover of mountains.'

Chapter Eleven

She looked up and her whole face lit from within at the sight of him and made his heart quicken. 'Oh, James, I knew I could rely on you.'

'Of course.' He put his hat and cane on a table and walked towards her, both hands extended. 'Mr Dependable, that's me.'

She didn't know why she did it but she grasped both his hands in hers and stood on tiptoe to kiss his cheek. 'Thank you.'

'Vinny.' He held on to her hands and raised them, one by one to his lips. There was no sign of the bantering, carefree young man who loved to tease. 'You shouldn't thank me. I have brought you nothing but grief.'

'How can you say that? You are my dear...' She stopped and looked up at him. He was waiting for her to continue, but she could not. The word 'brother' stuck in her throat.

He said it for her. 'Brother?'

'No. Not brother. Not even stepbrother. That was a game we played to amuse everyone.'

'And the time for games is past,' he said quietly, holding her hands to his chest, where she could feel his heart beating, almost as quickly as her own. He smiled. 'You know, I have been waiting for you to grow up.'

'Have you?'

'Yes.' He stooped and kissed her forehead and then each cheek in turn. The touch of his lips was like fire on her skin. It seared it with a strange sensation that spread through her whole body, making her heart beat so fast she thought it would burst, filling her belly and ending in the moist spot between her thighs. A huge sigh escaped her.

'Vinny?'

'Yes?' It was whisper; she hardly dare speak.

'Not now. Later. When the curtain comes down on the last act, I have something I want to say to you, something important. Will you promise not to do anything foolish like accepting Wincote until you have heard me out?'

'James, I—'

'Don't say anything now,' he interrupted her before she could tell him she had already turned the gentleman down. 'Leave it until later.' He suddenly became businesslike. 'Now tell me where these mountains are that you want shifting.'

She laughed and told him what needed doing. Together they worked side by side until the others began to arrive and she went to the ladies' dressing room to change. Her exhaustion had disappeared, there was a new sparkle in her eyes and a lightness in her step. James was only going to have one last try at dissuading her from accepting Lord Wincote, she told herself as a defence against disappointment. But would he have kissed her, would he have said he had been waiting for her to grow up if that was all he meant?

When she returned, everyone was assembled in the ante-room behind the stage. 'The ballroom is filling up,' Miss Hastings said, peering through a gap in the curtains. 'We shall have a full house, although there are some very strange characters taking their seats, not the sort you would expect to be interested in Shakespeare. Quite common looking, in fact.'

'I do not care what they look like, as long as they have paid,' Lavinia said, peering out over Emily's shoulder. 'I expect they are connected with the orphanage.'

'Who is that strange man with Major Greenaway? He looks decidedly smoky to me.'

The man was tall and thin, dressed in a suit of black clothes which was shiny with age. 'Oh, Papa asked Major Greenaway to take care of security. With so many strangers in the house, he wanted to ensure there was no trouble and no repetition of what happened to Lady Graham and Lady Willoughby. He is probably a Runner or something of that sort.' She turned away. 'We must leave the stage, it is nearly time for the overture.'

'Oh, dear, I am so nervous,' Emily said, echoing Lavinia's own thoughts.

They were all nervous, except Lancelot Greatorex's players, for whom it was just another night like every other. Even Lady Rattenshaw, who had arrived later than everyone else, was jumpy.

'My lord,' she whispered to James when she found him standing alone, watching Lord Wincote and Lavinia preparing for their first entrance. 'You wanted to know about a certain gentleman...'

'So I did.'

'He is as close as wax about his family. He said his grief over the death of his grandfather was too recent to talk about. I tried again to persuade him to throw in his lot with me but he refused, which has deprived me of a great deal of fun, not that I have not enjoyed my time as Lady Rattenshaw.'

James smiled wryly. 'It might not have been fun at all.'

'No, I realise that. In the face of my entreaties, he said that, though he would not leave Lady Lavinia for me, it was not because he did not love me but that it was expedient. Apparently he had been expecting the prosecution to pay him handsomely to hush up the evidence he had against the King. And when they refused he went to Lord Brougham, who also sent him away. He is desperate for money and he simply has to have Lady Lavinia's dowry.'

'The devil!' James said angrily. He had known it all along, but to have it confirmed was enough to make his blood boil.

'If you confront him, my lord, he will deny he ever said any such thing. He will put it down to the rantings of a spurned female. Hell hath no fury and all that…'

'It is of no consequence,' he said, smiling down at her. 'I think I might yet win the day without having to say a word against the gentleman.'

Lavinia saw the smiles they exchanged and her heart almost stopped beating. He was not going to ask her to marry him, he was going to ask for her felicitations on his engagement to Lady Rattenshaw. She had been right when she saw them with their heads together after that visit to the theatre, she had not imagined it; Lady Rattenshaw was James's secret love. He looked so pleased with himself, she had no doubt she was right. But why must she hear him out before giving Lord Wincote his answer? His lordship already had his answer, though he did not believe it. She looked across at him, dressed in his Lysander costume, but turned away quickly when he gave her a secret smile.

'Places, everyone,' Lancelot called as the hired orchestra began the overture.

The curtain went up on the opening scene, and the orchestra stopped playing as Sir Percy and Miss Hastings

entered. The moment Sir Percy spoke the very first words
no one had any more time for speculation or even ner-
vousness. Lavinia took a huge gulp of air to steady herself
and with an effort of will she did not know she possessed,
became Hermia, beloved of Lysander.

When the curtain went down for the last time, the ripple
of applause grew to a crescendo and cries of 'Bravo!' The
whole cast reappeared and took a bow. The audience
clapped and called 'Speech! Speech!' But though they
tried to push Lavinia forward to make it, she was spent.
She did not have an ounce of energy left, either physical
or mental, and simply shook her head.

It was left to Lancelot to thank everyone for coming and
raising the grand sum of five hundred pounds for the orphanage. He told his listeners that it had been his privilege
and his pleasure to join such talented actors and actresses,
who would surely make their marks if any of them decided
to tread the boards as professionals. And then it was all
over.

Behind the curtain everyone was talking at once, laughing and joking and dissecting their performances, looking
forward to the celebration party which the Duke was providing. It was all too much for Lavinia, who slipped away
to the bookroom where she sank into her father's armchair
to collect herself and her thoughts. The play was over, but
the bigger test was still to come. She had yet to convince
Lord Wincote that she had meant her refusal and would
not change her mind. And worse still, she had to listen to
James enthusing about Lady Rattenshaw and offer her con-
gratulations.

'Lady Lavinia, there you are. I have been looking for
you. Why are you hiding?'

She looked up to see Edmund standing over her. He had

already changed from his costume into evening clothes, a pair of black superfine trousers strapped under his shoes, a perfectly tailored coat and a purple brocade waistcoat. 'I am not hiding, my lord. I needed a few moments' quiet contemplation. It has all been so exhausting.'

'Yes, I understand,' he said, drawing up a chair opposite her and sitting down, so close to her his knees were almost touching hers. He leaned forward and took both her hands. 'We shall sit here quietly for a moment or two and you will soon be yourself again, ready to take on the world.'

She looked down at their linked hands, too lethargic to pull away, wishing with every fibre of her being that James would come and rescue her. James, who looked on her as a sister, not a wife. 'My lord—'

'Edmund,' he corrected her. He released one of her hands to reach out and touch her cheek. She shuddered. 'You are not afraid of me, surely?'

'No.'

'Then look at me.'

She raised her head and found herself looking into his dark eyes and could not tear her gaze away. She could feel his eyes boring into hers and his soft voice, soothing her. 'You are so tired after all you have done, so very, very tired, so we will rest here together, in quiet harmony…' His voice became a soft hum, like the sound of bees on a summer's day. Her eyes flickered and then closed…

James could not find her. He had gone to the men's dressing room immediately the play ended to change before returning to the ballroom, expecting to see her with the Duke and Duchess and the rest of the cast who were milling about, drinking champagne and congratulating themselves on the success of the evening, but there was no sign of her. No Wincote either. Surely the man had not cornered her already? She had promised to wait, but in the face of Wincote's persuasiveness, would she? Had they gone into another room? Left the house?

He was on his way to search for her when he saw Major Greenaway pushing his way through the throng towards him, accompanied by a seedy individual whom James had never seen before.

'James,' Donald said, as the two men met. 'A word, if you please.'

James looked about him. There was still no sign of Lavinia or Wincote. 'Not now, Donald. I have to find Lavinia.'

'This won't take long.' He took James's arm and drew him into a corner where they would not be overheard. 'This is Mr Theobald Tribble. He is a jeweller and receiver…'

'Sir, I protest!' Tribble said. 'I never knowingly—'

'Quite.' Donald cut him short and continued to address James. 'I brought him here tonight to watch the play—'

'And never understood a word,' the man said. 'I could have done what you asked without sitting through three hours of nonsensical verse.'

James looked from one to the other and wished they would get on with it.

He needed to find Lavinia, and quickly.

'I asked him to come tonight to identify the man who sold him Lady Willoughby's diamond clips,' Donald went on.

'And did he?'

'He did.'

'And was it—?'

'It was. I have a Runner standing by. He will be taken up as soon as you give the word.'

'I don't know where he is. Nor where Lady Lavinia is. I was just going to look for them.'

'Then I will help you. If he gets wind we are on his tail…'

He did not need to finish the sentence, James was already striding away, intent on turning the entire house upside down if he had to.

'Come, my dear,' Edmund said, very quietly but firmly, as if talking to a child. 'Everyone is waiting for us to announce our engagement. His Grace has champagne especially for the toast.'

'I am tired,' she said. 'I want to sleep.'

He stood up and bent over her to take her by the arm. 'So you shall, just as soon as the formalities are over, then you may sleep as long as you wish. Now, stand up like a good girl and take my arm.'

She was too tired to resist and stood obediently, though he had to support her.

'Now, my dear,' he went on, his voice low. 'You are to be your usual bright self and smile a great deal. You are very happy. The play has been a great success and you are to marry the man you love. Is that not so?'

'Yes.' She was smiling and apparently alert as he lead her from the room and across the wide hall in the direction of the ballroom.

'Vinny!' They were suddenly confronted by James. 'I have been looking everywhere for you.'

'You may congratulate me on my good fortune,' Edmund said, triumphantly, drawing Lavinia closer to his side. 'We are just returning to the ballroom to make the announcement of our engagement.'

'Oh, no, you are not! Vinny, tell me this isn't true. Tell me you have not accepted this…this charlatan's offer.'

'Steady, my lord,' Wincote warned him. 'That statement is actionable.'

'Not if I can prove it.' He turned to Lavinia. 'Vinny, do not do this thing. If you love me, do not do it.'

She looked up at him and smiled. 'I am going to marry the man I love,' she said.

He could not believe it. He reached forward to touch her. She almost shrank from him and the horror of it hit him like a physical blow.

'Corringham, I will thank you to step aside and let us pass,' Wincote said calmly. 'We are expected at the party. You may join us if you wish, but only as long as you refrain from bothering her ladyship, soon to be my wife.'

In a fury, James raised his fist, but before he could land the blow his arm was caught by Major Greenaway, who had come up behind him. 'No, Corringham, that is not the answer. Think of the scandal if you should come to fisticuffs under his Grace's roof.' He turned to Edmund. 'Lord Wincote, there is someone here I should like you to meet.' He waved Mr Tribble forward.

Edmund took one look at the man, grabbed Lavinia by the hand and dashed across the hall to the front door, pulling her after him. 'Come, my lady, I have changed my mind, we will not join the party after all.'

James was after them in the time it took to collect his scattered wits, but he was not quick enough. The street, when they reached it, was thronged with people. Many of them had been part of the audience and were streaming out from Stanmore House and climbing into waiting carriages and cabs. They mingled with others already on the streets: gentlemen and clerks, ladies of every degree, children letting off firecrackers, workers carrying banners, saying 'God save Queen Caroline'. But there was no sign of Edmund Wincote or Lavinia.

'Damn the Queen!' James said, trying to see over the heads of the multitude.

'What did you say?' demanded a little man, from the jostling crowd. 'Did I hear you damn Her Majesty?' He turned to his fellows. 'Here's a King's man, mates. He would have the Queen sent to perdition. I reckon he needs a seeing-to.'

They crowded round him belligerently. He tried pushing them away. 'For God's sake, let me through. There is a young lady in grave danger—'

'She would be if you had anything to do with it,' the little man said, laughing. 'But we aim to protect her. Come, lads, off with his coat and breeks and into the Thames with him.'

James fought them off, wondering where Donald had got to. He should have been at his side. His coat was ripped in the struggle and he lost his hat, and though anger lent him strength, it was not enough, he knew he was being overpowered. Suddenly he felt hands under his armpits and was hauled off his feet and bundled into a cab which had appeared from nowhere.

'For God's sake, stop struggling and get in,' Donald said.

James pulled himself up from the floor as Donald jumped in beside him and slammed the door shut on the enraged crowd. The horses set off, but in the mêlée could make little headway. The persistent little man ran along-side for a hundred yards until at last the road cleared a little and they picked up speed and left him behind.

'My thanks for the rescue,' James said, inspecting his torn coat. 'But where has that villain gone with Lavinia?'

'She seemed willing enough.'

'She did not know what she was doing. She was tired, exhausted, did you not notice her eyes—' He stopped and clapped a hand to his forehead. 'My God! Why did I not think of that before? He has mesmerised her. He has taken over her mind. She will do exactly as he tells her.'

'Can he do that?'

'He did it before. I witnessed it.'

'Do you think he has a parson standing by?'

'No, he did not expect to see you or that jeweller fellow, what was his name?'

'Tribble.'

'He recognised him and knew the game was up. He has changed tactics and has Vinny as a kind of hostage. It is a ransom, not a wedding, he is thinking of. They are either on foot or, like us, have found a cab.'

'I thought I saw the Loscoe carriage outside Stanmore House when I arrived.'

'Yes, the Duke sent it for my sister and her children. It would have been waiting to take them home again. It was unfortunate that Sir Richard had a prior engagement and needed their coach.'

'Did you notice it when we left?'

'No, I can't say I did. Wincote must have purloined it. It is a good strong coach with four of the best horses in London. We cannot hope to catch up with them in this ancient rattler.'

'No, but it will be easy to spot.'

'If we knew where they were heading. He would hardly take her home to Mount Street.'

'No, but he could take her to Cumberland.'

'Cumberland! My God! We must make haste.' He rapped on the roof. 'Corringham House, Duke Street,' he ordered. 'As fast as you can. Five guineas if you can do it in less than ten minutes.' Then, to Donald, 'We'll take my coach and horses.'

They were flung back in their seats as the cabdriver

whipped up the horses, shouting to the crowds to give way. 'Make way!' he yelled. 'Make way for Lord Brougham!'

In spite of his anxiety, James laughed. 'Very imaginative, our driver, but it seems to have done the trick.' The crowds were cheering them and then a new hazard presented itself because the mob decided horses were not good enough and they were going to unharness them and pull the coach themselves. It would take an age and when they discovered Lord Brougham was not inside, there would be a lynching.

'No, his lordship is in a devil of a hurry to see the Queen,' their driver shouted. 'Things to discuss before the hearing next week and her Majesty wants to go to bed.' This set up such a howl of laughter, they were allowed to proceed unhindered.

'If he has harmed a hair of her head,' James said, as they fairly flew along. 'I shall personally run him through and take pleasure in doing it. And the worst of it is that she will not have her wits about her to fight him off.' He thumped his knee with his clenched fist, hardly feeling the pain. 'Vinny, Vinny, where are you?'

She was dreaming. She was in a coach, going heaven knew where, and there was this dark shadow beside her and an ache behind her eyes which was stopping her from thinking clearly. Her limbs were heavy, and her face hurt from smiling in the dark. Why was she smiling? Was she happy?

'Lavinia, my dear, you will forgive me, I know. You will understand why, when you wake.' The soft voice droned on. It had been talking to her non-stop for what seemed hours, assuring her all was well and that she would soon be in bed. But she was in bed already; she would wake up in a minute to find Daisy standing over her with her morning chocolate. She tried to force her eyes open and then discovered to her dismay that they were open already.

Something stirred in her brain, something she must remember, something important. She tried to grasp it, but it eluded her. She groaned and put her hand to her aching head. 'My head hurts.'

'It will be better by and by,' the soft, unhurried voice went on. 'You have caused me no end of trouble, don't you know that? And so has Corringham. Too leery by far, that one, sharp enough to understand a man's need for blunt, but then he would, considering he's a gambler too. If Lady G.'s necklace had not been fake, I might have got away with it, had enough money to pay off my debts and appear the perfect match for you. She never felt it leave her neck, but the Willoughby woman's clips, that was more difficult. She set up such a din, I had to think fast and then I daren't sell them with Major Greenaway breathing down my neck. Had to in the end, what with Lady Rattenshaw not being the genuine article…'

There was something about that statement which worried her, but her head was too woolly to think about it. She looked out of the window. The coach was going at walking pace through dense crowds, all shouting and cheering. No wonder her head ached. 'What are they shouting about?' she asked.

'They think you are the Queen and are cheering you.'

'That's silly. The Queen is…' She shook her head, trying to clear it.

The carriage was jolted by the crowd pressing against it and suddenly she was herself again. She recognised the interior of the family coach, she recognised Lord Wincote. She looked down at herself and realised she was still wearing her ancient Greek costume.

'Sleep on,' he murmured. The voice was the same dull monotone she had been hearing all evening. No, not quite all evening. Since the play ended. She remembered the cheers and the clapping, just like the cheers and clapping that had roused her from her torpor just now. Had she been asleep? Had she walked out to the carriage in her sleep, still wearing her costume? Or was it just one more demonstration of his lordship's strange power over people's minds?

She sat quite still, trying to drag back the events of the evening to her conscious mind. James had been there. James had tried to stop her. James had kissed her, told her to wait for him, that he wanted to talk to her. Where was he now? Why had he allowed Lord Wincote to take her away like this? Suddenly the coach jolted to a stop, surrounded by men and women all making their way towards St James's Square where they meant to stand outside the Queen's residence and cheer her.

'Bang-up vehicle and no mistake,' one of them said, pulling open the door and filling the inside of the coach with alcoholic fumes. 'Prime horseflesh too. And more of the like inside.' He grinned toothlessly at Lavinia. 'What ho, my little leddy! Who are you?'

'Get out!' Edmund yelled, trying to push the man away, so that he could shut the door again.

'No call to get on your high horse,' the man said. 'We only want to know if the lady is the Queen.'

'Of course she is not.'

'One of her ladies-in-waiting, perhaps?'

'No, I am not,' she said, so forcefully that Edmund realised she had come out of her mesmerised state and was fully aware of what was happening to her.

'Do not be so quick to deny it, my dear,' he said calmly. 'They are very partisan and I could not protect you if they decided to turn nasty. Better to say you are part of the Queen's household and we can be on our way.'

'No. I would rather put myself in their hands than yours.' The mob was clambering all over the coach now, even on its roof and Tom Bagshott, who had not been at all sure he should have obeyed Lord Wincote's order to drive them and would not have done so if Lady Lavinia herself had not asked him, clung tenaciously to the reins. The vehicle began to rock alarmingly.

'They will have us over,' Wincote said. 'For God's sake, Lavinia, tell them you are on an errand for the Queen and they will let us go.'

'I do not know why you should be so afraid, my lord,' she said, doing her best to stay calm. 'You have been on her Majesty's side from the beginning. You tell them that.'

He tried, but someone had recognised the Loscoe coat of arms and they laughed in his face. 'That's a caulker if I ever heard one.' The man who was standing on the step laughed, his rugged face so close to Lavinia's she could smell the cheap Geneva on his breath as he looked her up and down, taking in her flimsy costume. 'I knew them gentry got up to some weird rigs, but I never thought to see it with me own eyes.'

'Jed, what's to-do?' someone shouted at him. 'Are we going to let them go or are we going to tip them in the river?'

'It is no good,' James said. 'We will never get through. Perhaps we should have rounded up some help before setting out.'

'We cannot go back so we might as well try and go forwards,' Donald said. Both men were sitting on the box of the Corringham carriage. James was driving, growing more and more impatient, while the major leaned down and endeavoured to force a way through, using his not inconsiderable voice.

'There is a great knot of people surrounding a carriage ahead of us,' James said. 'If they are not careful they will have it over.'

'Never mind that now. Can you get past it?'

'I don't know. The horses might take fright, they are nervous enough as it is.'

'It will make the crowd scatter, though.'

'True, but someone might be hurt.'

'Give the tits the order. I'll yell runaway horses at them. That should shift 'em.'

'And before you know where we are, they really will bolt and then what?'

'Oh, come, James, you are one of the best whipsters in the business, you can bring them up again.'

James gave the horses a touch of the whip. They needed no more. Already half-spooked, they set off at a gallop, almost dragging James's arms out of their sockets. The sound of the hooves and Donald's bellow of warning scattered the crowds. In a minute they had passed and were flying along the now empty road ahead of them.

'That was the Loscoe coach,' Donald yelled as they rattled past, but the horses were out of control and they could not stop.

'James!' Lavinia screamed, as the hurtling vehicle passed within inches of them. 'Oh, James.' He had been driving so fast, he had not recognised the coach and did not know she was inside. She began to weep silently. Tears coursed down her cheeks unchecked.

Edmund laughed crazily. 'He did not see us, but he has done us a service and scattered the mob so they have lost interest in us. Now you must settle for me, my dear.'

'Never! He will come back.'

'Give me leave to doubt it. He obviously has other things on his mind. Lady Rattenshaw, perhaps, though she is no lady.'

She was diverted enough to look sharply at him. 'What do you mean?'

'You did not know the so-called lady is an actress?'

'That's nonsense. You are mad.'

'Not at all, my dear. Shall I tell you her name? It is Marianne Doubleday, one-time paramour of Sir Percival Ponsonby. They thought they had tricked me, but I was at the whore's house one day, waiting for her—we were going out for a drive into the country—when I saw a playbill, rolled up on a bookshelf. I undid it, out of curiosity, you understand, and there she was, as large as life...'

'I am sure I do not know what you are talking about.'

'The plot Sir Percy and the Earl of Corringham hatched to discredit me. They dangled the actress in front of me, hoping to divert me from my purpose.'

'What purpose?'

'To marry you, of course.'

'I told you I would not marry you.' His revelation, intriguing though it was, mattered little against her need to convince him. 'Can't you understand that? Take me home at once.' She tried to sound firm, in control, but her head was still pounding and she knew that if it came to it, she was not strong enough to fight him off.

'Oh, no, my dear. You are too valuable a commodity to hand over without some kind of recompense for my pains. If I cannot have your dowry, I shall have your ransom. Now settle down and go to sleep, we have a long drive ahead of us.' He put his head out of the window and called up to the coachman. 'It is safe enough to proceed now.'

'No!' Lavinia shouted. 'Tom, you are not to move an inch.'

Infuriated, Edmund scrambled up on the driving seat. Lavinia seized her opportunity, jumped from the coach and ran, heading for the departing crowds. She would be safer among them than with her abductor.

Lord Wincote abandoned his attack on Tom and set off in pursuit. He did not look before dashing across the road in front of a coach and horses galloping at breakneck speed towards them. Lavinia, hearing the terrible sound of screams, splintering wood and neighing horses, turned just in time to see Edmund flung into the air like a rag doll, and the coach veering crazily, before embedding itself in a tree. Then there was a terrible silence.

She stood as mesmerised as she had been when Lord Wincote took her from the house. Some of the crowd turned and began to run towards the scene, taking Lavinia with them. Those at the front went to Lord Wincote. He lay in a crumpled heap, his lifeless eyes staring into nothing. 'He's dead,' they said.

Lavinia stood looking down at him, unable to believe what had happened. She had been frightened by him, terrified of his strange power, but never had she wished him dead. What was that other coach doing travelling so fast? 'Leave him,' someone said, drawing her away. 'Can't do nothing for him now.'

She looked up as the now sober crowd ran to the crashed carriage, its wheels still spinning. Some ran to free the horses, others to look for the occupants. She saw Major Greenaway pick himself up from the ground and shake himself almost as the same time as she recognised the Corringham coat of arms on the door. 'James!' she screamed, starting to run. 'James.'

He had been thrown off by the impact and was lying in a mass of broken branches. She thought he was dead too and her panic to reach him gave her the strength to push past everyone, tearing her costume on the splintered wood. 'James!' She sobbed his name as if repetition would bring him back to life. 'James, oh, James.'

When she reached him, Donald was kneeling beside him. He looked up at her. 'He's alive,' he said quietly.

'Oh, thank God!' She fell on her knees beside him, just as he moaned and tried to sit up. 'I thought you had been killed, too.'

He forced a grin. 'No…winded, that's all.' He reached up and touched a bump on the back of his head, wincing. 'I shall have a headache tomorrow.'

'Are you sure that is all?' Lavinia, with tears running down her face unchecked, threw herself into his arms. 'I do not know what I would have done if anything had happened to you.'

'I shall be as right as ninepence directly.' Still shocked, he looked round at the devastation and saw her torn dress, the scratches on her arms and his own aches and pains faded to nothing. 'You are hurt.'

'No, not at all.'

'What happened to Wincote? Did…?'

'It was not your fault,' Lavinia said. 'He ran right under your horses' hooves. Oh, you do not know how glad I am to see you. When I saw you galloping past and you didn't stop…'

'I could not. It took nearly half a mile to pull the horses up and calm them before they could be persuaded to turn the coach and bring us back. I was so distraught with worry, I drove hell for leather. I tried to pull up when I saw the man in the road. What was he doing there?'

'Chasing me. I was running away from him. James, he was horrible. I am sorry he is dead, but I was so frightened…'

'Dead?' He looked from Lavinia to Donald.

'Afraid he's a goner,' the major said.

'Oh, my God! I killed him.'

'It was no more'n he deserved, my lord.' Tom had left their coach and run to help. 'After what he did and the way he treated Lady Lavinia, I have no pity for him. I'd have strangled him with my own hands if you hadn't come along.'

'That's all very well,' James said, hauling himself to his feet and brushing leaves and twigs from his clothes. 'A man has died a violent death and I am to blame.'

'Brought it on hisself,' Tom insisted. 'You should have heard the things he was saying to her ladyship and her in such a state—'

'You can tell me later,' James said, looking down at Lavinia, who had put his arm round her shoulders to support him. He was perfectly able to stand, it was Lavinia who needed support. There was no doubt she had had a terrible fright; she was quaking like a leaf with shock. 'First things first,' he said, taking off his torn coat and draping it about her shoulders. 'Tom, take Lady Lavinia back to her carriage. I will join you directly when I have seen what I can do for Lord Wincote.'

But there was nothing to be done. His lordship lay where he had fallen. Someone had straightened his limbs and shut his eyes so that he looked as though he were asleep, except for the pool of blood under his head.

'I'll see he gets to the mortuary and inform the authorities,' Donald said. 'You take Lady Lavinia home. We can send someone to salvage the carriage tomorrow.'

He thanked his friend and made his way to the Loscoe coach, limping a little. Now the numbness was wearing off he felt as if he had been in a gruelling bout with Gentleman Jackson and come out the worse for wear. But he was better off than Wincote and whatever the man had done, he could not rejoice in his death. He went to join Lavinia.

She was sitting in the coach with the door open. In the meagre light, coming from the street lamps, he could see her face was paper white. 'Vinny, are you sure you are all right?'

'Oh, yes, now you have come.' She held out her hand to help him into the coach. 'My shining knight. You were coming to rescue me?'

'Someone had to pull you out of the bumblebath you had fallen into.' He managed one of his old smiles, then called out to Tom who was sitting with the reins in his hands, to take them to Corringham House.

'Corringham House?' she queried, as he pulled the door shut. 'Don't you mean Stanmore House?'

'No. You can hardly go back to that party looking like that and neither can I. Besides, I mean to have a few minutes alone with you, without interruption.'

'Oh.'

'I expressly asked you not to speak to Wincote until you had heard what I had to say. Why didn't you stay in the ballroom with the others?'

'I didn't feel like it. I wanted to be alone to think.'

'About Lord Wincote's offer?'

'No. I told him two weeks ago I would not marry him. I wanted to think about what I should do now the play was over.'

'You had already rejected him?' He could not conceal his astonishment. 'Why didn't you tell me?'

'I tried, more than once, but something always happened to prevent it and when I realised you were in love with Lady Rattenshaw—' She stopped suddenly. 'Lord Wincote told me she wasn't a lady but an actress.'

He turned in his seat so that he was facing her. 'Vinny, what are you saying?'

'Lady Rattenshaw is an actress. He told me her real name but I have forgotten it. He said you knew...'

'I did, but that was not what I meant. What do you mean, you realised I was in love?'

'You are, aren't you? Isn't that what you were going to tell me?'

'No, by heaven, it was not. At least, not that I was in love with Lady Rattenshaw. Wherever did you get that idea?'

'You often had your heads together and smiled at each other and... Oh, I don't know. I was confused.'

'Oh, Vinny, Vinny, how could you think I could love anyone but you? You are in every breath I take, waking and sleeping. You are part of me, my heart and lungs and head...'

Her thoughts were in a whirl and her heart was singing, she could hardly believe what she was hearing. 'Not your sister?'

'No, you goose.' He took both her hands and cupped them in his. 'I love you as a man loves a woman, and have done for years—ever since I set eyes on you when you were a spoiled, opinionated sixteen-year-old.'

She punched him playfully on the arm. 'I never was.'

'Still are.'

'No, I am not.'

'There you are,' he said, though he was smiling. 'Case proved.'

'I am no longer sixteen.' She was suddenly serious. 'You said you were waiting for me to grow up.'

'I did. And an unconscionable time you have been about it.'

'Growing up was painful. It was easier to stay as we

were and you did not help, roasting me and treating me like a little sister.'

'I thought that was what you wanted. But it was definitely not what I wanted, believe me. I wanted a grown woman.'

'James, I have done my growing up all in a hurry. And now—'

'You are the perfect age. May you never grow older. May you never change. I love you just as you are. Always and forever.'

It was unbelievable and she could not quite take it in. 'Do you mean it?'

'I was never more serious in my life.' He put his arm about her and drew her nearer to him, savouring the feel of her so close, her head on his shoulder. He could smell the scent of her hair and feel the warmth of her body against his as his coat fell from her shoulders.

'James, don't ever let me go again.'

He laughed, suddenly light-hearted. 'I would have to put you in chains, it is the only way, you know.'

'Don't be silly. I need no chains to stay at your side. A simple gold band would do.'

He turned to her in astonishment. 'Does that mean you will marry me?'

'You have not asked me.'

'Dear me, how could I have overlooked such a simple thing as asking the lady I love to be my wife?' He smiled down at her, with such tenderness that she was knew he was not joking, in spite his bantering tone. 'So, my love, will you marry me?'

'Oh, yes, please.'

He kissed her then, properly, mouth on mouth as a man kisses a woman—and it was all she could have hoped for, tender and sweet, but full of passion. They were still locked in each other's arms when the carriage came to a halt.

He helped her out and instructed Tom to go to Stanmore House and tell the Duchess what had happened. 'Let her know Lady Lavinia is unharmed and ask her to send some clothes for her,' he said. 'Say we will join the party later. I can rely on you to do it discreetly.'

'Yes, my lord.'

They watched him set off and he took Lavinia's arm to escort her indoors. The house was quiet, only a single lamp lit the hall. 'I told the servants not to wait up,' he said, leading her into the drawing room.

'Then don't wake them,' she replied. 'I need nothing until my clothes arrive.'

He lit the lamp which stood on the table by the hearth. Its warm glow illuminated only a part of the room, but she did not need to see it. Her eyes were filled with the sight of the man she loved, turning to face her, his arms outstretched. She ran eagerly into them and he held her tight, kissing her over and over again.

'Oh, James, I can't believe it. That we are here...'

'Which we shouldn't be, of course. We are alone in my house, in the middle of the night; if word gets out, your reputation will be in tatters.'

'I am sure it already is. After all, I went off with Lord Wincote.' She shuddered at the memory. 'I think—I am sure he must have mesmerised me. I have no recollection of anything until I came to my senses in that carriage. Oh, James, I was terrified.'

'It is all over now, my love.'

'Yes, and he is dead. I can't quite believe that. Such a waste of a life.'

'I regret that,' he said quietly, reminded of the story of Wincote's brother. Had Edmund really murdered him?

They would never know now, but if he had, he had been punished for it. 'But it was truly an accident. I did my best to avoid him.'

'I know, and risked your life to do it. Oh, what will Papa and Mama say about it?'

'They will be told the truth, but as far as the rest of the world is concerned it was no more than a tragic accident.'

'But what will everyone say when we tell them our news? There will be a dreadful scandal, coming so quickly on Lord Wincote's death.'

'Are you saying you want to postpone an announcement?'

She looked up into his face and her heart turned over all over again; he was gazing down at her with such love and tenderness in his eyes. 'What do you think?'

'I do not want to delay a single minute longer than I have to before I make you my wife.'

'That sounds good. Say it again.'

'My wife.'

She giggled suddenly. 'I can't believe it. Won't everyone be surprised?'

'I doubt it,' he said, smiling at her indulgently. Whatever she wanted, he would do his best to give her. But holding back would be hard. 'I have, according to Little Mama, been wearing my heart on my sleeve for weeks. She advocated laying it at your feet.'

'She knew?' she asked in surprise. 'She never even hinted, though she did tell me not to give up on you.'

'She said something of the sort to me. I had decided to take her advice and tell you after the play, but Wincote got there first.'

'We will not talk about him. Kiss me again.' She lifted her face to his and he obliged willingly, holding her close against him, feeling her heart beating through the flimsy material of the torn gown. His body responded uncomfortably as desire coursed through him, his passion doing battle with his innate sense of chivalry, which was not helped by the way she was kissing him back. There was an abandonment about it that told him she was a passionate woman who could and would satisfy him.

But it was not only passion but tenderness that held him in thrall, tenderness for her youth, for her feelings which could so easily be bruised. He wanted a good beginning to their life together, he wanted her happiness above his own desires. He held her gently away from him, as they heard a carriage drawing up outside. Tom was back.

'The party will be over,' she said, hearing it too and reluctant to come back to earth from the cloud she had been floating on.

'I doubt it,' he said, smiling. 'I believe it is set to go on all night. We need to change our clothes and make ourselves tidy, but if we are quick they might not even have missed us. We have been absent for less than two hours.'

Two hours! Was that all? It had seemed like the whole night, a year, a lifetime. But her life was before her and she was happy. She smiled and took his hand as they faced their future together.

* * * * *

Historical Note

The so-called trial of Queen Caroline was resumed on the third of October when Lord Brougham made a masterly speech for the defence, which everyone, even his opponents, applauded for its persuasion and eloquence. It made such a strong impression that many peers, hitherto for the motion, debated whether to continue to support it.

Defence witnesses were every bit as convincing as the prosecution and the trial lasted for fifty-two days. The majority in favour of the bill on its second reading was twenty-eight. On November the eighth, the divorce clause, the most contentious of the issues, was carried and on Friday, November the tenth, the bill came up for its third reading. This time there was a majority of only nine. When the result was announced, Lord Liverpool rose and announced that had the third reading been passed with the same majority as the second, the Government would have felt it their duty to send it to the Commons. However, with the opinion so evenly balanced, it was his intention that the question 'that bill do now pass' be changed to say 'this day six months', a procedural device which had the effect of abandoning it. His motion was carried, amid loud cheers.

Given the ferment of support for Queen Caroline in the country, it was the wisest, perhaps the only thing he could have done. In effect, the Queen had been found guilty but had escaped the punishment of divorce. Everyone breathed a sigh of relief that revolution had been avoided and the population went wild with celebration. The Queen, her victory a hollow one, was refused a palace and went to live in seclusion at Brandenberg House while the King, not altogether pleased by the result, put in hand the arrangements for his coronation which took place on July the twenty-ninth, 1821.

Caroline made a last-ditch attempt to attend but was turned away at the doors of Westminster Abbey. The King was crowned alone. Afterwards he went on a state visit to Ireland and it was while he was out of the country, on the evening of Monday, August 6, 1821, that his Queen died. The King was said to be jubilant. He did not marry again and died in 1830, to be succeeded by his brother, William IV.

* * * * *

Modern Romance™
...seduction and
passion guaranteed

Tender Romance™
...love affairs that
last a lifetime

Sensual Romance™
...sassy, sexy and
seductive

Blaze™
...sultry days and
steamy nights

Medical Romance™
...medical drama on
the pulse

Historical Romance™
...rich, vivid and
passionate

27 new titles every month.

*With all kinds of Romance for
every kind of mood...*

MILLS & BOON®

MB1

books and a surprise gift!

We would like to take this opportunity to thank you for reading this Mills & Boon® book by offering you the chance to take TWO more specially selected titles from the Historical Romance™ series absolutely FREE! We're also making this offer to introduce you to the benefits of the Reader Service™—

★ FREE home delivery
★ FREE gifts and competitions
★ FREE monthly Newsletter
★ Exclusive Reader Service discount
★ Books available before they're in the shops

Accepting these FREE books and gift places you under no obligation to buy, you may cancel at any time, even after receiving your free shipment. Simply complete your details below and return the entire page to the address below. *You don't even need a stamp!*

YES! Please send me 2 free Historical Romance books and a surprise gift. I understand that unless you hear from me, I will receive 4 superb new titles every month for just £3.49 each, postage and packing free. I am under no obligation to purchase any books and may cancel my subscription at any time. The free books and gift will be mine to keep in any case.

H2ZEA

Ms/Mrs/Miss/Mr ....Initials...............................
                                                          BLOCK CAPITALS PLEASE
Surname ....
Address ....
....
....Postcode...............................

Send this whole page to:
UK: FREEPOST CN81, Croydon, CR9 3WZ
EIRE: PO Box 4546, Kilcock, County Kildare (stamp required)